Book Three in the Audrey Markum, Photographer Series

FILLING *in the* SHADOWS

I0561943

LINDA COTTON JEFFRIES

MILFORD
HOUSE

an imprint of Sunbury Press, Inc.
Mechanicsburg, PA USA

MILFORD HOUSE

an imprint of Sunbury Press, Inc.
Mechanicsburg, PA USA

For information about special discounts for bulk purchases, please contact Sunbury Press Orders Dept. at (855) 338-8359 or orders@sunburypress.com.

To request one of our authors for speaking engagements or book signings, please contact Sunbury Press Publicity Dept. at publicity@sunburypress.com.

FIRST MILFORD HOUSE PRESS EDITION: October 2025

Set in Adobe Garamond Pro | Interior design by Crystal Devine | Cover by Victoria Mitchell | Edited by Gabrielle Kirk.

Publisher's Cataloging-in-Publication Data
Names: Jeffries, Linda Cotton, author.
Title: Filling in the shadows / Linda Cotton Jeffries.
Description: First trade paperback edition. | Mechanicsburg, PA : Milford House Press, 2025.
Summary: Once, Audrey Markum's keen eye for detail led to the discovery of a child's body and the identity of his killer. Now an adult, that early skill has her working as a photographer for weddings and the Pittsburgh Police Department. She is thrilled by her first destination wedding but hidden danger is building in the city that threatens Audrey and everyone she loves if she and boyfriend, detective Rod, can't stop it in time.
Identifiers: ISBN : 979-8-88819-330-3 (paperback).
Subjects: FICTION / Mystery & Detective / Women Sleuths | FICTION / Action & Adventure | FICTION / Crime.

Designed in the USA
0 1 1 2 3 5 8 13 21 34 55

For the Love of Books!

For David, whose patience for construction
slowdowns far exceeds mine.

CHAPTER

1

The notice always came in the mail, Wade Marconi thought as he rubbed his hand through his short, bristly hair. No one ever said anything to your face. Just the official 'we regret' and 'does not meet our needs at this time' crap that had been in every other letter he'd received during his career with the Pittsburgh police. From high school, he'd gone straight into the Marines, but an injury had knocked him out of basic training. After that, he'd pulled himself back together and gone into the police academy. He'd expected to rise in the ranks just as his father had, but the times had changed, and he knew exactly who was to blame. For every promotion he'd been denied, he could picture the person who'd gotten it instead, and he had an epithet to describe every fucking one of them, blacks, women, college boys, Hispanics, the list went on and on. There was no way up for a hardworking white man, none at all, not anymore. He'd had to take on extra work as security for Dwayne Ellerby, a local businessman, just to get ahead.

It was all going to pay off soon, though, Marconi reassured himself as he twisted the letter in his hands. Once it was the size of a pencil, he lit it from the gas burner on the stove, held it for a moment, and then dropped it into the sink, watching the opportunity burn away before finally washing the ashes down the drain. Ellerby had the funds and the means, and together, the corporation they'd formed and the camp they'd built were going to start the revolution. Their numbers were growing, too, a little slowly but growing all the same. Marconi was hoping to recruit a young man in his squad, a tall, athletic white man who reminded Marconi of himself at a younger age. John Washington appeared to be a loner, never mixing in with the crowd of young cops in the precinct. Marconi knew Washington had gone the same route he had, skipping college and going into the academy. Washington was also more fit and capable than a lot of their members, many of whom were closer to retirement than not. Plus, Marconi thought, what could be a better revolutionary-sounding name than John Washington? Marconi figured he'd be perfect.

The camp was well hidden, he had to give them that. They had driven nearly an hour east from Pittsburgh, through farmland and scattered small towns until they'd reached this dense stand of woods. For the last ten minutes, the road had wound gently upward until they'd stopped by a narrow driveway that led off to the right. Two short stakes held a metal chain across the weedy track, a small rusty padlock hanging on the left end. Officer John Washington watched as Marconi, who was driving the pickup in front of them, got out and looked around before nodding quickly and getting back into his truck. Instead of Marconi opening the padlock as he'd expected, John watched as the driver beside him reached up and pushed what looked like a garage door opener. Immediately, the stakes folded down flat, and the two trucks drove over them easily.

"Slick," John said, nodding to the driver whose name he still wasn't sure of.

"Get a load of this." The driver gestured ahead of them with his chin, and John watched as the door on a decrepit-looking garage began to rise. He would have guessed that the rundown structure didn't even have electricity, but apparently, that was the point. As the door slid up, he could see that a second door on the back of the building was also going up. The two vehicles pulled into and then through the garage before emerging onto a smooth, blacktop drive that led further into the woods. John looked at the side mirror and caught sight of the doors sliding back into place before trees surrounded them once again.

"Unbelievable!" He congratulated the driver but, inside, fear stirred to life. If this assignment went south and they took him out, it would be years before anyone found his body—if they ever did.

"Militias can be crazy," the captain had warned him when they'd talked about the possibility of him going undercover. "Are you sure you're ready to take this on, Washington? No one's pushing you to do it." The man was right; no one had pushed him into it. At least not out loud.

About a month ago, John had been in the break room at the precinct when Police Corporal Wade Marconi first approached him. He'd had only a few encounters with Marconi before that, straightforward conversations about shifts and duty assignments. So, Washington was surprised when two patrol officers, a white woman, and a black man, stepped out of the break room and Marconi leaned over and whispered, "Fucking shame, isn't it?"

"Huh?" had been his reaction, unsure what the older man had meant.

Once they had the break room to themselves, Marconi had spoken more freely. "We got blacks and women patrolling our streets now? It makes me sick, I tell you. When my dad was on the force, nothing like that would ever have gone on."

"Really?" John had mumbled, not sure how to meet such a casually racist and sexist comment. He didn't think he'd spoken two words to the corporal before then. Marconi was a belligerent sort of man with a crewcut, athletic build, fading tattoos on his forearms, and a military bearing despite his age.

"Not for long now, though." Marconi touched his hand to his sidearm and leaned forward. "Come Halloween, we'll be setting the record straight. Just wanted to give you a heads up is all."

John still had no idea what to say and was relieved when another pair of cops came in looking for coffee. Marconi had given him a quick wink before leaving the room. That's when John had gone to the captain and found out about the task force working to gather information on the local and state militias that were rapidly multiplying.

"Do you think you could work your way in?" The captain had asked.

"I'm not sure." Washington had admitted to the captain with a bit of embarrassment.

It had taken every bit of nerve that he had to pretend to blend in and join Marconi's group. Now, as they drove deeper and deeper into the woods, Halloween was just over three weeks away, and more than one clock seemed to be ticking.

"So, what's your favorite thing about kindergarten, Far?" Audrey and Far were walking up the steep front steps to Rod's house. It was the final day of moving for Audrey, and Rod had 'hired' his young nephew to help while his moms went to the doctor for Gina's first ultrasound. She was five months pregnant, and they were hoping that in addition to a good health report, they'd also learn the baby's sex.

Far's voice was a little muffled by the bed pillows he was carrying, but he called out a quick "Art".

"That was fast. You made a friend named Art?"

Far laughed. "No, silly. My friends are Talia and Peter. Art is a *class*, not a person."

"Oh, I get it. What makes you like it so much?"

He was using his butt to hold the front door for Audrey while she carried in a wide box filled with computer components. "I like Mrs. T a lot, but I really like the stuff she has us do. It's not the baby stuff we did in preschool, like making things out of string and cardboard. Mrs. T shows us *real* art like paintings and statues, and we get to use real paint and clay. I told her I like to draw, and she said that an artist should always have a sketchpad so that they can draw whatever they want."

"That's awesome. So, did you get one?"

"Yep, Memma got it for me. Want to see it?"

"Yeah, I'd like to, but let's finish bringing these things in from the truck first. I borrowed it from my friend Oscar, and I have to get it back to him."

Rod walked into the living room then and smooshed Far's face between the two pillows. "Who's this minion you've got helping here anyway?"

Far giggled again, and Audrey looked at Rod. With a mock serious tone, she said, "I'll have you know, Mr. Franklin Avery Rodriguez is an excellent mover-inner."

Audrey watched as Rod picked up his young nephew and swung him in a circle before setting him down. At six, Far was a wiry little bundle of energy and she was reminded again how much Far looked like his uncle. Rod was nearly six feet tall with a similar slim, athletic build and with the same honey-colored skin, short dark hair, and warm brown eyes. They made a handsome pair. "Glad to hear it, buddy. You're earning your money today, huh?"

Far set the pillows on the couch and then jumped to sit on top of them. "Are you paying me in real money, Uncle Rod?"

"Of course, I am. What makes you ask?"

"Well, I know Mama G had a doctor's appointment today, and they didn't want me going along, so I thought you were just pretending." He dropped his arms down in his lap. "Is something wrong? She's been pretty tired lately."

Rod crouched down in front of the boy and rested his hands on Far's knees. "Buddy, I don't think there's anything wrong. It's just a checkup. It's normal for mommies to get tired when they're carrying a baby." Rod stood then and pulled Far to his feet. "Okay, who's ready for a snack break?"

"Me, me!" Far jumped up and down.

"I'll be with you in a moment, once I set this box down upstairs." Audrey headed up the stairs and maneuvered the box into the bedroom on the left. She loved watching Rod interact with his nephew, but the box hadn't gotten any lighter as she'd been standing there listening.

When Rod had asked her to move in with him, Audrey had been a little nervous, but, for the most part, she'd been happy to agree. After she'd experienced the double trauma of being beaten and dragged from her apartment and then later having to testify against her attacker in court, panic attacks had begun making it more and more difficult to feel comfortable in her old apartment. Rod had bought his house up on the hill in the Brookline neighborhood of Pittsburgh years ago, and, although he had completed most of the remodeling that was needed on the first floor, he hadn't gotten around to the upstairs yet. So, Audrey and Rod had used the time that was left on her lease to prepare one of the upstairs bedrooms for her to use as an office. Audrey's wedding photography business required space for cameras and equipment, as well as a complete computer setup.

At the moment, the room was a mess, but all the things she needed were finally in the same place. She caught sight of herself in the narrow mirror on the wall and paused to pull some packing material out of her straight dark hair. She tried to fluff it up a little bit, but the fact was that in her messy T-shirt and fraying jeans, she looked like she'd been moving all day. She was never very fussy about her appearance, so she didn't pay too much attention to it now. She did notice that the room still smelled a bit of paint, though, so she opened the windows a crack before heading downstairs. She spotted Far spinning happily on one of the stools next to the kitchen counter while Rod poked around in a cabinet, so she headed back out to Oscar's truck. Happily, there wasn't much left to bring in. There were two lightweight bags of linens that she slung over either shoulder before pulling out the last of the boxes. She shut the door with her hip and then headed back up the steep set of steps, pausing at the top to look around for a moment. She loved the look of Rod's neighborhood, now her neighborhood, too. Mature trees turning red and gold filled in between the tiers of houses on the hillside. Like many others, Rod's house was a two-story mixture of brick and siding. It sat on the top tier, which meant steep steps in front but a nice, flat yard in the back. With both a front porch and a back porch, Audrey knew she was going to love the change from apartment living.

When she got to the front door, she called in through the screen, and Far came running to open it for her. "Thank you, kind sir." She sang to Far, and the little boy began to giggle once more. Audrey quickly dropped the bags and box in the bedroom and went out to join Rod in the kitchen. She plopped down on the stool next to Far and swiveled it slightly back and forth. "Okay, I am officially done moving in. Everything's a mess, of course, but . . ." She shrugged and turned to Far. "Can I see your art now?"

"Oh, yeah!" He gave a surprisingly deep yell and ran to the living room.

Half an hour later, the three of them were still in the living room when the two women returned. Rod's sister, Emma, a long-haired beauty who looked surprisingly like her brother, was holding a short stack of pizza boxes. She gave him a one-armed hug while Gina, fair-haired and sporting a volleyball-sized middle, got one from Far, before they swapped places and began moving into the kitchen. "What can I get everyone to drink?" Rod asked, and a deep male voice called out in answer.

"I'll have a margarita if you're pouring!" Oscar Wilder-Jones was standing at the front door peering in, a wide grin on his face.

"Oscar, come on in!" Audrey moved quickly to open the door for him. Audrey's childhood friend Sandy and her husband Oscar had experienced a year just as traumatic as Audrey's when their infant Rosey had been kidnapped. Within a few days, Rod and his partner Smitty had successfully located the infant, but her disappearance and the subsequent death of her daycare worker had left them reeling. Given all of that, Audrey was especially glad to see the big smile on his face now.

Oscar stepped into the room. "I was over this way on a job, so I had a buddy drop me off."

Audrey protested, "I was going to drop your truck off later. You didn't have to come and get it."

"It's no sweat." Oscar gave Audrey a gentle squeeze on the shoulder.

"Well, I don't have any margaritas, but how about a beer and some pizza?" Rod moved forward, smiling and stretching out his hand to clasp Oscar's.

"Nah, that's okay. I just wanted to say a quick hello. How's everyone doing?" He shook hands and then turned to Audrey. "You get everything moved?"

"Yep, I'm good. I appreciate you letting me use your truck today while Rod's is in the shop. How are Sandy and the girls?"

"Good, they're all good. Rosey and Martha are looking a lot more alike now that Rosey's past the colic and eating up a storm. They're both scooting all over the place, too. It's bedlam, but we love it." He glanced over at Gina then. "You're not having twins, are you?"

"Are we?" Popped up Far.

Gina and Emma laughed. "No, buddy, I'm sorry but it's just one." Gina stroked her rounded belly before leaning down to Far's level. "We did find out one thing, though."

"What?" he asked.

"You're going to have a little sister. What do you think about that?"

Rod moved quickly to scoop Gina into a hug before turning to give Emma one as well. "One of each, huh, Sis? That's terrific!"

Audrey watched Far's face but couldn't decipher what the little boy was thinking. He looked around at the adults scattered about the room before turning back to face Gina. "I guess that's okay. First, I wanted a dog and then I wanted a baby brother, but I guess a sister will be okay." He shrugged, and Gina pulled him into a warm hug.

"I like how honest you are," Rod added. "It's a lot of change, I know, but I can promise you this: having a sister can be awesome!" Emma laughed and accepted another hug from her brother before gathering them all around the table to eat. Audrey saw Oscar to the door before joining them.

It wasn't long before the group had polished off the pizza, and Far and his mothers were ready to go. Rod opened his wallet and extracted a ten-dollar bill, which he presented to Far as they were packing up. "You worked hard, little buddy. I'm glad we had your help today!"

"And your company!" Audrey added. The little boy beamed and made a point of holding the door until all three of them were through it. "Thank you, Uncle Rod. See you later!" he called.

It wasn't until she and Rod were cleaning up the kitchen that Audrey spotted Far's sketch pad at the end of the counter. "Oh no, look, Rod. He forgot it."

Rod picked it up and flipped through the first few pages before looking up at Audrey. "Am I just a besotted uncle or are these pretty good? You can really tell that these are dogs he's been drawing, and that one even looks like Simple Simon to me."

"I think you're right. I don't know much about kids' developmental stages, but I certainly don't think many kindergarteners draw that well. Plus, it looks like Simon but not like any of the photographs you have of him. If he's drawing him from memory, that's even more impressive. Do you think we should drive it over to him tonight?"

"I don't know. I'll check with Emma." He sent a quick text and then started the dishwasher, while Audrey went into the bedroom to begin sorting enough of her belongings to clear the bed. She had just finished folding some clothes into an empty drawer when she heard Rod call from the other room. She hadn't heard exactly what he'd said, so she moved back into the living room. She was surprised to see him holding two champagne flutes.

"What's this?" She laughed.

"Emma says Far has another pad, so instead of driving across the city, I thought we'd celebrate a little here!"

While he held his arms wide, a glass in each hand, Audrey clasped her arms around him and reached up on tiptoes for a kiss. Then, she stepped back and accepted a glass. "To us!" She toasted, and Rod echoed her.

"To us and many, many more nights together after this." Audrey beamed and, after they'd both taken a sip, they joined hands, turned out the last light, and headed to the bedroom, champagne bottle in hand.

"Hey! Banana bike! Get the hell out of here!"

Jerry raised his eyes from his phone and turned at the sound of the harsh voice. He'd been leaning against a brick wall while he waited for his friend Carlo. His sort-of girlfriend was texting some new rant about school, and he was glad to be distracted from it. When he looked up, though, he realized that it had gotten a lot darker. It surprised him that the man had seen him at all until he noticed the way the yellow bike seemed to glow against the dark wall.

A squat, greasy, tattooed man with a disturbing bulge at his waistband was standing by a big, open garage bay and smoking a cigarette. Jerry thought about yelling back at him, but before he could, a bike tire squealed to a sudden stop beside him. He snorted, "'bout time," as Carlo came up beside him. Out of the corner of his eye, Jerry spotted the greaser guy gesturing at them to move, and he quickly pocketed his phone. "C'mon, let's get out of here before that guy has a coronary. What are we meeting here for anyway?"

Jerry and Carlo peddled down the middle of the narrow alley, dodging around the scattered trash and leaves that filled the rutted sections of pavement. "I was just dropping off something for my mom at Bishops . . ." Carlo was interrupted by the appearance of a dark, heavy-duty truck looming toward them. The truck, with its top coated in exhaust soot and a headlamp held in place with strips of black tape, filled the narrow section of the road.

The boys peeled apart, nearly scraping against the walls on either side of the alley as the truck grunted past. The night turned two shades darker once it was alongside them, and Jerry paused to watch the taillights as it turned into the garage bay that the guy had been guarding. Curiosity overcame his natural timidity, and he turned to follow in the truck's path.

"Where are you going?" Carlo asked, but Jerry hissed back at him.

"Quiet. I want to see what's in the truck."

"Are you kidding?" Carlo followed but kept his voice quiet. "It's probably just something boring like plumbing parts. Why would you care?"

Jerry pulled up against the wall where he'd first been standing, and he motioned Carlo back into the shadows behind him. He whispered, "With a guard on the door? I don't think so."

As the truck pulled into the bay, the room filled with light, and the guard was met by an older, heavier man who drew a thick wad of keys from a loop on his belt. He flicked through the assortment before selecting one and using it to remove a padlock from the back of the truck. As the truck's rear door lifted with a lumbering grind, the fat man gestured at the guard to close the bay door.

At the same moment that Jerry's mouth dropped open at the sight of the truck's cargo, the guard spotted the two boys and drew the gun from his waistband. A shot blasted the wall just to the left of Jerry's head before both boys leapt onto their bikes and began tearing away, standing on the pedals to gain as much speed as they could. The sound of another shot filled the air, and Jerry felt a sting in his left foot, but they continued to fly and were soon around the corner and racing down a wider street.

They heard nothing more but continued to pedal hard until they found themselves in front of a small market. It was still open, its light pouring onto the sidewalk. Gasping for air, they leaned their bikes against the front display window and sank to the concrete. "What the hell was that, Jerry?" Carlo demanded once he had enough breath to talk.

"Jesus, I'm not even sure. Did you see what was in that truck? It looked like a body!"

"I don't give a shit about that truck. He shot at us." Carlo paused, then pointed at Jerry's shoe. "He shot you!"

"What?" Jerry followed Carlo's finger until he spotted the pool of blood forming under his foot. Then he turned away. Air and circulation were returning after their mad ride, and suddenly his foot felt as though it was on fire. "Oh my God." He leaned forward and began untying his shoe, but Carlo grabbed his forearm.

"No, remember that movie with the train? His foot got hurt really bad, but the guy told him not to take off his boot. He wrapped his whole foot and boot up with tape."

"But we're not busy trying to stop a train." Jerry leaned forward again, but Carlo was already pulling a roll of tape out of his backpack. Jerry looked up, puzzled. "You carry duct tape in your school backpack?"

"Nah, man. I told you, I was dropping an old lazy Susan off for my mom at Bishops. I thought I might have to tape it to the back of my bike, but after I emptied my pack, I was able to stick it inside."

Jerry laughed, in spite of the pain. "Are you kidding me? Why didn't she just drive it over in her car?"

"Who knows? Whenever my dad leaves on a deployment, she starts to get these crazy ideas about what I might get into, like I'm some kind of drug-king wannabe. So, she comes up with these ridiculous tasks for me to do that she thinks will fill up my time and keep me out of trouble." Carlo dug around in his backpack until he found an empty plastic bag. He shrugged his shoulders and then returned to the job. "Ok, I'm going to put this all around your foot and then tape the whole mess together tight."

"Oh, jeez. It's really starting to hurt."

"Can you call someone to come and get us, get you, I mean, and take you a hospital? I forgot my phone at home."

Jerry pulled out his phone, wincing as Carlo began tightening the tape. He looked through his contacts, and then sank back, unsure who to call in the middle of such a bizarre situation. He wanted his mom, of course, but she was gone until late that night, busy with some work deal that Jerry couldn't remember. Confusion seemed to be creeping into his brain as he forced himself to focus on the list once again. He was scrolling to his dad's number when his finger slipped and started dialing his older brother instead. His head felt fuzzy as he waited for the call to connect. Just before he was going to hang up and try for his dad, he heard a quick "What?"

"Joe, it's me. You're not going to believe this."

Jerry felt himself falling onto his side and lost his grip on the phone. He thought he saw Carlo pick it up, but soon everything was as black as the stupid night.

Keller couldn't believe how many times Bo had waddled out from the office to check and see whether or not the truck had come. "Nothing yet?" The man squeaked out, his high, pinched voice contrasting sharply with his heavy stature.

"Nah," Keller pulled at the cigarette in his mouth and resumed looking out the garage bay. He was getting sick of watching that idiot kid across the street. How long could someone stare at their phone without turning into a complete moron? It didn't look as though he was paying attention to anything else, but with the truck due there any minute, Keller felt he had to get the kid out of there. "Hey! Banana bike! Get the hell out of here!" He watched as the teen looked up briefly before returning to his phone.

He was about to yell again when the kid was met by another teenager on a bike, and the two of them turned and rode away. Keller was turning toward the back of the garage when he thought he heard the first rumblings of a truck. It was a piece of shit truck that they'd been using forever and, now with its muffler nearly gone, it could be heard from quite a way off. Bo came out again, and the two of them stood watching while the truck maneuvered its way through the doors. The silence when it was shut off was shocking.

The driver, a man named Marconi, had left with a quick nod after talking with Bo and handing over what looked like some kind of medical supplies. Then Bo pulled out his ring of keys and began flipping through them. Finally, he settled on one and inserted it into the thick padlock on the truck's back door. It turned easily, and Keller helped him shove the door up. There were boxes everywhere, the neat stacks having shifted in transit, but on the floor in the back lay a form, the hands and legs tied with a dirty nylon cord, the head covered in a flowered sack like someone would take to a market. As Bo stepped back toward the cab, Keller went toward the bay doors to close them and caught sight of the teenagers pressed against the nearby wall, watching. Without thinking, Keller pulled out his gun and fired. They were on their bikes in an instant and, although the first shot had missed, he thought he might have clipped one of them with the second.

"What the fuck are you doing, you idiot? You're firing a gun in the city? Do you know what could happen?"

"But they saw the truck." Keller pointed toward the wrapped form. "They saw that!"

"Right, and if you hadn't shot your gun at them, they'd have taken off and told a story that no one believed. Now, people have heard you. You didn't hit either of them, did you?"

Keller couldn't be sure if his second shot had connected with one of the kids or not, so he shrugged, hoping to deflect Bo's question. Instead, the man grabbed him by his shirt front and shoved him against the wall. "What? I don't know if I hit them or not. Maybe."

"Maybe, my ass, get out of here. Get your truck and go after them. Find out for sure. Jesus, the number of fucknuts in this organization is unbelievable."

Keller thought that he heard a groan coming from the form in the back of the truck, but he didn't stop to check on it. Instead, he pulled his keys from his pocket and left through the side door. His pickup was parked nearby, and he moved off quickly. He had to guess which way the boys had gone, and after wandering around for a block or two, it dawned on him how impossible it would be to find them. They could have ridden off anywhere. He moved slowly down one street, turned, and then tried another. He began moving in a kind of grid out away from the garage but couldn't see any sign of the kids, especially in the growing darkness. After what felt like forever, he spotted a convenience store and pulled up along the curb in some deep shadows beneath a broken streetlight. He sat quietly watching for a moment before getting out and going into the store. He figured he could try and calm Bo down by bringing him a case. God knew a six-pack wouldn't be enough. As he stepped up over the curb, his eye caught on a dark stain that spread along the sidewalk. Then he noticed that bicycle tire marks cut right through it. A faint trail led off away from the store, so he quickly got back into his truck and pulled out onto the street.

It was growing darker, and in this part of town, more streetlights seemed to be out than lit, but as he moved forward slowly, a flash of yellow flared and then disappeared before flashing again when a motion detector light clicked on. Someone was walking a couple of bikes, one of them bright yellow. "Gotcha, you little shit." Keller pulled ahead of the kid and then thrust his truck toward the far curb, trapping the boy and the bikes. He jumped out of the cab and lunged, knocking him forward so that the boy collapsed into the tangle of bikes. As the kid scrambled to get up, Keller used the butt of his gun to knock him in the head. With him unconscious, it was easy to throw the kid and the bikes in the bed of the pickup truck. He didn't think the kid would come around too quickly, but he didn't want to take any chances. He noticed a roll of tape looped on the kid's arm, so Keller ripped off a strip and slapped it across his mouth before using some more to secure his hands and feet. Tossing a tarp over the kid and bikes, he made a turn and headed back to the garage. Bo would be impressed, he felt sure.

A leaf caught in an air current twisted lazily before continuing its slow descent. Audrey stood watching, her camera held loosely in her hand as she waited for the bride-to-be to set down her phone. They were half an hour into the planned engagement photo shoot, but Sylvia's fiancé had yet to appear. Audrey had taken several pictures of the young woman leaning against the wooden railing, her long, blonde hair artfully arranged over her left shoulder. It was beautiful out, the autumn leaves making a stunning backdrop, but time was slipping by, and Audrey needed to wrap things up.

"Sylvia, I think we'll need to reschedule."

The young woman pocketed her phone and walked up. "I'm so sorry, Audrey. I have no idea what's going on. When I talked with John yesterday, everything was all set for today. Now he's saying he can't get away from work. Is it going to be hard to reschedule?"

Audrey tucked the camera away in her bag and collected her other gear as she thought about the coming month. Her biggest wedding job yet was coming up that weekend. After setting her stuff down on a nearby bench, she pulled out her phone and checked her calendar. To make ends meet as her photography business grew, she continued to work as a photographer for Pittsburgh's police department. Her shifts with the police department generally took up two or three days a week, so there wasn't a ton of availability left. She looked up at the frustrated young woman. "Could you do Thursday morning? I have no idea what the weather will be like, so I can't promise that we'll be able to come back here, but that's about all I've got for now."

Sylvia retrieved her own phone and scrolled through it for a moment before looking up. "Okay, I can do it then. I'll get in touch with John and make sure that he's free, too. I'll get back to you as soon as I can. Is that okay? I'm sorry this happened." She looked around at the dazzling autumn colors and the beautiful late afternoon light. "It would have been perfect, I know."

Audrey tried to smile reassuringly, knowing that Sylvia was right about the missed opportunity. "It'll be okay. If the weather's not nice, we'll find some other gorgeous spot to take the pictures." They moved toward their cars, and Audrey took her time stowing her gear as Sylvia pulled away. Audrey worked hard not to show her frustration, but on the inside, she was pissed. The photo shoot had been planned at one of the city parks, but not one that was near Audrey and Rod's place. In order to manage all her gear and a few props, she'd gone to the expense of renting a car to get there. She'd charge some part of the fee for the missed session, but her conscience wouldn't let it be too much, probably not even enough to cover the cost of the rental.

She climbed into the unfamiliar vehicle and made her way back through traffic to drop off her stuff before returning the car. Now that she was living way out in Brookline, she was going to have to break down and buy a car. It was time to sit down and have that talk with Rod about finances, to make some sort of formal plan for sharing expenses. He'd put her off every time she'd brought it up before, but it couldn't wait any longer.

Smitty threw himself into his chair, startling his partner, Rod, at the next desk. He looked up, surprised at the level of anger in Smitty's voice.

"Has Washington always been an asshole?"

"What, who?"

"John Washington, tall, skinny, white guy, light brown hair?"

Rod's partner in the homicide division, Demetrius Smith, was usually a pretty even-tempered guy, so the outburst took Rod by surprise. "I haven't talked to him much, but I have no reason to have a bad opinion of him. Why? What'd he do?"

"I was in the break room getting some coffee, and, while I was stirring some sugar into my cup, he made this whole show of emptying out the pot and washing it before starting a new one."

"Geez, I wish more people'd start a new pot, much less wash out a carafe. I mean usually people just leave the dregs for . . ."

"No man, it wasn't like that." Smitty slammed his hands down on the arms of his chair. "There was half a pot left. This was deliberate. The pot was hot. So, what he was making a show of was washing the handle that I'd just used. That bastard Marconi was at a table laughing about it."

"Well, shit. You know that guy's an asshole. I'm sorry, man." Rod turned toward his friend, not sure what else there was to say in the face of that kind of treatment. As an African American man on the force, Smitty had always come up against barriers, some obvious, others less so, but somehow, he'd managed to hang in there despite it all. With his Hispanic background, Rod had faced some issues, of course, but the burden that Smitty bore each day was on a whole other level.

"I tell you, there are more days than not that I wonder what the hell I'm doing working here."

"Don't say that, Smitty. I'd be nowhere without you. We're a team. C'mon. Let's get out of here. We can grab a bite to eat."

"All right, but this isn't over between him and me. Just so you know."

It killed John Washington to overhear the conversation between the two men. He'd left the break room not long after the embarrassment with the coffee pot. Marconi had headed for home, and John finally felt as though he had a minute to himself. He felt filthy every time he had to deal with Marconi. And now, hearing how angry the detective was, he felt even more like shit. Once the two detectives left, he checked the hallway and then slid into the captain's office.

"I fucking hate this duty, Captain. I really do."

The captain leaned back in his chair, rubbing his hand along his smooth head. "What happened?"

"I just made an asshole of myself insulting Detective Smith for Marconi's benefit. Here the man was shot in a raid that netted us three murderers and then, while recovering, he helped locate a kidnapped infant. The man's a fucking role model." He tapped his chest. "He's a role model to me, and I just insulted the shit out of him."

The captain lowered his chair back to the floor and leaned toward the young officer. "Listen, if you want out of this undercover job, just say the word and you're out. Last month Butler had one of its undercover officers go missing. This is a nasty, dangerous group, and I'm guessing Marconi isn't even the worst of them."

John lowered his face into his hands and thought about what was at stake in the job he'd agreed to take on. He felt his spirits sag but forced himself to sit back up and face whatever was coming his way. He squared his shoulders before addressing the captain again. "I'm sorry for coming in here complaining, Captain. What do we know about the guy who's missing? Anything? Should I be looking for him?"

As he climbed into his car an hour later, John caught sight of the string of texts that Sylvia had sent after he missed the photo shoot. It had been hell trying to figure out shifts that would allow him to overlap with Marconi but also provide opportunities to update the captain. He checked his schedule before texting her back. '*I'm sorry again for messing up today. Thursday morning is fine. I'll meet you there.*' He was about to set the phone down when a bit of the fear he'd been swallowing reared its head once again. As a failsafe measure, he texted one more message. '*If I miss Thursday's appointment, please ask Audrey to contact Rod and the captain.*' Then he headed home for a quick shower before he had to 'train' with the assholes once again.

In the two weeks he'd been training with the Brotherhood, as they liked to call themselves, John Washington had come to know the camp well. The paved drive behind the old garage took them more than two miles into the deepest part of the woods before stopping at a perimeter marked with a seven-foot fence. It was constructed of a flimsy-looking wire mesh, but Marconi bragged it had 10,000 volts running through it, almost twice what you'd need for cattle. The way into the camp was through a fortified gate that someone manned whenever they were actively training. A closed-circuit video surveillance system took over when they were not there.

The camp was off the grid and included one long, low building that was powered by a gas generator that hummed constantly in the background. A set of outhouses was located on the far edge. In constructing the camp, Marconi had explained, they'd planned on having a solar array, but it hadn't proved feasible once they decided to maintain as much of the upper tree canopy as they could in order to hide from possible aerial views. John had heard a few of the younger members complaining about having to haul gas back and forth, but otherwise, little was said about the logistics of keeping the place going. Between the front fence and the building, an obstacle course had been set up. Marconi had taken John and two other young men through it a few times, but with so few of the 'brothers' having any level of physical fitness, it got much less use than the gun range.

Although he was well trained in gun use by the police department, it was the gun range here that disturbed John more than the rest. Part of it held the traditional paper silhouettes on a pulley system for practicing at a variety of distances. Rather than targets or featureless outlines, however, these sheets had been altered to feature African American men, women, and children, women in headscarves, as well as a variety of same-sex couples. All of the Brotherhood's hatred was literally on display in their gun range. There was another area that had been made to look like an urban street with some junked cars and false walls that had been painted in racist, sexist, and homophobic graffiti that was so graphic it made him sick to his stomach. When they weren't inside the building drinking and spewing anti-government rants, this was where the bastards hung out.

On the surface, they didn't seem like a very formidable group, but when he'd taken a moment to sneak a look at a closed-off section of the building, John had seen a weapons stash that could have supplied an army fifty times their size.

"Pretty impressive," Marconi slapped him unexpectedly on the back. "Don't you think? We've got a local guy, a businessman, helping us bring them in."

John was so startled to be found snooping around the building that he briefly hesitated before grinning back at Marconi and rubbing his hands together in anticipation. "Do these guys know how to use weapons like that?"

Marconi pulled the door closed behind them and gestured John toward the backdoor. "Aw, those automatics do all the work. They don't need to know much more than how to load and pull the trigger. They've got that part down pat."

Marconi gave John another look, and John swallowed hard, worried that he might have given something away. But if his cover had been blown, he figured he might as well ask the questions he wanted answered now and pray that there would be some way to get the word back to the station. "So, you mentioned Halloween. That's coming up soon. Is there a plan that we're going to be working on? I noticed the chairs were arranged like a classroom when I came through the front room this morning."

"Yep, in about fifteen minutes, Bo's gonna help me walk everyone through it. You'll want to be sure and get yourself a good seat." He nodded once more at John before walking back around toward the front of the building.

"You bet," John called after him and turned toward the outhouses in the back. A moment to himself, that's all he wanted. The fear had begun bubbling up inside him again, and he needed to get a grip before he made any more mistakes. Once inside the rough, wooden building, a narrow rectangle cut into the upper back wall allowed a bit of light to enter the small area. Having seen the sort of routine, electronic sweeps they did at the camp entrance, John had argued hard against trying to bring any sort of phone or electronic tracker into the camp with him. Instead, Rita Banks, their genius tech guru, had fitted him with a small, voice-activated lapel-style video camera. In the dim light, he took a moment to check the components. The battery life looked good, and it indicated that the memory card still had plenty of space on it. He hoped that if Marconi or one of the others did get to him, the tiny setup might survive and provide clues that other, more capable officers could follow. He heard someone holler out to the men, so he made one more check that the unit was on and in place, squared his shoulders, and tried to force the fear back down inside. "Please God, don't let me fuck this up," he whispered before stepping out and joining the others as they traipsed inside the building.

Forty-five minutes later, when Marconi and Bo finished their presentation. John was shocked by what he'd heard, but the fact that he'd been allowed to hear it led him to believe that perhaps Marconi didn't suspect him after all. Around him, the men in the room began shifting chairs and breaking into twos and threes, discussing their small group assignments. John was about to get up and join the nearest group when he spotted Marconi and Bo moving toward him. His gut clenched, but he forced his breath out slowly, trying to maintain a calm appearance.

"So, what'd you think?" Bo asked. John still hadn't learned much about this lumbering, heavy-set retired steel worker. Someone had said he was part owner of some sort of Pittsburgh garage that the group used, but, other than that, John'd gotten few details. The men approached, and Marconi spun two chairs around so that they faced John, Marconi on one side, Bo on the other. John tried not to panic as his gaze shifted back and forth between the two men. "You know we're going to be counting on you and Marconi here to back us up. We're committed supporters of the police, and we expect them to have our backs in this." Bo paused. "They don't? There'll be hell to pay. You know what I mean?"

Inside, John thought, hell no. This was the part he understood the least. How could they constantly talk a big game about being on the side of law and order, while at the same time planning to shatter every bit of it? Instead, he just nodded. "I'm in Bo, shouldn't be any trouble to get the shift arranged so that I'm available."

Marconi nodded then, but the look that crossed his face made John shudder inside. "Got the captain in your pocket, do you? Get any shift you want arranged? Is that right?"

"What? No. I just meant . . ." Before he could finish his sentence, two fists shot forward in rapid succession, one straight at his gut and the other alongside his head. The double blow knocked him backward into the chairs behind him. The air he needed left his lungs completely, and he tried desperately to pull more in before the chairs collapsed beneath him. Then, his head hit the concrete floor, and he was out.

"Jesus, you moron. Why would you do that?" Bo shoved Marconi in the shoulder as he struggled to stand back up. "He's a cop for fuck's sake."

"I know that, the fuck you think I hit him for? You didn't see him looking at the armory earlier. He's a plant, I tell you, and we don't want him reporting back on what we're doing!"

"Then why the hell not take him out before the damn presentation? I thought you were one of the brains in this outfit. Now it turns out you're as dumb as the rest."

"Bo, I swear . . ." Marconi looked around then and spotted the crowd of men watching them. Instead of lashing out at Bo, he turned instead to two young men he'd been training earlier. "Get him tied up. Use something strong and get a bag over his head so that we can transport him somewhere." The young men moved to either side of the body and began dragging Washington from the room, his heels scraping and bumping on the rough floor.

"Uh, I've got some nylon rope in my car, but I don't have a bag. You mean like a plastic bag from the store?" The young man, seventeen at most, Marconi thought, looked a little green.

"Not a fucking plastic bag. He's a cop from my precinct for God's sake. We're not planning to murder him."

Marconi looked from the young men back to Bo who lifted an eyebrow before turning away. "I've got a bag on the front seat of my car," Bo called out. "Get him tied up and bagged and then finish loading the truck."

The pair left the room, and Marconi turned to the remaining observers. "You've all got jobs to do, so get to it. The truck that's going to haul the weapons into the city is here, so get it sorted out. Remember, what we said. Small stuff goes in your own vehicles, larger stuff in the truck." The group scattered to their various tasks, and Marconi sunk into a nearby chair. Once the room was cleared, he dropped his head into his hands and swore softly. What the fuck was he going to do with Washington? Had he overreacted? Was it possible the man didn't know anything, and they'd just lost one of their few able-bodied members? When he'd walked up behind Washington looking at the weapons cache, he'd just intended the slap as a joke. But the look that flashed on the man's face had signaled trouble. Right or wrong, Marconi thought, he'd done what he'd done, and it was time to move on.

Marconi sat up straight and looked Bo directly in the face. "We are not murdering another cop. That's final. Especially not one from my precinct. People saw us talking together. I'd be implicated immediately. We just need to hold onto him until after our demonstration on Halloween. You've got space above your garage in the city, right? Keep him there and, in the meantime, I'll work out a plausible story to explain his absence from work. It's only for a few days after all."

"All right. I hear you. Once they've got him tied up good, have them put him in the back of the truck. Keller can keep an eye on him at the garage, but you have to figure something out. I'm not taking the fall for this, and I'm not letting it interfere with our plans. Halloween is just the beginning. We've got a lot bigger plans for after that."

"Fair enough. I'll go see to the loading now. Once it's ready, I'll drive it to your place. You've got to have my car ready, though. I need to turn around and get back out to Ellerby's before Friday noon."

"We're set. We're just leaving a few out here at the camp to cover it for the weekend." Bo turned and began heading toward the door. Marconi wasn't sure if he'd heard correctly or not, but it sounded like Bo had finished by adding "Let's hope some other moron doesn't fuck up."

When Jerry woke up, he was being pulled into the back seat of his brother's car. He lifted his head and turned to see Joe at one door, Carlo at the other. "You're awake!" Carlo grinned down at him while holding up his injured foot as Joe pulled him into the car by his armpits.

"Ow, that hurts so much!" Jerry growled at his brother.

"Don't get mad at me. I just came to help. C'mon, we're heading to the hospital. It isn't far from here."

"But my bike! I can't just leave it here. Can't you fit it in the back or something?"

"No way, I don't want that disgusting thing in the back of my car. In fact, you better not be getting any blood in there either."

Carlo leaned in before closing the passenger door. "I've got it, Jerry. I'll walk them both back to my place, and you can pick it up later."

Jerry nodded with relief and then lay down on the back seat of his brother's car. It was the left foot that had been hit, so he held it off the seat, over the floor mat. Carlo had wrapped it up good, but Jerry wasn't sure if it was still bleeding or not.

When they arrived at the hospital, Joe pulled into the curved driveway that led to the emergency room door. He hopped out and came around to open the door by Jerry's feet. As he tried to ease him forward, an attendant in blue-green scrubs appeared with a wheelchair and helped Joe lift Jerry onto the seat. The man flipped up one leg rest and gently set Jerry's foot on it before releasing the brake on the chair. He turned to Joe as he began moving back toward the car. "Are you next of kin? Do you have insurance information for him?"

"I'm his brother, but I don't have that kind of stuff on me. Okay if I drive home to get it, see if my dad is home to come back with me?"

"No, park your car and come on in. He's a minor, and he needs someone with him. You'll have to contact your Dad by phone."

As the man began wheeling him to the door, Jerry watched as his brother pulled away. "I've got a picture ID from my school in my wallet if that helps. My mom works at the Art Institute, but I'm pretty sure our insurance is through my dad's work. He's a financial guy at First National Bank." Jerry offered as the doors whooshed open.

They made their way into the emergency department, and a tall woman dressed in maroon scrubs helped the attendant lift Jerry onto a rolling bed. A blood pressure cuff was wrapped around his arm, but before it finished filling with air, everything went blank again.

"Okay, okay. I've got you." A woman spoke kindly as Jerry's mind swam back to the surface. A pillow had been placed under his head, and an IV poked into the back of his hand. Jerry was pretty sure he didn't mind having missed all that. A small woman in a white coat, who looked a bit like his mom, was leaning over him speaking quietly. "You're going to be fine. You're experiencing some shock, so we've started an IV, and we're going to keep an eye on your blood pressure. Can you tell me what happened?"

Jerry noticed that she had brought out some weird scissors and was cutting through the bag and Carlo's tape, as well as the side of his shoe. She had a stack of gauze pads beside her and was dabbing at the blood as she worked. "My friend Carlo thought it was a good idea to wrap it all together. He saw it in that movie about the runaway train."

She smiled. "That was an excellent idea. I think you'd have lost a lot more blood if he hadn't thought to do it that way." Once everything was cleared away, she turned and looked at his face. "Were you shot?"

Suddenly, the fear that he'd felt when they were racing away came pouring back over him, and it felt as though he couldn't quite breathe. He ended up just nodding at her, unsure what to say about the strange circumstances that had led him here.

"All right. I'm going to make a call to the police right now. That's protocol. I have to do that for any gunshot injury. While we wait for them, though, we're going to get you to X-ray, so that we can get a better look at that foot." She padded the foot with additional gauze and then set it back down on the bed.

"I hope my dad gets here soon."

The woman smiled at Jerry again and directed a heavyset older woman in another set of blue-green scrubs to steer the bed down the hallway. "He'll probably be here by the time you get done. I'll see you in a few."

There was a long ride down one hallway and then another before the woman parked him by a door that said X-ray. Then there was a wait. Jerry wished he could have his phone, but it was in a bag somewhere under the bed where he couldn't reach. Without it, he closed his eyes and thought back over what had happened, trying to remind himself how everything had looked. It was a good distraction, but it didn't help that much with the pain. Finally, a tall, thin man in a black shirt brought him into a cool, dark room. He steered the bed back and forth underneath some machinery before finally setting the brake and looking Jerry in the eye. Without saying anything, he moved down to Jerry's foot and reached his hand under the heel, adjusting its placement, apparently lining it up with some sort of camera line. It hurt so much having it moved, but Jerry was embarrassed to say anything. Instead, he held his breath and tried to wait until the man set his foot back down. When the man ducked behind a glass partition and called out "Hold your breath," Jerry had already been holding his breath long enough that he felt like he was about to explode, but the procedure happened quickly, and the man emerged from the cubicle. "Breathe. Good work. I'm going to move the machine now and see if I can get a look from a different angle. Try not to move, let me move the foot for you."

Inside Jerry's head, he was screaming, 'Please don't touch it, please don't touch it,' but on the outside, he managed to stay quiet. It hurt like hell as the man lifted and turned the foot, and Jerry held his breath once again. The man stepped back into the glass room briefly before coming back out. "Okay, you're done." He opened the door. The same woman was there to push his bed back down the hallway. She had a sweet face and seemed friendlier than the X-ray guy, but Jerry didn't feel much like talking. He let his head sink into the pillow and tried to rest, hoping that his dad would be in the emergency room once he got back.

Just as the woman parked his bed along a wall, Jerry spotted his brother Joe standing nearby. He lifted his hand in a little wave, and Joe followed them, standing on one side of the bed as the woman pulled a curtain around on a track, shielding his view from the rest of the emergency department. Jerry couldn't quite decide whether it was better to be able to see all the scary stuff going on around him or to just hear it. There was a baby shrieking somewhere, as well as an old man who sounded like he was in horrible pain, his moans filling the cool air. Jerry still couldn't reach the plastic bag with his stuff, and he was about to ask Joe to hand it to him when the small woman doctor reappeared, pulling the curtain back slightly as she entered. He tried to sit up in order to speak to her.

"Here, let me." The doctor pushed something on the side of the bed, and it eased him up until he could see everyone around him. A deep male voice screamed out, "Where's my son?" Jerry looked up at the doctor.

"That'd be my dad."

The doctor stepped forward and held the curtain aside as Jerry's dad came barreling into the enclosure. He looked at Jerry propped up on the bed and immediately smacked Joe against the head. "Christ almighty, Joe, you could have told me it was his foot." He clasped his hand to his chest. "I think I'm having a heart attack."

"Sir, have a seat here." The doctor pulled a metal chair forward and ushered him into it. "I'm Dr. Singh, and I'd prefer to just have one emergency at a time here if we can help it." She paused for a moment as he caught his breath. "Okay, now that everyone's here, I'm just going to confer with a colleague of mine while we take a look at the X-ray." She touched Jerry's knee very lightly before turning to go. "I'll be right back. I promise."

The curtain was pulled closed behind her as she left, and Jerry turned to look at his dad. "Hi, Dad. Uh, thanks for coming."

"Son." DJ Kominski was a tall, athletically built man, but as he bent over to hug Jerry, the boy thought that his dad looked older than he remembered. It was a stupid idea since he'd seen him at breakfast that morning, but now there was something kind of tired-looking in his eyes, and it made Jerry feel bad. "How in the hell did you manage to get shot?"

"I'm so sorry, Dad. I never meant for anything like this to happen."

"What did happen?" Joe stood next to their dad, clearly as confused as ever about the whole situation.

"I was waiting for Carlo down on that alley near Bishops and . . ."

Just then a woman's voice said, "Knock, knock," before pulling back the edge of the curtain. "It sounds like someone is about to explain, and I thought I'd step in. I'm Officer Laura Katz." A surprisingly young-looking woman in uniform with red hair pulled back into a bun reached out to shake Jerry's hand before turning and reaching out to his father.

"I'm Jerry, Jerry Kominski. This is my dad DJ and my brother Joe."

"It's nice to meet you all, I'm just sorry about the circumstances."

"He was about to tell us what happened."

"Great! Now you'll only have to go through it once." She pulled a thin notebook from a back pocket and a pen from another. "Go for it, Ace."

"Well, it was just starting to get dark, and I was in the alley back behind Bishops repair shop waiting for my friend Carlo. I was messing around on my phone when this guy yelled at me. He was standing by the open door of a garage. It was a big one, like a really big door, not just for cars. I kind of ignored him, because I wasn't doing anything wrong, and he yelled at me again. He called me banana bike and told me to get out of there."

"Banana bike?" Officer Katz raised an eyebrow.

Jerry's brother Joe leapt in to comment. "The Dork has this neon yellow bike that he rides everywhere." Jerry's dad touched Joe's shoulder to quiet him and then nodded for Jerry to continue.

"I didn't say anything to the guy and Carlo showed up then, so we started to ride away. But we were still in the alley when a big old truck started coming toward us." He held his hands out wide. "It was like it filled up the whole street, so Carlo and I split apart and pressed ourselves against either side of the alley to stay out of the way. But it made me mad, plus, I was a little curious about why the guy had been guarding the garage and yelling at me. So, we followed it."

"Are you kidding me?" Jerry could see the horrified look on his dad's face, so he turned back to the officer without answering him.

"We were careful. It was getting even darker, so we kind of snuck up and leaned against the wall of another building. Sure enough, the truck pulled into that big bay and a big, heavy-set guy showed up with a huge set of keys. He undid some kind of lock and then pushed the truck's door up. When it was open, Carlo and I could see it was filled with a bunch of boxes, but there was also a body lying inside of the truck, not moving. I think maybe Carlo, or I, made some kind of sound because the first guy noticed us and pulled a gun out of his belt. There was a loud sound, and a piece of the brick wall broke just above my head. We jumped on our bikes and tore off, but he shot again and hit me in the foot. Carlo and I kept going, though, as hard as we could until we got to the little market on Butler St. and realized there wasn't anyone following us. That's when I called Joe, and Carlo taped up my foot."

"Wow, that's quite a story. I'm sorry that happened to you." She turned toward his father. "Mr. Kaminski, has anything like this ever happened before?"

"No, no, no. Never. Jerry's a good boy." Joe made a snorting sound, but his father continued. "You be quiet. Jerry isn't into anything bad. He likes to draw, and he likes to ride his bike, not much else."

The curtain pulled back once again, and the doctor reappeared. "I'm sorry to interrupt but we've come to a decision. Jerry, the bullet went all the way through, but the wound needs to be cleaned out thoroughly and a cracked bone needs to be addressed, so we'd like to go in and take care of that. Mr. Kaminski, we'll need your insurance information, as well as written permission to do the surgery. Jerry, we'll be using a local anesthetic, not a general one."

"Wait, I have to see it? That's gross!"

"No," she shook her head. "You'll be lying down, and there'll be a drape so that you don't see anything. It'll be okay, I promise." She rested her hand on his knee once more. "Mr. Kominski, one of our admins will be in to take care of the paperwork with you in just a few minutes."

"Here?"

"Yep, we try and make it as easy as we can. Jerry, I'll see you in a little while."

Officer Katz folded her notebook shut and reached into a shirt pocket to extract some business cards. She handed one to Jerry and another to his father. "I'm going to get going now; let you all get on with things. Jerry, my partner, and I are going to go and check out that garage but I'm also going to write up my notes and share them with some detectives in my department. I'm pretty sure they're going to want to talk with you some more about what you saw. You mentioned that you like to draw. Once you get home, if you feel up to it, maybe you can try and draw a little bit of what you saw, help us figure out what might be going on." She nodded goodbye and then stepped out.

It was fully dark when Keller returned to the garage with the boy and the bikes in his truck. The big bay doors were closed so he pulled up next to the side door and lowered the back gate on his pickup truck. He lifted the boy out and balanced him on his shoulder as he pulled open the door. He noticed that the door of the big truck was still open although the body had been moved.

"What's this?" Bo asked as Keller approached.

Keller grinned, proud of having located the teen. "It's one of the kids. I've got the bikes in my pickup."

Bo's voice screeched in response. "One of them? What the fuck good does it do to have one of them?"

Keller stopped, lowering the boy partway to the floor before dropping him the rest of the way. "What do you mean?"

"Did you talk to him? Do you know where the other one is?" Bo asked, pointing at the boy.

"Well, no. I had to knock him out to grab him. I didn't chat with him first." Keller spat out, frustrated at bearing the brunt of Bo's anger once again. Then he noticed the other body as it lay against the side wall, the nylon cords still in place. "Who's that guy anyway? What are we going to do with him? Is he still alive?"

Bo stepped over and nudged at the man's abdomen with his foot. "He's a cop. Marconi says he's a plant."

"So why not kill him? Get him out of the picture? Why bring him here?"

"That's what I thought, but Marconi said it was too risky since they're from the same precinct." Bo held up a plastic bag with a syringe in it. "He gave me some stuff to dose him with if he wakes up." He looked up at Keller. "Look, if you hit the other kid, cops are going to know about it."

"What do you want me to do?"

"Get your pickup away from the door while I grab the keys." Bo moved toward the office, calling back over his shoulder. "Then get them both upstairs. Tie them up and make sure they're both still out. I'm going to drive the truck over to my place for now and shift it out to the plant later. Marconi's not going to come for it until the weekend."

Keller looked at the stairs and the distance he'd have to go to carry both bodies up to the second-floor area. It was no surprise that the real work was falling on his shoulders once again. He stepped over and unlocked the bay door, then watched as Bo hefted his considerable bulk into the cab of the truck. When he was ready, Keller moved to open the bay doors.

Bo leaned out the window as he drew even with him. "And get rid of that fucking gun for God's sake."

Keller waited as the truck pulled away before closing and locking the bay doors. Shit work again, he thought as he checked that both hostages were still out. He pulled his own keys out as he moved toward his truck. He fastened the tarp down tight before shoving his gun well under the seat and parking a block away. Once he was back inside the garage, he moved the boy first, slung over his shoulder again as he stepped cautiously up the stairs. He'd grabbed a set of handcuffs from his truck and used them to secure the boy's arms around a support pole that came up into the center of the attic space. He double-checked the tape on his legs before going back downstairs and fetching the other body. This one was considerably heavier, and Keller was winded by the time he had him in place. He was checking the cords when he heard a knock on the door below.

Keller's eyes swept back and forth as he descended the stairs, but he saw nothing that he thought might give them away. A second, sharper knock sounded from the side of the building, so he called out. "I'm coming."

The light over the door was broken but he could see by their silhouettes that two policemen were standing there. "Sir, may we come in?"

The first voice asked, and Keller was surprised when he realized that one of the officers was a woman. He stepped back and gestured for them to enter the now-empty bay.

"Can I help you with something, officers?" Once inside, the woman seemed to take the lead.

"Can I have your name?" She pulled out a notebook.

"Nathan Keller. Is there something wrong, Officer?"

"We had a report of a gun being fired from this garage earlier this evening."

"A gun?" He shook his head back and forth and held his arms out at his sides. "I haven't heard anything at all."

"Have you been here all evening?" He noticed her studying him, the enormous bay, the chaos of the bench areas, and the blackened floor in the center. The second officer was drifting around, studying the perimeter, but luckily showed little interest in the back stairs.

"I went and got some dinner earlier, but I got back here around eight-thirty I'd say."

"Anyone else here with you?"

"No, just me. I keep an eye on the place in the evening sometimes."

The woman looked at her partner as he completed a circuit of the space. The man gave a quick shake of his head. "Are you the owner here?"

Keller started to say yes. He'd been the owner after his pop passed, but the brotherhood owned it now. He decided to tell as much of the truth as he dared. "Uh, I used to be the owner, but business wasn't doing so well so I sold it, couldn't afford the taxes, you know?" He paused. "I'd like to get on home, now, though, if you don't mind. It's getting late."

The woman snapped her notebook shut and gestured to her partner. They started toward the door, but she paused and pointed at Keller. "We'll be going now, but I don't think this matter is finished."

He waited until he heard their cruiser pull away before locking the door and leaning back against it. Jesus, what were they going to do now?

Audrey looked at the charger set for her hearing aids. Once again, the light had been green when she went to take them out but had then quickly switched to red, indicating they weren't ready. "Dammit!"

Having just arrived home from work, Rod stopped by the door of the bedroom and peered in. "Hey there. What's wrong?"

"It's the charging station. It crapped out again, and now they're not ready. I don't know what's wrong." She was surprised to look up and see Rod looking a little sheepish as he stepped closer to speak to her.

"I did the wiring in here and I've had a little bit of trouble with that outlet. Maybe I should have someone in to look at it."

"No," Audrey looked away and shook her head. "I've tried it in three different outlets now, and it's inconsistent with all of them. I've had this set for a long time, and I think the charger is wearing out. I'm due for a checkup, so I can ask the audiologist to have the lab take a look at it." She looked up at him in frustration. "I'd just been hoping to delay the expense."

Audrey unplugged the unit and carried it and the dead aids to an outlet near the kitchen counter where she could keep a better eye on them. She plugged it in and jostled the hearing aids in their foam until the light glowed, indicating they were charging.

Rod pointed at the wall beside her and waited until she was facing him again. She'd been working at home that day and hadn't bothered with her backup aids, so she appreciated the fact that he tried to enunciate very clearly. "I actually had a contractor and his electrician in to do the kitchen, so if it'll work anywhere, it should work here."

FILLING *in the* SHADOWS

Audrey turned back to the charger. "Okay, you crappy piece of electronics, do your job or you're toast." Then she felt a light hand on her
shoulder and turned to face Rod as he spoke once again.

"Are you on duty this evening, going out?"

"No, luckily. I was planning to work a little longer on my computer
so it shouldn't be an issue. But listen, I'd like to talk to you about money.
I want to figure out a budget, and I need to know how much I should
be . . ."

"Okay, tomorrow should work." He glanced at his watch and spoke
quickly before she could finish her sentence. "I'm just going to grab an
apple and then catch the game."

"All right, tomorrow'd be great." Audrey leaned in and kissed him,
pleased when his arms came around her rather than shifting toward the
fruit bowl. God, it was so great living here now. She leaned her head back
to speak when she saw his eyes dart toward the phone lying on the counter.
He held the hug a moment longer and then stepped over to take the call.

"Hey, Gina, what's up?" He paused for a moment listening and
then appeared to explode. "They did WHAT?" He bellowed before his
voice changed to an animal scream that even Audrey could hear. She was
shocked to see the phone smash against the wall as he grabbed his keys
and tore out the front door.

Audrey could see Gina's face on the shattered screen, blinking before
going black. Then her own phone began flashing with an incoming call,
Gina's face now appearing on her screen. Audrey quickly stopped the call
and texted Gina 'give me one sec'. She ran for the bedroom and dug out
her other aids. Once they were in, she made a video call back to Gina.
"Gina, what's wrong? What's going on?"

Gina's face was red with anger, but she seemed to be shifting from
anger into frustration. "Goddammit, Emma told me not to call him, but
I was just so mad, I couldn't stop myself."

"What's wrong?"

"Far came home from school yesterday in tears and said he's never
going back there."

"But why? He was raving about it a few weeks ago when we were together. He was going on about his teacher, his friends . . ." Then Audrey
saw Gina's tears and realized she was struggling to speak.

"They had some kind of lockdown drill, and it terrified him. He says he got yelled at for making a noise when someone banged on the door to their classroom."

Audrey jumped to her feet. "They put a kindergartener through that? Are you kidding me? My God, no wonder Rod tore out of here. I'd like a piece of whoever thought that was a good idea." She saw Gina's face turn to the side as she heard squealing tires through the phone. "Uh oh, I think he used his light. I'll let you go, but please give Far a really long hug from me!" Gina nodded, and then the call ended.

Audrey sank back onto the stool and leaned her head on her arms. How cruel, how utterly cruel to do that to a young child. Why had the world come to this, where barricading schools and terrorizing children was seen as the remedy for a country gone crazy with guns?

Rod tore across town with his light flashing. It was a good thing cars were getting out of his way because he wasn't thinking clearly. He was nearly blind with rage at what Far had been forced to experience. Rod knew guns. They were part of his job. But, because he knew them, he also knew what had gone wrong in the country with regard to guns. Police and military officers trained constantly and followed meticulous instructions for maintaining and storing guns safely. But the gun discipline of the military and the police bore no resemblance to the insanity of the current gun market. Crazed gunmen had armories in their own homes for God's sake. But rather than deal with that, with the real problem, some bureaucratic morons had decided that lockdown drills and active shooter simulations were the way to keep school children safe.

He screeched to a halt in Emma and Gina's driveway, cut off the flashing light, and stowed it back inside the car. He forced himself to take three deep breaths before stepping out of the car and walking quickly up to the door. His sister-in-law opened it, but Emma was right behind her, blocking his way. "Rod, stop. You can't come in here acting crazy. It won't help." She paused to make sure he was settled before reaching out and taking his hand, pulling him gently toward the sofa.

He looked from one woman to the other, at the pain and grief on their faces, and then sank into the sofa, resting his hands on his knees. "I'm sorry. How's he doing?"

The two women sat together on the end of the couch, their hands clasped together. "I asked Gina not to call you because I knew you'd go ballistic."

"It's just that I'm so . . ."

Emma rested her hand on Gina's shoulder before continuing. "I know. We're both upset, just like you. But we need to focus on Far, not on how we feel about the school or their policies or the general insanity in the country right now. He's sad and afraid, and he doesn't want to go back to school. We kept him home today. We both took off work to be with him. We've talked with him and reassured him the best we can, but, honestly, we haven't made much headway."

Gina's voice was calmer now. "A few minutes ago, he said he's afraid you'll be angry with him."

Rod shot up. "Me? Why in the world would I be angry with him?" Then he spotted a small face peering around the corner at the three of them. Rod started toward him but quickly knelt down to Far's level instead. He gentled his voice and reached out his hands. "Buddy, I couldn't be mad at you. Why would you think that?"

Far hesitated before moving closer and finally falling into Rod's arms. He held the boy until Far was ready to let go, then sat down on the floor and settled him into his lap. Emma handed Rod a tissue, and he dabbed at the little boy's face. "I got in trouble at the drill, Uncle Rod. We were supposed to be super quiet, but there was this loud bang on the door, and it scared me. I started to cry, and the teacher got mad at me. She said that the bad men would be able to hear me, and then we might all get hurt."

Rod pulled Far to him again. "Oh, buddy, you didn't do anything wrong. There is no reason for me to be mad at you. That's a scary situation you're describing. I think I would make noise too."

"Really?"

"Really. I've been in situations where I was really scared, and I know how hard it is to be quiet. What's making me sad, though, is that your moms tell me you don't want to go back to school. When you were helping Audrey move, you were telling us how much you like school."

The little boy was quiet then, and Rod waited, rocking him ever so slightly as they sat together on the floor. Finally, he seemed to come to some sort of decision. "Uncle Rod, could you take me to school tomorrow and talk to my teacher? You could tell her that I didn't mean to make noise and that it's hard to be quiet when you're scared."

"I could do that if it's okay with your moms." He looked up at the two women, and they nodded in response.

"I'd like us to go as a team, Far." Emma smiled and reached her hand out to the little boy. He stood up and melted into the arms of the two women. Then he giggled.

"Team Far," he said, laughing.

Rod stood and rubbed the top of the little boy's head before poking him gently in the stomach. "Team Far it is. What time should I be here tomorrow?"

While Far tore off back down the hall to play, Emma walked Rod to the front door. "Thanks, Rod. I'm sorry you risked life and limb tearing over here, but I," she looked back at Gina. "We, really appreciate your coming over. If you can be here by 8:00, it'll give us a few minutes to talk with his teacher and make sure he feels okay in his classroom." She paused then, worry crossing her face once again. "I don't think we should assume that we're done with this issue, though. I think it's going to take a while for him, for all of us to process it." Emma reached up and kissed her brother on the cheek.

"Well, I'm here whenever he needs me." He hugged her again, waved at the two women, and headed out. Rod sat in his truck for a minute or two, swallowing a few more deep breaths before he felt like he was ready to move. He reached for his pocket thinking that he'd send a reassuring text to Audrey before driving home, but it was empty. Dammit, he thought, I bet I'm going to have to buy a new phone.

The next morning, Rod was up and out early in order to go to school with Far and his mothers. The principal seemed nice enough and explained the city's requirements regarding drills, but Rod remained angry about the whole situation and found himself stewing about it as he drove back home. The hardest thing was feeling so powerless about the whole situation. When the assault rifle ban had gone into effect years ago, many police officers had come out in favor of it, but the nature of conservative politics in America had left Rod and some of his fellow officers in a discouraging minority when it came to views on gun control. He liked to think that rabid gun enthusiasts were an aberration in the force, but sadly, that just wasn't true anymore. It was hard to put Far's situation aside and move forward.

That morning, Audrey was scheduled for a shift with the police, but there had been no calls that required her camera, so Rod was glad to have her with him as they pulled up and parked in front of a modest, three-story apartment building.

"He's in this one." Rod gestured toward the front of the building where two columns of doorbells flanked the deep red door. He pushed the buzzer marked Kaminski and, after the click, opened the door and ushered Audrey in. Rod moved toward the staircase. "They're on the second floor." At the landing, he paused for a moment and kissed Audrey on the cheek as she stepped up beside him. "Thanks for coming, Scout. I really appreciate it. We haven't been out together on a call in a while, have we?"

"You're right, we haven't. It's nice to be out working on something with you." She smiled, and they continued up the remaining flight of stairs.

A beautiful brass knocker marked the doorway to 2B, and Rod's sharp rap brought someone to the door quickly. A slender, dark-skinned woman with a halo of curly brown hair greeted them at the door. "Hello?"

"Good morning, Mrs. Kaminski, is it? I'm Detective Rodriguez. We just spoke on the phone?"

"Certainly, yes. Come on in. I'm Kalisa." She stepped back to reveal a gangly, mocha-skinned teen sprawled on a recliner. "This is my son, Jerry. I'm afraid my husband and our older son are both out."

"That's all right. We can catch up with them later if we need to. In the meantime, Kalisa, Jerry, folks call me Rod, and this is my friend, Audrey." They moved into the room and sat down on an oversized sofa across from Jerry. "How's the foot feeling?"

Jerry shrugged, lifting the bandaged foot a foot inches before settling it back down on the foot of the recliner. "It's starting to hurt a bit more, but it's ok." He looked up at his mom, who stood by his chair. "She doesn't want me on any of those super scary painkillers, so . . ." He shrugged again, but his mom just rested her hand on the top of his head.

"I think you'll get by just fine on the over-the-counter stuff, especially if you keep busy and don't think about it. But, if it's too bad, we've got some of the Tylenol from the ER you can take." She patted him on the shoulder and then looked at the pair. "I made a fresh pot of coffee after we talked on the phone. Would you like some?"

"We don't want to be too much trouble, but that sounds great."

"Perfect, I'll be right back. Jerry, do you want anything to drink?"

"No thanks, Mom." Once she'd left the room, he grinned sheepishly at Rod and Audrey. "Too much to drink and . . ."

"Not much fun hobbling to the bathroom, huh?" Jerry nodded and seemed to relax back into his chair a bit. "So, Jerry," Rod began. "I know you talked with Officer Katz at the hospital."

"Yeah, I was told that any gunshot wounds get reported to the police."

"That's right. Often that's the end of it, especially if it's the result of an accident. But she was concerned about what you and your friend saw."

Kalisa came into the room holding a wooden tray with a carafe, three mugs, and a sugar bowl. She settled it on a low coffee table between the sofa and chairs, then poured them each a cup.

Audrey took a mug and sat listening to Rod and the teen.

"This is great, thanks!" Rod said as he accepted a mug as well.

"I'm sorry I don't have any cream or milk for it."

"Black is fine. Thanks." Rod took a sip and then placed the mug on the table and turned back to Jerry. "Can you tell me your story one more time?" Rod held up the pad of paper he'd borrowed from his nephew Far. "Officer Katz said you like to draw?"

Jerry and his mom looked at each other and laughed. "You can say that again!" Jerry looked at his mom again. "Could you bring me my pad from the bedroom?"

Audrey pointed to the walls around them and asked. "Who's the photographer and who's the sketch artist?" Rod followed Audrey's gaze around the room, embarrassed that he hadn't noticed the stunning artwork when he first walked in.

Jerry pointed at a pair of photographs across from him, one a tree-lined beach at sunset, the other a broken archway from what looked to be an ancient church. "My mom's the photographer. She teaches at the Art Institute. Those were both taken in Jamaica where she grew up." Then he twisted in his chair to point at a detailed pencil sketch of a kitten that was framed beside the door. "That one's mine. I'm starting with pencils for now, not sure where I'll go next." His mother returned carrying a broad artist's sketch pad.

Rod laughed and set the child's pad on the table. "Guess I don't need this!"

Kalisa helped Jerry settle the pad on his lap so that he could page through the sheets to show what he'd done. "It was my mom's idea for me to draw out what I saw, to treat it as an exercise and try to remember everything that happened." He lifted the cover page to show a city alleyway at dusk. A detailed garage bay with a broken sign over the door filled the center. The middle of the bay was empty, but the sides and back were all filled with trash. A few tools hung on a side wall, and what might have been a workbench in the back was buried under a jumble of auto parts and rags.

"I think I've seen that garage. It's a few blocks in, north of the river, not too far from Mercy Hospital, right?"

Jerry nodded. "I was waiting for my friend Carlo. We were meeting there because it's behind the repair shop where he had to go." Jerry turned the page to show a closer view of the garage with a man standing in front of it, his mouth open as though he were yelling.

Audrey leaned in. "Wow, Jerry, you're really something. The detail is amazing."

"Tell me about this man," Rod took a long sip before setting his mug back down and pulling out a small notepad. "You told Officer Katz that he yelled at you first, is that right?"

"Yeah, I was just standing there, leaning on the side of a building and looking at my phone. I wasn't doing anything to him." Jerry turned a page, and a bright yellow bike stood out against the deep shadows, the dark form of the boy standing beside it.

Rod noticed the boy's mother, clearly proud of her son's work. "I've been teaching Jerry about light and to think about a scene from a 360° perspective."

"The rest is just black and white," Audrey asked as she pointed at the bike. "What made you decide to use the color here?"

Jerry shrugged. "I just got this nice set of colored pencils, but I haven't done much with them yet. When the guy yelled at me, he called me 'banana bike,' and it stuck in my head, I guess." He flipped over another page, and a detailed drawing of a truck filled the center of the page. "Once my friend Carlo got there, we started riding away, but this big, ugly truck came barreling toward us, and we had to hurry and split to either side of the street so we wouldn't get hit." Then Jerry looked at his mom again before turning another page. "I know it was wrong, but it looked like it was going to the garage that the guy was guarding, and I was so curious. I felt like I had to follow it." Jerry flipped another page. Now the garage bay was filled with a back view of the truck, its rear door opened to the top. It held boxes and wooden crates, but what drew everyone's eye, was the form that lay in front of them. "This is why Officer Katz called you."

Rod nodded. "Tell me more. Who is this?" He pointed at the fatter, older man who had his hand on the truck's bumper and appeared to be holding a bunch of keys.

"We saw that guy unlock the back of the truck. I didn't get as good a look at him, because it was just after that when the guy yelled and shot at us. Carlo and I took off and rode as hard as we could." He closed the pad and laid it across his knees. "That's all I've got."

"May I?" Rod stood and took the sketchpad from Jerry, shifting aside the coffee tray so that he could lay it flat on the table. "These drawings are incredible, Jerry. Is it okay if Audrey takes some photographs of them?" He paused as Jerry nodded yes, then stepped aside to let Audrey have a good angle. "What did you think about what you saw? When you picture it now, do you get the feeling that it was a dead body?"

"I've been wondering about that a lot. I think it was a man, and I could see what looked like nylon rope wrapped around part of him, but I didn't see any blood. There was a bag over the head that kind of scared me."

"Was it plastic, like a shopping bag?"

Jerry shook his head. "No, it was cloth, like with a pattern on it. Kind of girly, actually, which seemed weird to me." He leaned back in his seat. "I'm sorry I'm not being very helpful."

Rod exploded with a laugh. "Are you kidding me? You are hands down the BEST witness I have ever talked to."

Audrey laughed as well. "He's not kidding. I work as a police photographer, and I've seen some of the people he's tried to talk to."

"Police photography? How did you get interested in that?" Kalisa asked, turning to Audrey.

Audrey shook her head for a moment before answering. "Some days, I don't even know! I have my own wedding photography business, but I'm still getting it up and running, so I work for the police to help pay the bills." As she sat down, Audrey gestured around her at the beautiful photographs. "Is your work on display anywhere? I'd love to see more."

A knock sounded at the door, and Kalisa stood to get it. "You're too kind. I have some up around the Institute but nowhere else, I'm afraid." She opened the door and led a woman inside who appeared to be near tears.

Jerry leaned forward in his seat as the woman approached him. "Ms. Rizzi, are you okay?"

She pulled a worn tissue from her pocket and dabbed at her eyes. "Jerry, do you know where Carlo is? He didn't come home last night."

Jerry moved to try and stand up quickly, but the pain stopped him. "What do you mean? He taped up my foot for me, and then he left to walk our bikes back home." He turned to Rod. "He lives in the apartment building across the street. We've been friends forever."

Rod flipped to a clean sheet in his notepad and began writing down the details. "Ms. Rizzi, I'm Detective Rodriguez. I've just been talking with Jerry about what the boys saw last night. Is it unusual for Carlo not to come home? Could he be at a friend's house, maybe?"

She shook her head quickly. "No, he's never done this. If he's not at our apartment, he's usually here at Jerry's."

"What does he look like?" Ms. Rizzi was an interesting contrast to Jerry's mother, fair where she was dark, plump where Kalisa was slender.

"He has light brown hair and glasses. He just got his hair cut short, though. I have a picture." She pulled her phone out and began swiping through the photographs before settling on one and showing it to Rod and Audrey. "Here he is. This was just last week." She handed the phone to Rod. "I asked him to take a broken lazy Susan over to Bishops to get fixed. I haven't seen him since."

"Oh no!" Jerry leaned forward suddenly and shouted. "Banana bike, that's what the guy called me, and Carlo was walking it home." He looked at Ms. Rizzi. "Carlo and I were watching this garage, and a guy shot at us. That's how I hurt my foot."

Ms. Rizzi seemed to pale, and Rod quickly stood to offer her his seat. She looked up at the group around her. "There was a shooting?"

"It just hit my foot. Carlo was fine, Ms. Rizzi. He helped me call my brother and get to the hospital."

Rod closed his notebook and nodded as Audrey stood as well. He tucked his notepad away and turned to face the group. "I don't want anyone to leap to conclusions. I know we're all anxious, but we're going to go back and get to work on this. Ms. Rizzi, if you'll send me that photograph of Carlo, I'll get everyone busy looking for your son."

While the photo and contact information were being shared, Jerry stood up, his hand on the arm of the couch as he balanced on one foot. He reached for Far's discarded drawing pad but only succeeded in knocking it to the floor in front of him. It fell open to reveal a handful of drawings of various dogs. He bent over further and picked it up, handing the pad to Rod with a smile. "Looks like someone else likes to draw, too."

Rod took it from him and tucked it under his arm. He reached out to shake Jerry's hand before turning to the two women. "It belongs to my nephew Far. He's in kindergarten and has a real thing about dogs."

Jerry's mother reached out her hand to shake Rod's. "Well, it looks to me like you've got a budding artist on your hands."

"Thank you, I'll keep that in mind. Jerry, ladies, I'll be in touch. I appreciate all your help today."

Audrey thanked the group as well and followed Rod out to the car. She took the pad onto her lap as Rod finished buckling his seatbelt. "You and I thought Far's drawings were good. Isn't it interesting to hear some real artists confirm that?"

Rod grinned before turning to start the car. "I guess we know what to get him for Christmas this year!"

After the interview with Jerry was over, Rod dropped Audrey at home before heading to the precinct. She allowed herself an hour for car hunting online before deciding she'd better get to work. She was nearly finished with a photo package that she was putting together, and, with a deadline approaching, it was time to dig in.

By lunchtime, with no police calls to interrupt her, Audrey was feeling happy with what she'd accomplished. She had sent the completed file to the couple, and, since the groom worked at one of the local car dealers, she'd sent him an additional text asking if he might be able to help her locate a good car. She'd liked the couple and felt that if anyone could give her an honest deal, he'd be the one.

With her aids fully charged, she showered and dressed before calling for a ride. She was meeting her friend Sandy for the first time in weeks. The twins were back in daycare two days a week now, and, as much as Audrey loved spending time with the little girls, she was looking forward to having her friend to herself. They had split the distance and were meeting at a sandwich shop between Sandy's office and Rod's house. Or was it her house now, too, Audrey wondered?

As Audrey typed in the tip for the driver, she spotted her friend walking into the shop. She hurried up and was able to catch the door before it closed behind Sandy. "Hey, you!" She called, and Sandy turned, catching her in a quick hug.

"Hey, you back. How're you doing?"

"I'm good, but you look awesome. You're so dressed up!"

Sandy pulled at the edge of her sweater, a beautiful deep red that suited her pale complexion and long dark hair. "You think so? I've been working so hard to lose the baby weight, but it's tough, and my baggy old clothes weren't helping my state of mind at all. Oscar got tired of hearing me whine about it and bought me this outfit."

"I love it. I think you look great. Let's order and then find a table." They stepped up to the counter and ordered their lunches before settling into a table near the front window. "So, first baby pictures and updates, and then we *will* talk about other things."

Sandy laughed and reached for her phone. "Okay, five minutes, and I promise I am done." She flipped through the photos until she found the one she wanted. "Okay, here you go. This was taken last week after my mom's surgery. We were trying to keep the two of them from crawling on her, so we set up a little fence around her recliner."

The photo showed two little girls holding onto the top of the railing, both with milk mustaches and cereal stuck to their chins. "Oh, man, they're standing up! When did that happen?"

"You, my friend, have not been over to visit in a little while."

"I know. I'm sorry. We were working on fixing up my office in Rod's house, and then the move. I do want to see them, though." Audrey pointed to the twin on the right. "How's Rosey doing after that whole ordeal?"

Sandy laughed. "My God, even in a photo you can still tell them apart. You're amazing. Between you and me, even Oscar can't tell them apart in a photograph."

"It's something she does with her head." Audrey demonstrated, tilting her head slightly to the side.

Sandy laughed. "I hadn't thought about that, but you're right. Anyway, she's doing great. We're so lucky that the bastard who kidnapped Rosey had a wife who took good care of her. Now, the colic is gone, and her appetite is good. Her whole temperament seems better, happier, you know, now that she's feeling better."

"How's it been having them back in daycare? Is that hard, given what happened?"

Sandy took a moment before answering. "It was hard at first, and we even went around and looked at a lot of other centers. We just didn't like any of them as much as we did the first one."

"Wow, even after Rosey was taken?"

"Did you ever see the movie *The World According to Garp*?"

"Sure, but I don't remember it."

"So, they're looking at buying this house when a plane flies into it. Garp says they'll take it, that it's been pre-disastered. I think that's how we feel about the daycare center. It's probably the safest place they could be."

"Wow, that's not something you hear every day. Pre-disastered, huh? Too bad that didn't work with my apartment."

"Aw, you should have gotten out of that place a long time ago, before you were attacked. Now, you have a whole house to live in!" Sandy tucked away her phone and waited while the waitress set down their plates. "How is it?"

"The house? I love it. The front steps can be a killer, but the porches are great. Right now, the neighborhood is especially pretty with all of the fall trees."

"I'm glad you like the house, but what I meant is, how is it living with Rod?"

"It's good, great even. There's stuff we're still figuring out, of course, but I really like being with him." She paused then, unsure whether to share more or not. She'd known Sandy forever, though, so she found herself going ahead. "Actually, last evening was a little overwhelming. Rod got a call from his sister-in-law Gina about his nephew Far. Instantly, Rod slammed his phone against the wall and went tearing out of the house. I'd never seen that before."

"Wow! What happened?"

"Gina called me back and told me that they'd had a lockdown drill at Far's school. He's just in kindergarten, and he'd been frightened by the teacher fussing at him."

Sandy's hands dropped to the table. "A lockdown drill for kindergarteners? Are you kidding me? How in the world do they talk to kids that age about something like that? I can't imagine."

"Me either. It just seems cruel. It does nothing to stop the insane state of guns in our country. Instead, it just terrorizes our children."

"Wow, no wonder Rod got so mad." She paused and took a sip from her drink. "Well, aside from that, any glitches yet? Any horrible habits you've stumbled upon? I know my first year with Oscar had more than one nightmare in it."

Audrey leaned back in her chair and set her fork on the edge of the plate. "It's not a glitch, really. It's just that I can't pin him down about money issues. I want to talk about what I can contribute, and he keeps putting me off. Just this morning, I decided I want to get a car, but I have no idea what my price range should be because everything is so up in the air."

Sandy shrugged. "People can be funny when it comes to money. Plus, you've both been making your own way for years now, so finding how to put things together can be tricky. You'll figure it out. I'm sure. You know, though, even if you two were to call it quits, we're so grateful to him and his partner for finding Rosey that we might decide to pick him over you."

"Oh, great! Well, thanks for that vote of confidence. I guess I know where I stand."

Audrey laughed as her friend reached across the table and clasped her hand. "You know I'm just kidding, right? Although I can't make any promises about Oscar's allegiances."

"Hopefully, neither of you will ever have to choose between us. We're still very much in love, and I'm pretty sure we're going to be able to weather the conflicts that come up. At least I hope so. Hey, you mentioned your mom's surgery. How's she doing?"

Sandy held up her left hand, the first two fingers crossed together. "So far, so good. The doctor said that the first surgery went so well, they plan to schedule the second knee in about three months."

"That'll put us into winter. Will that make it harder to rehab?"

Sandy shook her head. "No, we got her a membership at one of those cheap gyms, and she's been going faithfully. Did you know your mom's been going with her?"

"No, I didn't. That sounds good for both of them."

"The hope is that with both knees done, my mom will be able to get back into her studio to paint in the spring. I think that's proving to be a pretty good motivator for her."

A few minutes later, with their meals finished and Sandy's lunch break winding down, they headed outside. Audrey pulled up her phone to arrange a ride and spotted a text from the groom in the car business welcoming her into his dealership. "Sandy, would you have a second to drop me off at this car dealership?" She turned her phone around to show the address and map.

"Sure, that's not far at all. I wish I had time to stay and car shop with you, but we've got a client coming in soon."

"That's fine. I appreciate the ride." It was just a few blocks to the dealership, and Audrey gave Sandy one last hug in the car before stepping out. "I will be over soon, I promise, to see you and your girls."

"Sounds good!" Sandy called as she waved and pulled away.

Audrey was happy to see that Henry was already walking to the door to welcome her. "No snap decisions, now." She silently scolded herself before stepping into the appealing showroom.

After their interview with Jerry, Rod made his way back toward the alley
and the repair shop that had been mentioned. He thought about going
to the station first but decided that a quick stop while everything was
fresh in his mind couldn't hurt.

He pulled down the alley first, noticing the garage with the broken
sign that Jerry had drawn so well. No light shone from inside, and its
bay doors were now fully closed with a padlock on a chain hanging between them. He had read over Officer Katz's description of their visit
to the garage the night before, so he thought it futile to approach the
garage again directly, at least not until they had enough information to
secure a warrant. Instead, Rod turned and saw the area where Jerry had
indicated he'd been waiting, the back of a big brick building that fronted
the main street. There was a spot right above head height where a bit of
paint was missing, revealing a glimpse of red brick. Rod looked overhead,
hoping to spot some cameras that might be useful, but the two he could
find both looked like someone had taken a BB gun to them, their lenses
splintered and the plastic shattered. He pulled over behind the back of
the repair shop and parked, grabbing his notebook before stepping out
and locking the door. A sidewalk extended from the alley to the main
road between the brick building and the repair shop, and he took that
route to the front door.

He'd been here before, Rod remembered. Ten years ago, he'd been a
uniform cop when Bishops repair shop was broken into and ransacked
by vandals who'd covered the shop windows with the vilest kinds of ra-
cial epithets. As he pushed open the shop's heavy metal door, Rod was

transported back to that morning when the front door's old, rippled glass lay shattered around his feet, even as the little bell tinkled above his head when he walked in.

At that time, Bishops had been operating for more than ten years. It was a funny sort of place, an old hardware store that had been converted into workshop space, one side focused on wood and furniture repair, the other side equipped for small engine work. Each side had a wide worktable, as well as machinery, cabinets, and shelving that ringed the sides of the large room. Rod learned that Amos Wright, a tall, thin, dark-skinned African American man, was the carpenter, and Bob Gallagher, a thick-waisted, acne-scarred white man, was the mechanic. The two were standing behind their shared counter area, having a beer and arguing, when Rod walked in. He thought that the topic was whether to stay or go.

As the three of them talked that afternoon, Rod heard the story that few in the neighborhood had ever known. The two men, born just weeks apart, had grown up together in rural Georgia. Amos's father had been a farmer, struggling from season to season and making ends meet by taking on work at a local garage. Bob's father had been the garage owner, although anyone with half a brain could see that Amos's father was the one keeping the shop running. "My dad was a drunk," Bob stated flatly. "A drunk, and a mean one at that. He paid Amos's dad dirt wages, while rarely even bothering to get up and pump gas for folks." Bob looked over at Amos, a look passing between them before Bob took a deep breath and continued. "My mother took off when I was eight. She'd had enough of his treatment by then, and I guess she figured I was bound to grow up just like him. At any rate, she didn't bother taking me with her, and I never laid eyes on her again. Amos knows," He nodded at his old friend. "More than once after my father'd taken a strap or a belt or whatever he could find to me, I'd sneak over to Amos's house, and his mama would fix me up."

"One night, Amos and I were in the garage cleaning up. We were about twelve, I think, and I saw flames in the window of our house next door. I tore off, ran up onto the front porch, and threw the door open, but a wave of smoke pushed me back. Amos called the fire department and begged me not to try and go in there, but I wouldn't listen. I pulled my shirt up over my mouth and nose and went in. At first, I couldn't see anything, then I heard this choking sound off to the right. I got down on my hands and knees and crawled toward the sound. By that time, the flames were all around the living room, and I was so scared . . ." He took a long breath and leaned back in his chair. "Sorry, it's been a long time since I've told this story. You'd think it'd get easier over the years, but . . ." Rod waited as Amos set a hand on Bob's knee and waited for him to continue.

"My dad was blackout drunk, half falling off the couch, a couple of empty bottles on the floor around him. I stood up into the smoke and tried to get my hands under his armpits and pull him out." He shook his head slowly. "That's when the ceiling gave way." He pulled his sleeve up, baring his arm to show a long, wide scar that disappeared under the shirt above his elbow. "A beam fell on me, knocking me to the floor. I couldn't hold onto him, couldn't see anything. I was choking and coughing myself by then. I passed out, and the next thing I knew, Amos was pulling me down off the porch. Firefighters had arrived then and went to work, but there wasn't much they could do other than take care of Amos and me."

"They managed to save the garage," Amos added, and Bob nodded in agreement.

"Amos, his dad, and I worked the garage for a few more years, and I lived with them while we finished high school. We sweated out the end of the Vietnam draft for a year and then headed north to DC, once we figured we weren't going to be called."

Then Amos took over the tale. "Bob found work up there right away, and he paid for a shitty-assed apartment where we lived for about seven years, long enough for me to study carpentry and furniture work with one of my dad's brothers. When we figured we had enough for a stake in something, we came up here and opened our own shop. Been here ever since."

"Have people bothered you here before this?"

"Oh sure, from time to time." Bob looked at Amos, and something unspoken seemed to move between the men again.

Then Amos answered the question that was hanging in the air. "People around here pretend like they don't care, but they do. They don't like seeing a black man and a white man working together."

"But you've owned this place now for ten years, right? Has something changed recently?"

"We haven't changed," Bob added, "but the neighborhood has. There are a lot more drugs, jobs are scarcer, and people, both white and black, are struggling. We try and keep our heads down, not make waves."

Amos pointed to the ceiling. "We live upstairs over the shop. That bothers people, too, I think."

Rod looked from one man to the other and then blinked. "Okay, well I think you've answered all of my questions, so I'll get going now. If you need some help cleaning this mess up, I'm off shift at six. I'd be happy to come back and help." He shook both men's hands and turned toward the door.

"Thank you, that's very generous of you, officer, but we'll be okay." Bob rested his hand on Amos's shoulder and nodded goodbye.

Now, as he pushed the heavy metal door in, Rod found himself missing the beautiful, old glass door. The wide display windows that once held posters for all sorts of community events were now coated with dust and sported thick metal bars. But when he walked in, Amos and Bob were there, standing behind their shared counter, arguing again. Today's argument though, seemed to be focused on sports. "They played like crap, and you know it!" Amos cackled as he folded a twenty-dollar bill into his wallet.

Rod walked up to the counter and reached out his hand. He shook hands with both men before looking first at Bob. "Don't tell me you bet on the Penguins. They've been on a losing streak lately, haven't they?"

The man shrugged. "What can I say? I thought they were due. I'm Bob Gallagher. Can I help you?"

Rod opened his badge wallet and showed it to both men. "You may not remember me, but we met about ten years ago."

Amos rested his hand on Bob's shoulder. "You were in uniform then, weren't you? Officer Rodriguez, is that right?"

Rod smiled. "On the money." He answered. "I made detective since then, homicide, so I haven't gotten down here in a while."

"Oh no, I hope there hasn't been a murder." Bob gasped and looked at Amos.

"No, no. But there is a teenage boy missing. That's why I wanted to talk with you both."

Amos walked out from behind the counter and led the group to a set of three chairs situated around a short refrigerator. "C'mon over here, and let's sit down. Can I get you something to drink?" Rod and Bob sat down while Amos leaned over and opened the door. "We've got some soft drinks here, would you like one?"

"Sure, that'd be great, thanks." Amos handed around three cans, and once they'd all been cracked open, Rod spoke again. "Do you still live up above the shop here?" He gestured toward the stairway behind the counter.

"We do, actually. Thought about moving a bunch of times, but we've got it fixed up just the way we like it now, so we use our money for travel rather than putting it into some old house." Bob smiled over at Amos. "Bermuda at Christmas! Isn't that right?"

Rod laughed as Amos and Bob knocked their cans together in a toast. Amos raised his can then. "Yessir."

"Well, before you go . . ." Rod smiled, but then changed his tone of voice to one more serious. "I'm wondering first if you two were home last night."

"Yes, we were upstairs watching the hockey game. Why, did something happen?" Amos looked at Bob as he rested his can on his knee and leaned forward.

Rod nodded. "Two boys, teenagers, were in the alley behind your shop last night. One of them said he had dropped off a repair earlier?"

"Let me check." Bob got up and moved to the counter, where he pulled out a wide ledger. "We still do it old school around here, I'm afraid." He ran his finger down the page before stopping. "Oh, that's right. I remember. Carlo Rizzi dropped by with an old wooden lazy Susan for Amos to work on." Bob laughed then and gestured to Amos. "Remember, we were just getting ready to close up when he came in?" Bob returned to his chair.

"So, you know the boy?"

"A little. He's been in before. Is he all right?"

"That's my worry. He didn't come home last night. I spoke with his friend, Jerry, and he said that they were in the alley when a big truck came. They scattered to either side of it and then got curious. The other boy had seen a man guarding the garage, and he wanted to know why."

Amos snorted. "I bet I know who that was, racist bastard."

Bob reached out his hand and set it gently on Amos's arm before turning to Rod. "Most likely, it was Keller, Nathan Keller, who was doing the guarding. Tatted up, greasy-looking guy. I've seen what looks like a gun tucked into his waistband."

"Has he threatened you two?"

"No," Amos shook his head. "It was never proven, but we always suspected that he'd had something to do with the break-in and vandalism that you looked into for us."

"I noticed that the cameras back there don't look like they're working."

"How many times do you think we've replaced them, Bob? Three? Four?"

"Four, I think. Every time we get them up and running again, they get busted." He lifted his arms in the air in a gesture of surrender. "We finally gave up."

Rod nodded and made a note before turning back to the two men. He thought about telling the men the story about the truck and the body, but it seemed ill-advised. Instead, he kept his focus on Carlo. "In addition to the boy Carlo being missing, the other teen is at home with a gunshot wound to his foot. He says that someone from the garage yelled at the boys and fired two shots. One hit a wall, the other hit the boy's foot."

Both men looked at each other and shook their heads sadly. Amos spoke first. "We didn't hear anything over the game. I'm afraid my hearing isn't what it used to be, so we keep the set up pretty high." He turned back toward Bob. "You were right, though, we should have gotten out last year."

"Why last year? Did something happen then?" Rod turned to Bob.

"There was never anything we could put our finger on to report, just this sense. Last winter, we thought we caught sight of some militia-type guys the night before our cameras were shot up the last time. It was too dark for us to be positive, but we had a feeling there were men with guns meeting up in that garage. There were cars and trucks with Confederate flag stickers and other hateful slogans."

"And recently? Have you seen anything lately?"

Bob stood and collected the empty cans, dropping them into a blue recycling bin near the door. Then he turned and briefly lowered his head. "Nope, we're ostriches. We decided to be ostriches."

"Meaning?"

Amos got up and stood next to Bob, reaching out to take his hand. "We decided to look the other way. We increased our security with the metal door and those bars on the windows, and we go in and out of here by the front door onto the main street, never around the back. It was a matter of self-preservation."

Rod leaned back in his seat and shook his head. "I'm so sorry to hear you've been subjected to all of that, that you can't feel safe in your own home and business." He paused and looked around the shop, items waiting for repair with small red tags on them, and what looked like finished work nearer the door sporting green tags. Then he looked at both men. "You're handy guys, right? Any acting skills to speak of?"

Both men laughed. "You mean other than acting straight for all our lives?" Amos laughed, and Bob patted him on the shoulder. "Why, what are you thinking?"

Rod stood. "This is the last place that the boy Carlo was seen, so I'd really like to get a look at what's going on with that garage. I'm wondering, if our lab were to bring over a small but powerful camera, could one of you act like you're starting to repair one of your cameras and then sort of give up?"

Amos grinned. "But actually, install the little camera in the mess of tape and stuff?"

"Yeah." Rod nodded. The two men looked at each other and then at Rod. "I'm sure we could do that," Bob responded. "Think we could keep the camera after you're done with it?"

Rod laughed. "I'll see what I can do." He reached out and shook each of their hands as he moved toward the door. "I appreciate your help. I'll have someone from the lab get in touch with you soon to set it up. In the meantime," he paused, "keep yourselves safe. I'd rather have a couple of live ostriches than a pair of dead busybodies."

Rita Banks didn't think she'd seen the repair shop before, but, with Rod's directions, it was easy enough to find. She'd been working as a technician for the police for several months but hadn't gotten to go out into the field until now. It didn't sound like a big job, but she was happy for the change in routine. When she'd spoken with Detective Rodriguez that morning, he'd cautioned her to go in the front entrance and not pull through into the alley behind. Luckily, when she arrived that afternoon, someone was just pulling out of a parking space two doors down. She parked quickly and grabbed the backpack that held her gear.

The repair shop might have been nice at one time, but if it had ever had any glory days, they were long gone now. The windows were grimy and partially blocked by a stack of boxes. The metal door, heavier than it looked, screeched on its hinges as she pushed against it with her hands and feet. Once she was inside, however, she was pleased to see that the interior of the shop looked a lot better than the outside. The wide space was divided into two, tidy sections, each with a sizeable table. Cabinets lined the walls on two sides and items with red and green tags lay scattered around the side of each table. The scent of sawdust immediately took her back to her uncle's woodshop where she used to sit at a high stool and watch as he worked. She heard a quick cough and the rasp of sandpaper as an older man looked up to greet her.

"Good afternoon. Can I help you?" The tall, thin, older man stepped from behind the wide table and moved forward with his hand outstretched.

Rita set her bag on the floor before shaking his hand. She liked the feel of his calluses on his friendly handshake. "I'm Rita Banks from the police department. Detective Rodriguez sent me."

"Hello, well that was fast. I'm Amos Wright." He looked over his shoulder where a white man was coming down the stairs. "Bob, come and meet Rita from the police department."

He held his hands up apologetically. "Bob Gallagher. I'm sorry, they're still a little bit greasy. I can't find my lava soap this morning."

"I think it's over on that back sink." Amos offered, and Bob headed toward the back.

"That's okay." Rita lifted her bag and moved further into the room. "So, I didn't entirely understand what Detective Rodriguez had in mind, but he mentioned the need for a very small video camera. Is that right?"

"Come on over here. Set your things up on this table." Amos moved aside a battered dresser drawer and brushed the area with a small whisk broom as Bob returned to the front. Once the area was clear, she pulled out the items she'd brought and held the camera up for the two men to see.

"Wow, that's a camera? Really?" Amos held the camera in his hand while Bob leaned over his shoulder to see it. "That's not much bigger than a shot glass, is it?" He looked over at Bob before turning back to Rita. He pointed a figure at her laughing, "but you wouldn't know anything about that, would you, missy?" The black plastic disk felt surprisingly light. He handed it to Bob so that he could examine it as well.

"Nope, never seen one," Rita laughed and then opened her laptop to show them the feed that was already running. "It's small, and its signal is wireless, so we think it'll be the best model to hide."

Bob stepped around the table and went to retrieve a cardboard box. He gently poured the contents onto the table. Broken in pieces before them lay the next-to-last camera that they had installed above the back door. "This is the kind of model we'd been trying." The front lens of the camera was shattered, but the wire was still attached. "You can see. Rather than tear it down . . ."

"Which probably would have been more work than they were willing to do," Amos interjected.

Bob nodded. "Yep, instead they shot out the lens. This one's case survived better than some of them."

Rita leaned over the broken camera and began examining it. She reached for a nearby roll of electrical tape and tilted the damaged camera back and forth, trying to determine the best angle to attach the new camera. "I think we can make this work. Do you have a piece of glass that we could use to replace what was shattered?"

"Let me look." Bob moved to a tall set of cabinets that were built into the back wall. He pulled out a few drawers before he found the one he wanted. Inside were bits and pieces of glass from a variety of projects over the years, and he quickly found two contenders. "Here we go."

He brought them to the table and, within just a few minutes, had replaced the shattered glass with a new disc. If someone looked closely at the camera, they'd easily tell that it wasn't an actual lens. But, from the ground level looking up, it'd do. Rita continued fiddling with the unit, adding and removing tape before making adjustments and then re-taping it. She held it up for the two men to inspect. "What do you think?"

Amos looked at the unit and then the other two men. "It'd convince me. What do you think, Bob?"

"I think it looks good, but I'm not sure how we're supposed to play this. We don't want them to think it's a working unit because we don't want them shooting it up again."

"Yeah, I'm not sure the new camera would withstand that sort of thing."

Amos moved across the room to a drawer in a back table and returned with a pair of small hinges. "What about this? What if we hide these hinges in the tape, and once we get it in place up there, we act like the bracket broke and leave the thing hanging? These can hold it in place."

"Sounds like a plan to me." Rita smiled. Then she removed the camera, and the two repairmen worked to make both the real and the false attachment for the base. When they held up the new arrangement, she reinstalled the small camera, hiding it once again within the black electrical tape. "All right. I think this might work. Now, how are you going to get it up into place?"

"Rock, paper, scissors?" Amos asked, and Bob nodded. With a one, two, three movement, Bob's hand was extended flat while Amos's was balled in a fist. "Dammit, I never learn, do I?"

Bob chuckled, and the two of them moved toward the back of the shop where a long ladder was suspended above the door. "I'll help you set it up and hold it still while you work, Amos. I've got you."

"All right, all right. But don't get mad when I yell at you while I'm putting the damn thing up. It's called acting, and I don't want you taking anything too personal." Bob snorted with laughter as they opened the back door and began maneuvering the ladder into place. Rita was careful to take her laptop and slip back out of sight of the door. She watched the image on the screen as Amos slipped a tool belt around his waist and mounted the ladder. He began heckling his friend Bob almost immediately. "You hold that bastard steady now, you hear me?"

"I will. I will." Bob called up, his grip on the old wooden ladder as firm as he could make it.

Within a few minutes, the image on the screen stuttered as she heard Amos call out. "Dammit to hell, the bracket broke!"

"Well, can't you fix it? You're supposed to be a repairman after all."

"I'm a repairman, not a damn magician, you fool!" Amos hollered down.

Inside, Rita watched as the screen stuttered and then cleared, showing a good view of the garage across the street. She stepped nearer the door and spoke softly. "Bob, it looks good. The angle's perfect."

Bob acted like he hadn't heard a thing, but he called up then. "Oh, forget about it. Just leave it. Somebody'd probably just break it again. Come on down."

"You sure? I might have another bracket somewhere." Amos called down.

"Nah, don't worry about it," Bob called up, giving Amos the signal that the arrangement was working.

Amos began descending the ladder after which both men hung it back up, closed and relocked the backdoor before moving to the laptop. Rita looked up at them. "We're in business now. That was excellent!"

"Look at that view. It's so clear!"

Amos nodded. "I'm impressed. Okay, so you're going to send the feed to our computer, too, right? We have an old laptop upstairs."

Rita nodded. "Go ahead and bring it here. I'll show you how to log on and see the feed. I need to call the station for a minute and make sure they're in as well." While Bob disappeared up the stairs, Rita called in, pleased that she was able to reach Rodriguez so quickly. "Log in and see if you're getting it, would you, Rod?" She waited for a moment while he logged in. "See it now? Yep, it'll be in color as long as there's enough light. Then it'll be more of a grayish feed." Rita looked up to see Bob returning with an older laptop, so she finished with Rod and returned the phone to her pocket. "Well, this has seen a few days, hasn't it?"

Amos and Bob both laughed before Amos responded. "Listen here, little sister, it works just fine for the two of us. We don't need anything fancy." She laughed as she worked her way through the older model's search system until she was able to pull up the feed. "You have any kin down in Georgia?" Amos asked as he watched her work. "You remind me of a cousin I had growing up there. She was smart as a whip, too."

"Who, Leyla?" Bob asked as he took another look at Rita. "I can see that."

Rita laughed. "No, as far as I know, my family's been here in Pennsylvania for quite some time. Oh, here you go." She pivoted the laptop around until they could both see the feed.

"Wow, none of our other cameras ever had that good a view."

Rita grinned as she began packing up her laptop and stowing it in her bag. "Only the best for you two gentlemen. Only the best! I imagine Detective Rodriguez will get in touch with you later to follow up. Nice work!" She smiled before letting herself out the front of the shop.

Amos and Bob began cleaning away the tools and other materials. "When I was a kid, I thought I wanted to be a spy. Guess you're never too old, huh?" Bob asked, and the two men laughed as they finished setting the shop to rights.

18

Late Wednesday afternoon, Keller pulled his truck up to the big bay door and honked once. Bo opened the left-hand door, and he pulled up partway. Then Keller went around to the back, lifted the tarp, and pulled out the bags of food that he'd picked up at the convenience store. With the bags, he gestured toward Bo. "Want me to take this stuff up?"

The man grunted and shook his head. "Nah, you'll have to move them first. I don't want any of those cops coming back and finding anything."

Keller was irritated again. It sounded like he was going to be stuck with the work. "Where am I going to put them?"

"Use the storeroom in the back of the coffee shop next door."

"Someone will see me taking them in."

"Nah," Bo separated a thin set of keys from his larger set and then jerked his arm over his shoulder to indicate the back of the building. "Here's a key to the door in the back." Keller looked up and spotted the connecting door near the back of the short hallway. He didn't think he'd even noticed it before. "Get those bikes in there, too, and make sure you clean up the attic area. Then throw some stuff in front of that door so it doesn't look used. I'll be back this evening."

Keller watched as the man lumbered back out of the building and climbed into his car. Jesus, the work always fell to him. He shook his head and got back into his truck, pulling it further into the garage before closing and locking the big door.

It was late before he had the bikes moved, both of the hostages shifted, and the attic area cleaned up. The cop was still out cold and stank like an outhouse, which made transferring him hell. But the boy was awake and frightened enough that, with a knife against his back, Keller was able to walk him to the new location. He tossed the bag of food at him before turning to lock the door behind him. "You keep quiet, and I'll be back with dinner a little later. You make a sound," He paused, drawing his knife across in front of his throat. "Any sound and you're done. You hear me?" The boy nodded quickly, and he shut the door.

Keller took his time checking out the attic area once more before moving a trash bin and a crate of broken glass back in front of the door he'd just used.

CHAPTER
19

Late in the afternoon, Smitty returned from the coffee room with two cups of coffee and a grin on his face.

"What's up?" Rod asked, taking the offered cup of coffee from his hand.

"First, it was an asshole-free break room and, second, they got him!"

"Who?"

"Ellerby, the guy running for state rep."

"How? What did he do?"

"You're gonna love this. They got him for tax fraud, just like Capone! Remember the wife of that monster who stole Rosey? After we left the house with the baby, they went in and did a thorough search of the place. Turns out she's a CPA, and when they raided the house, they confiscated all her tax records. Apparently, Ellerby's were particularly juicy."

"Are they picking him up now?"

"No, not until Monday. He's got some sort of big family deal out of town this weekend, and they don't want to get into the middle of that. Once the family gets back into town, they're going to grab him."

"Oh, shit. It's a wedding. The daughter is getting married. It's some big weekend-long deal in the mountains. Audrey is photographing it."

Smitty tilted his head. "Is that a problem?"

"I don't know. Arresting him for tax fraud is a great idea, but we both know that's not what's wrong with the guy. They think he may have ties to countries we'd rather not be dealing with, and he's suspected of bringing all kinds of shit into the state. I'd rather Audrey wasn't near any of that business."

Smitty nodded but didn't say more as the two men returned to writing reports. After being shot in the spring, months of rehabbing, and a stint working on missing persons cases, Smitty had finally been returned to his desk in the homicide unit. Finding baby Rosey had been the highlight of his temporary assignment, but for the most part, it was a disheartening duty to pull. Drug issues, runaways, and a box of cold case files had taken up most of his time. He'd held on to one last case, though, when he moved back to homicide, frustrated that he still hadn't made any headway on it. A police officer named Stevens from the suburb of Butler had gone missing while on a camping trip in the woods outside the city. The weather had been mild, and his wife reported that he was an extremely capable outdoorsman, having been an Eagle Scout in his youth and currently serving as an Outward Bound instructor. Smitty had begun to feel the lack of progress as an added weight as time crept forward.

Then, around noon, a farmer and his dog had been out looking for a lost calf when they stumbled upon the body. It was still with the lab, but the on-scene officers had felt sure that the cause of death was a gunshot to his gut. They reported seeing what looked like a trail of blood leading back into the woods, but how far back, they hadn't been able to determine. Someone from that jurisdiction had called the captain and he'd asked Rod and Smitty to check into it. In just a few minutes, Smitty and Rod were heading out to look at the site.

20

Rod's nerves were already on edge way before he reached home. He recognized that now that he and Audrey had had their first fight and the self-awareness that might have helped the situation had arrived at least thirty minutes too late. Speechless, she had given him a look made of equal parts anger and defiance and left the house on foot. Dammit, he was an idiot. Maybe a well-intentioned idiot, but an idiot all the same.

It was the site where the body had been found that had set him off. He and Smitty had taken the time to follow the blood trail as far as they could. Although neither man was a great woodsman, a local sheriff's deputy helped direct them further along the trail. The group had gone nearly half a mile before they located what they thought was the scene of the shooting. In a narrow clearing, a slender pine stood broken, its trunk split roughly in half, while what looked like blood was splattered on a flat section of rock. The sheer distance that the wounded man had covered while steadily losing blood was astounding. Rod and Smitty had both stood at the site, speculating about what they were seeing and feeling sicker by the minute.

Finally, they'd made their way back out, and Smitty had taken on the unpleasant task of going to discuss the situation with Stevens's widow while Rod was free to go home. As he pulled into the driveway, Rod was reminded again of how much he missed his dog, Simon. On days like this, with only the dog to see him, Rod would bury his face in Simon's soft fur, finding comfort to combat whatever nastiness the day had held. He would breathe in and out slowly, scratching at the dog's ears and rubbing his stomach, saying out loud all the things he wanted to forget, to purge everything from his system, if only for the night.

But there was no Simon to greet him at the door. Instead, Audrey was there, and, although it was natural to reach for her and to hold her tight, there was not the same sort of mindless calm that the dog had so easily offered. Suddenly, she was talking about cars and money, her friend Sandy, and her twins. He tried to keep up as he moved from the door to the kitchen, searching for the coffee carafe, in case there was half a cup from the morning that he could toss in the microwave. But the carafe was washed and standing upside down, draining in the sink. He looked around then and noticed that every item from breakfast seemed to have been cleaned and stowed away out of sight. He knew it was a kindness that she cared for their place and helped to keep it nice, but for an irrational moment, it felt like some sort of scolding, as if the way he'd always run his life hadn't been good enough. Then she mentioned the Ellerby wedding.

"Don't do that wedding." Rod had turned to face her finally and was surprised to see the puzzled look on her face.

"What? Why are you saying that?"

"I just don't think it's a good idea, is all."

"Are you crazy? This is the biggest job I've ever had. I know it's not Hawaii or New York City, but it's an awfully fancy resort that I've been invited to. They're even sending a car for me. Besides, it's an entire weekend of events with a lot of highbrow guests."

"I just don't think it sounds very safe, a resort up in the woods like that. Anything could happen."

"At a wedding? Are you kidding me? Plus, do you know how long ago I booked this job? My business would be over if I backed out of it at this point. Why are you asking me to do this? Don't you trust me?"

"Of course, I trust you. It's that family. You hear things . . ."

"What things?"

Rod knew he was sunk at that point. There was no way on earth he'd risk the case against Ellerby. In fact, he'd probably said too much already, so he quickly changed the subject. "Nothing. Do you know when you'll be back?"

"I'm not sure. I'm invited for the weekend, so I imagine I'll be back when they decide that they're done. It'll probably be finished Sunday morning sometime, but if it finishes Saturday night, I'm not getting into a car with some drunk-assed driver just because you're worried about me." He could see the level of anger rising and regretted having said anything. "You said you thought I was brave, that I was tough to stand up to what happened to me. Why are you doubting me now? I don't understand."

Rod fell back onto the stool by the counter and scrubbed his hands across his face. "Forget it, forget I said anything." He lifted his head then and was shocked to see her turning away from him.

"Dammit, first you won't bother to talk about money with me so that I can start to figure things out, and now you're telling me what jobs I should take. I need some air and some quiet."

Before he knew it, she'd yanked out her hearing aids, tossed them on the counter, and stormed out the front door. He started to call out after her but realized the futility of it. Instead, he grabbed up the clean coffee pot and shoved it into place, nearly breaking the glass. Goddammit, where was Simon when he needed him?

Audrey's heart rate started to slow as soon as the silence washed over her. But she had made it down the steep hill and back up before she felt the anger finally begin to let go. It'd been stupid to leave the house the way she did, especially since she was already wishing she'd grabbed a sweater, but she'd been going for the effect. She began making her way back down the hill one more time, figuring she could use the exercise, as well as a few more minutes to think.

When he arrived home, she'd been so excited to tell Rod about the cars she'd been looking at. There was a hatchback that she'd especially liked, small enough to park in the city but with a trunk area that would be easy to get her gear in and out of. If she could get some sort of budget figured out for herself, she was pretty sure she had enough in her savings to make a good down payment with reasonable monthly payments after that. But Rod hadn't heard any of that. He'd just walked away and then started telling her not to take the weekend photography job. The attack in the spring, in addition to nearly killing her, had shredded the self-assurance that she'd been working so hard to build, first as a student, then as a businesswoman and a photographer. Counseling over the last few months had helped her to find some of that inner strength again, but, as evidenced by both the fight and the flight, it was still a bit fragile.

Audrey made the turn at the bottom of the hill and began walking back up one more time. The wind was picking up, and the light was beginning to fade, but the autumn leaves were beautiful, some still on the trees, others falling in swirls around her. In the quiet, her eyes caught on a particular cluster of bright red and orange tucked into the slats of a short wooden fence, and she couldn't help wishing she'd at least brought her phone with its camera. Anger and photography were never a good mix, she mused, catching her breath before climbing the front steps to the house. She paused at the mailbox and gathered the pile of junk mail and ads, a bill or two folded into the mix.

She didn't see Rod immediately, as she dropped the mail onto the kitchen counter. The items scattered apart as they fell, and a red *overdue notice* caught her eye. She picked it up, surprised to find that rather than some cheesy sort of come-on, it was an actual overdue notice from the water department. Was Rod short of money? Was he broke, and that's why she couldn't pin him down into a conversation about it? Crap, she'd probably been misreading the situation all along and making him angry by asking about it. Her hearing aids were right where she'd left them on the counter, so she tucked them back into place and went looking for Rod.

When the house turned up nothing, she stepped out into the backyard. Rod was crouched at the back of the yard, fiddling with something. When he stood up, she could see that he'd been straightening the small cross that Far and Gina had made for Simple Simon. Audrey waited, giving him a moment alone with his thoughts, before stepping forward out into the yard. He must have heard her coming because he turned swiftly and caught her up in his arms before she had a chance to speak. "I'm sorry . . ." She started.

"I'm sorry I snapped at . . ." But Rod was apologizing at the same time. The silliness inherent in the dueling apologies seemed to hit them at the same time. Rod stepped back but kept his arm around Audrey's waist. "Would you like a cup of coffee and a reasonable conversation?"

Audrey laughed. "Yes, I believe I would like both."

Once they were inside, Audrey took a seat on one of the stools while Rod went to the cupboard and pulled out a mug. He filled it from the fresh pot and handed it to her across the counter. As he was reaching, the scattered pile of mail caught his gaze. "Oh, shit. I missed one."

Audrey hesitated but felt that she had to say something. "Rod, is money an issue? Is that why you haven't wanted to talk about it with me? You know I want to contribute."

Rod came around the counter and sat down on the stool next to her, spinning them both slightly so that they were facing each other. "No, I don't have money troubles. Or rather, I do have money troubles, but it's not what you're thinking. I didn't want to talk about it because I'm embarrassed about it." His shoulders seemed to sink.

"Embarrassed? Why?"

He paused, swiveling on his seat as he thought. He took a deep breath. "So, my dad was a great guy. Gone way too soon. But he was proud, too proud in some areas—money in particular. The subject was totally taboo. I remember being with my dad at the toy store one time, and there was this remote-controlled car that I wanted. I asked my dad if I could have it, and he said we couldn't afford it. The thing is, the one that was out of the box to play with had its label torn partway off. I could see there was a five on it. So, I asked, was it five dollars or fifty dollars, maybe even five hundred dollars? I was a kid, so I had no idea, but he refused to even answer the question. Money was not something to talk about." Audrey watched him flip the bill back and forth as he talked before laying it back down on the counter. "Then he died. There was insurance money, and my mom worked, so we were okay, but she had never had to take responsibility for managing the household finances, and it was a struggle. One day, after Dad had been gone a few months, I remember my uncle Roberto coming over one afternoon and sitting with my mom, showing her how to handle everything. They set up a notebook for her with the different bills in it, each with its own page, and she'd sit down and write out the checks at the end of the month."

"Sounds like my mom. I still remember sitting on the couch with her, learning how to balance a checkbook and keep track of everything."

Rod smiled. "You were lucky to have someone who was willing to explain it all to you or," He paused, a look of chagrin on his face. "Or rather, someone who realized how important it was for you to sit down and learn it. Me, I had no patience for it. My mom tried, but she was gone before I finally matured enough to understand that I might need to know all of that." He picked up the bill one more time. "I never figured out a good system. Bills come in, and I write the checks, but I don't pay much attention to it and, sometimes, they get by me."

"Do you have a checkbook? Could I see it, maybe help you figure it out a bit?"

"Uh, not really."

"What do you mean?"

"Well, I have checks, but when the register ran out, I never bothered starting up a new one. I just glance at the statements each month, make sure there's still money in the account, and let it go at that."

"Wow, I don't know what to say. I've never had enough money in the bank *not* to worry about it. I keep super careful records because I operate on such a slim margin most of the time. Plus, I have to keep all sorts of receipts for the business in order to report out for taxes." She looked up at him then, unsure how to proceed. "I don't want to seem rude or presumptuous here," She paused. "But would you like some help?"

"Are you kidding me?" He opened the envelope and pulled out the overdue bill. "Look, the fine is forty-five dollars. If I give you forty-five dollars, could you help me out?" Audrey laughed at his candor and wrapped her arms around his neck before pulling him into a kiss.

When she let him go, she spread her hands out wide, clearing a section of the counter. "Okay, champ, bring me what you've got, and we'll sort it out. No more late fees, I promise." He returned with a battered cardboard box that was filled with a mound of bills, piles of check receipts, and at least two takeout menus. She held one up in the air. "You can keep your forty-five dollars unless you'd like to spend it on some take-out while we figure out this mess."

"I'm on it!" he laughed as he stepped back into the kitchen to retrieve his new phone. "Thai food okay?"

"Sounds perfect."

Although the food was indeed perfect, sorting out Rod's finances had turned out to be a more difficult task than she'd anticipated. She'd finally given up around ten-thirty, and they were talking about it later as they were getting ready for bed. "So, here's an idea. We already use the same bank. What if we open a separate, joint account just for the household expenses? We can both put money in each month, and it can be set up so that the bills pay automatically. For now, I'll contribute the equivalent of the rent and utilities I was paying before if you think that's enough."

"I think that'd be plenty."

"Okay. I can show you how to track your account online as well so that you don't have to worry about writing checks or keeping track of a checkbook."

They climbed into bed and drew each other close. Rod spoke first. "Thank you for working on this with me. I'm sorry I let my workday ruin things earlier."

"I'm sorry I stormed out like that. But," She pulled him closer. "We'll get better at all of this, I'm sure." She drew her finger through the soft line of hair at the back of his neck as he brought his lips to her ear.

"I love you, Audrey."

She slid over on top of him and nuzzled against his ear. "I love you, too, Rod." He reached beneath her bottom and brought her close as Audrey clicked off the light. Later, she'd fallen asleep quickly, numbers dancing around her head in the dark. It wasn't until the next day that she remembered the other part of the argument, the warning about that weekend's wedding. That was still to be dealt with.

When she got the call at eight-thirty the next morning, Audrey was re-lieved she hadn't yet rented the car for the rescheduled shoot. This time, the bride-to-be sounded more anxious than irritated with her fiancé.

"Audrey, I haven't been able to get John on the phone since Monday. He told me he'd be busy with work, so I didn't think too much about it. He promised he would get back to me last night, but I still haven't heard anything."

"Well, we can reschedule again . . ." Audrey began before she realized that Sylvia was still talking.

"I'm looking back at the text he sent after he missed on Monday, and it's weird."

"How is it weird?"

"It's like he knew he might miss. It says, '*If I don't show, ask Audrey to tell Rod and the captain.*' What do you think that means?"

"I'm afraid I've got no idea. I was planning to head into the station this morning, so I'll be sure and pass on the message. Do you want to reschedule again now?"

"No, I think I'll wait until I see him, and we can look at our calendars together."

"Sounds good. Keep in touch, and I'll let you know if anything comes of my talking to them at the station."

"Thanks, Audrey, I'm sorry to be such a pain in the butt about all of this!"

When the call finished, Audrey stashed her phone in her backpack and returned to the kitchen. Rod was just setting the carton of juice back in the fridge. "Can I catch a ride with you to the station? My shoot just got canceled and I've got some image files that the captain wants sorted out."

"Sure. I'm ready, you?" Audrey nodded, and the two of them filed out the door. "Was the call anyone I know?" Rod asked once they were buckled in.

"Do you know Sylvia Brown? She's marrying someone from your department, a guy named John Washington. Do you know him?"

Rod shook his head. "I know of him, but not in a good way."

"That makes this even weirder, then. On Monday, after he missed our appointment, he sent her a text saying, if he missed again to tell you and the captain."

"Me? Why would you tell me? That doesn't make any sense."

They discussed several possibilities on their way in but hadn't come to any conclusions before they reached the captain's office. "Captain? A word?" Rod spoke as he knocked on the open door frame. Captain Fischer had overseen the precinct for years before Audrey was hired. A warm, caring man, he was in his mid-fifties now and took a keen interest in his squad. Audrey had no qualms about sharing the odd text with him.

"What's up, Rod? I see you've got company."

"Good morning, Captain." Audrey offered. "I'm the one who wanted a word, actually. I got a strange message this morning."

"From who?" The captain leaned forward in his seat.

"Sylvia Brown, do you know her? She's marrying one of your officers, and when he missed an appointment for engagement photos on Monday, we rescheduled for this morning. But he told her that, if he missed again, he wanted her to ask me to tell you and Rod."

"Who's she marrying?"

"John Washington is his name."

The captain jumped to his feet. "Oh, God. When did she last hear from him?"

"Monday afternoon, I think."

"Captain?" Rod asked, surprised by the captain's sudden alarm.

"Smitty, get in here." The captain barked as he held down the intercom button. Then he looked up at Audrey and Rod once again. "I was afraid something like this was going to happen."

Smitty was there within a few moments. The captain gestured them all into seats before closing the door to the office. Once he was behind his desk again, he resumed. "John Washington is missing."

"That guy." Smitty made a sound of disgust, but the captain held up his hand. "It's not what you think. He's not that guy. He's been undercover on an assignment." The captain looked directly at Smitty then. "Monday was the last I talked to him. You have to know how uncomfortable he was with the role he was having to play."

"Racist asshole, you mean?" Smitty was shaking his head, then looked up in surprise at the captain's sharp tone.

"Exactly. He told me he'd had to insult you in front of Marconi, and it made him sick." The captain paused, his thumbs drumming a rapid beat against the desk. "He called you a role model."

"Captain, what's going on here?" Rod interjected.

"End of last month, Marconi approached Washington here in the precinct, made some crude racist and sexist remarks, as well as some veiled threats when they were alone in the breakroom. Washington came to me immediately, and I told him about a task force that's been looking into unauthorized militias in the area. They had just lost an officer from Butler and were hoping to recruit someone else from within the force."

"Oh, shit. The missing person's case, Dan Stevens. That's why they called you. He wasn't on a camping trip. He was undercover?" Smitty leaned forward, both hands gripping the edge of the desk.

"That's right. The site you two found in the woods is the closest we've gotten to locating their camp. Washington had gotten some footage of it but wasn't able to carry in any sort of tracking device. The woods there are so dense that we . . ."

He was interrupted by a knock on the door. He paused while Rita stepped into the room. "Oh, sorry for interrupting." She looked at the group. "Is it okay to speak, Captain? I think I've got something you're going to want to see."

"Gentlemen, Audrey, this is our tech specialist, Rita Banks. She's been working with us on the task force. Rita, I think you've met Detective Rodriguez. This is his partner, Demetrius Smith," he paused, chuckling. "And his other partner, Audrey Markum." For half a second, the tension in the room broke, and everyone seemed to take a breath. "Okay, what've you got?"

She looked first at Rod. "I've been looking at the feed we're getting from the camera behind Bishops. It's dull stuff, not a lot of coming and going, but I just spotted this from yesterday afternoon." The captain turned his monitor so that they could all see it while Rita tapped in the information that would bring up the recorded feed. One of the tall garage bay doors was open, a heavyset man holding it while a pickup pulled partway into the space. As they watched, the pickup driver got out and lifted back a tarp before pulling out three plastic grocery bags. They appeared to be bulging with food and looked heavy, but the bigger man made no move to help, maintaining his stance by the door instead. Rita paused the feed and looked up at the group.

"Captain, I've seen that big guy before. He was in the last footage that I downloaded from Washington's camera. He told me his name was Bo something."

"Rod? Smitty? That name mean anything to either of you?"

Both men shook their heads. "The only name I heard from the guys at Bishops was Nathan Keller. They thought he might have been behind the vandalism at their place years ago. I think that's the guy with the food bags."

"Can you run it again from the beginning?" Audrey asked, her gaze fixed on the screen.

"Sure." Rita cued up the footage, and they watched the silent footage again as the door opened and the pickup pulled in. When the man tossed back the corner of the tarp, Audrey pointed.

"There. Freeze it there."

"What are you seeing?" Rod asked, turning his gaze to Audrey.

"It looks like a yellow bike to me," Audrey answered. "What do you think, Rod?"

"Is there a significance to a yellow bike?" The captain asked, and Rod explained.

"Late Tuesday afternoon, two teenagers were hanging out around that alley when a big truck pulled into the garage. Jerry, the boy we interviewed, said that when they opened the back of the truck, they saw a body. Someone fired at them, and they took off, but he caught a bullet in his foot. While we were interviewing him yesterday morning, the other boy's mother came in and said that her son never came home that night. He had been walking their bikes back home while his friend went to the emergency room. Jerry, the boy who was shot, said that he has a yellow bike."

Audrey picked up the story then. "Jerry is an amazing artist. He showed us the drawings that he had made of the scene." She pulled up the photographs that she'd taken and transferred them to the captain's screen. Audrey pointed at the first man Jerry had seen, the one he said had fired the gun. "It looks like the same guy to me. He didn't get as good a look at the second guy, but he did say he was older and kind of fat."

"What have you got?" The captain asked when he noticed Smitty had been searching for something on his phone.

"I'm trying to access information on the ownership of the garage. It looks as though through last October, it was owned by a Nathan Keller, apparently inherited from his father, a Randolph Keller."

"But October? What happened then?" The captain asked.

"Ownership was transferred to a corporation, ICB Incorporated." Smitty looked up at the faces around him. "That ring any bells with anyone?"

"No, but in Katz's report from her interview with Keller, she said he told her he'd sold the garage, couldn't afford the taxes on it with business so bad," Rod spoke to the group around him.

"I'll look into it. See what I can find, Captain." Smitty offered. "In the meantime, though, what do we think those grocery sacks mean? Do we think Washington and the boy are there?"

"I don't know." The captain responded.

Rod gestured toward the screen, "Is this enough to get a warrant to search the garage, Captain?"

"I'm sure it is. I'll get a judge to sign off as fast as I can and then send Katz and her partner back over there." He looked up at Smitty. "In the meantime, keep digging into the finances." He shifted his gaze then. "Rod, did the kid you interviewed think he'd seen a dead body?"

Rod shook his head. "He wasn't sure." He looked at Rita. "Could you bring back up the drawing of the garage and the truck?" Once the image reappeared, he leaned in and pointed at the head of the body. "He told us that he thought it was a man, that he saw what looked like nylon rope around his arms and legs and a bag over his head. We asked if it was like a plastic bag from a shop, but he said no, that it looked like a cloth shopping bag, with a pattern to it." He pointed to himself and Audrey. "We thought that sounded more like a hostage than a dead body. If Washington and the kid . . ."

Audrey inserted, "Carlo Rizzi is his name."

"Thanks, if Washington and Rizzi are being held captive there, it might explain the need for groceries."

The captain leaned back in his chair, clasping his hands behind his head. "Why keep hostages, though? Now that we've got the body of the officer from Butler, we know that they're capable of murder." He shook his head. "I hate to think it, but it seems more likely that Washington was left somewhere out in the woods the same way. Taking him hostage doesn't make any sense."

"But what about the body the boys saw? Where's Marconi now, Captain?" Smitty asked. "Do we have any surveillance on him?"

"No. Washington was our surveillance. Marconi had a shift last evening, but he's not on the clock again until Tuesday. He said he had some sort of family commitment over the weekend and needed some time off for it."

Rod stood, and Audrey and Smitty rose with him. "Captain, I understand what's at stake with the task force, but it seems to me, we have to make Carlo Rizzi and John Washington our priorities now. Audrey's on the clock with us today. All right if she and I head over to Bishops and see if we can get a closer look at the garage while we wait for the warrant?"

"That sounds good to me." The captain answered and then turned to Smitty. "I'm going to forward you everything I've gotten from the task force and let them know you're going to be in touch, then I'm going to call Butler's captain and let them know what we've found. Fill the task force in on what we've got so far on this garage and see if they've got any more information we can use."

Smitty nodded in agreement. "Will do. I'll also dig into the corporation angle. Maybe I can get some more information on who's behind all of this. Always follow the money, right?"

The captain nodded in agreement, and Rita offered. "Captain, why don't I go along with Rodriguez over to Bishops and see if we can't get some cameras in closer to the garage, maybe from a different angle?"

The captain stood then and leaned heavily on the desk in front of him. "Sounds like a plan. Report back to me as soon as you have something and, in the meantime, watch each other's backs. This is a nasty bear we're poking at here, one that seems to be getting ready to attack."

"Oh, thank God, you're not dead."

John Washington's head felt like it was two or three times the size it should be. The air inside the bag was warm and stale as he twisted to try and loosen it from around his nose and mouth. He paused. "Who said that?"

"I'm Carlo, Carlo Rizzi. You haven't moved in a long time, and I was afraid you were dead. My hands are handcuffed, and I can't move much, but I can see. If you can sit up, about three inches to your left is a nail sticking out of the wall that might help you pull that bag off."

As John tried to sit up, nausea threatened to make the bag situation even worse, so he paused and moved as slowly as he could until his back was against the wall. He shifted his weight onto his left hip and scooted over a few inches. When he raised his head, he could feel something poking into his hair through the bag. He felt it catch and tilted his head back and forth until he felt the bag begin to slip. A few more contortions and he was finally free of it.

"Oh, Jeez. What happened to you?" Washington could see the look on the kid's face and figured that meant he was in bad shape. However, the youngster had his own goose egg and black eye, so it didn't look as though he was in terribly great shape either.

"I think I got beat up, same as you. Maybe drugged a little after that if you say I've been out such a long time. What are you doing here? I never saw you around the compound."

"Compound? What are you talking about?"

John lowered his voice to a whisper. "You're not a militia member or trainee or whatever?"

"No way." Carlo laughed, then lowered his voice as well. "I'm in high school. My buddy Jerry and I were riding our bikes when we almost got run over by this big truck. We doubled back to check it out, and when we saw your body lying in the back, we freaked. We took off on our bikes, but some guy shot at us and hit my friend in the foot. We made it to a little market, and when Jerry's brother picked him up to take him to the hospital, I started walking our bikes back home. Suddenly, this pickup truck came out of nowhere and cut me off. I fell into the bikes, and then I think he hit me with something. Next thing I knew, I was sitting upstairs in some kind of attic watching you passed out on the floor."

"When was that?"

"Uh, Tuesday night."

"And what day is it now? Do you know?"

"I'm pretty sure it's Thursday morning now. Yesterday, I was allowed to get up and use the bathroom a few times, and then this guy moved us both in here and gave me some junk food. He said he'd bring me some dinner later, but he never showed. You must be starving."

John nodded slightly, aware that the fog and nausea seemed to be clearing a bit. "I am pretty hungry, but I'm afraid I . . ." He gestured at his crotch, which was wet and dirty.

"I'm glad that's what I was smelling and not some dead body."

John tried to stand, but the ropes attaching his arms to his legs didn't have enough slack in them to allow the movement. He looked over at Carlo. "Any idea where we are?"

"We're in a storage room next door to the garage that we saw the truck pull into."

Then John thought to survey the area around him more carefully. "Do you think there are any cameras on us in here?"

Carlo followed John's gaze around the room and shook his head. "I don't think so. The guy with the tattoos who brought me the food and water told me to holler if I needed to go to the bathroom . . ." He hesitated. "Or if you woke up."

"Okay, let's give that just a couple more minutes. Can you tell if the top button on my shirt is still there?"

"Looks like it to me. Why?"

John lowered his voice once more. "It's a camera with some important information on it. We need to get it to the police as soon as we can."

"How are we going to do that?" Carlo held up his hands and feet, which were both secured, his wrists handcuffed around the handle of a wide metal freezer. He let his head fall forward. "My mom must be so scared right now."

"Because you're not home? Will she and your dad come looking for you?"

"No, my dad's deployed in the Middle East right now. He's a logistics guy for the army. He's supposed to be finished before Christmas, but . . ." Carlo shrugged his shoulders. "It doesn't always work out that way. Whenever it's just me and my mom, she gets worried at the slightest thing. I'm afraid this will tip her over the edge."

"We need a plan to get you and the camera out of here. What can you tell me about the bathroom?"

"The bathroom has a window that I've been working on getting open, but I haven't had any luck yet."

By noon on Thursday, Keller was dead tired and fed up with the whole situation. Bo still hadn't been back to the garage, and he'd been stuck babysitting the hostages. He hadn't even been allowed to go home to have dinner with his wife the night before. Stuck with the same kind of crap that he'd taken the boy, Keller was working up the nerve to call Bo and put his foot down when he heard pounding on the outer door.

The two officers from before had returned, this time with a search warrant. Keller stood in the middle of the bay reading it over while they began their search, noting that it mentioned only the garage and not the shop next door. He was surprised to see that the warrant did include the back of his truck, so he had to admit to himself that Bo's instructions had been smart. Good thing he'd swept it out once he'd moved his gun and tossed the bikes.

The search seemed to take forever as the two cops picked through several different piles of trash on the main floor before going upstairs. He waited, trying not to hold his breath, and praying that he'd been thorough in his clean-up. When he saw them back near the door that connected to the coffee shop, he turned and fixed his gaze on the front, bay door, praying that his hostages would stay quiet and waiting to see if the officers would notice anything. Finally, they came back downstairs. The woman leaned over, looking at the stairs to the basement area. "What's down here?"

Keller hadn't been down there in ten years or more, so he was able to answer honestly. "I've got no idea."

"You got a key?" Keller shook his head. The two of them looked around before stepping down the stairs and trying the door. Keller noticed her talking to her partner, but neither of them said any more. He looked up as they approached.

"So, we done here?"

"For now." The woman nodded and paused, looking at him for a moment, before gesturing her partner ahead of her out the door.

Keller locked the door behind them and then collapsed into the chair in the office.

"Wow, we're getting to be quite the popular spot!" Amos announced as Rod, Audrey, and Rita entered the shop. Bob turned from his work at the long table off to the right and moved to join Amos at the counter.

"What can we do for you folks?" Bob asked as he folded up a tattered towel.

"Hi Amos, Bob. You've met Rita Banks before. This is Audrey Markum." The group nodded hello, and Rod continued. "We wanted to talk with you two again, maybe pick your brains a little bit more."

"Sure," Amos answered, and Bob returned to the back of the shop, emerging a moment later with a couple of folding chairs. "Why don't we all sit down over by the window? Can I get anyone a soft drink?"

"No thanks. We'll try not to take up too much of your time." Rod acknowledged as the group settled into chairs. "First, we want to thank you for letting us hook up that camera outside. Have you looked at the feed recently?"

Both men looked a little sheepish before Bob answered. "Sorry, once it was up, we didn't pay it a whole lot of attention."

"That's okay. Can you tell us any more about the man you called Keller? I know you suspected him of being behind the vandalism years ago, but have you had any conversations with him since then?"

The two older men looked at each other and shook their heads at the same time. Amos spoke for them both. "No, we keep our distance."

"Did you know that the garage had been sold? It used to be owned by a man named Keller, but in October, it was bought by a corporation, ICB Incorporated. Does that name mean anything to either of you?"

"No, makes me think of Iron City Beer, to tell you the truth," Bob answered.

Amos lifted his eyebrow. "Maybe it stands for Iron City something else."

"That's an idea," Rod answered and made a note. "You mentioned that you'd seen pickup trucks with Confederate flag stickers on them, that sort of thing, right? Have you seen a lot of them, or do you think it's a few appearing over and over again?"

"It was mostly in the winter, and I've never been one to notice car or truck brands. You have any idea, Bob?" Amos turned to ask.

"I don't think I've seen more than four or five different vehicles, although I can't say for sure. Keller drives an older Ford F-150, I know that much. There certainly isn't much auto work going on at the garage. Not sure how they're making any money," He looked up at Rod. "But you said that the garage was sold. That doesn't make any sense to me. If they're not working on cars and trucks, then what are they keeping a garage for? City rents and taxes aren't cheap, you know."

Audrey spoke up then. "I noticed that a number of the buildings on this block are connected. Are there actual passageways between any of them?"

"There used to be, but years ago, the city cracked down on some of the fire prevention codes, and we had to pay to have improved firewalls installed between our building and the one we're connected to on our left. Cost a pretty penny, too."

"But we do feel safer," Amos added.

"That's true." Bob turned to Rod again. "Based on the grumbling I heard, I'm not sure that everyone followed through with the city's demand, though."

"I'd be willing to bet that cheapskate bastard Keller never did, although maybe the corporation insisted on it before buying it," Amos added. "There might still be a connecting passage." He shrugged.

"Any idea who owns the building that connects to the garage?" Rita asked. "We were hoping to maybe get some cameras in a little closer."

"Well, let me think." He leaned back in his chair. "When we first got here, there was a bakery next door. Then it was a coffee shop for a while, but that didn't take either." Bob looked up. "I'm afraid I've lost track of the businesses that've been there."

"The storefront is still closed, but the door next to it leads to apartments upstairs, I believe," Amos added. "Maybe you could talk to some of the tenants about setting up a camera."

"That sounds like a great idea." Rod stood, and the others quickly followed suit. "Thank you for your time, gentlemen. You've been very helpful." They moved toward the door. "We'll be in touch."

"Please do," Bob added. "We're going to be worrying about Carlo until we hear from you."

"Agreed," Rod added before the group shook hands and took their leave. Once they were on the sidewalk again, the three studied the buildings across from the garage before moving across the street to get a better look at the alley, the garage and the building next to it. "Okay, ladies, I don't think we should stand here in plain view for too long. Let's get back in the car to talk about this."

"Take us down the block and back again and then drive down the alley a ways, won't you, Rod?" Rita asked before turning to Audrey. "Can you get your phone out and shoot some video on your side while I do the same on mine?"

"Sure thing." In the end, they risked just two passes down the street before driving back to the precinct.

Once back at the station, they stopped at the captain's office. Rod leaned in. "Did they get the search warrant?"

The captain shook his head. "They're on their way back now. They got in and had a good look but they didn't find anything." He raised his hands in frustration.

"Dammit," Rod smacked his hand on the desk, then focused back on the captain. "We're looking at the area around the garage trying to figure out how to get better surveillance on it. We'll let you know what we come up with."

The captain nodded and the group headed to Smitty's and Rod's desks to pull up the footage and consider the possibilities. Smitty walked in as the two women were sending the images to the wide monitors. "What's the word on the search? Did they find anything?"

"Nothing. You learn anything?"

"Not much yet, I'm afraid. The task force hadn't heard of the corporation at all."

"Amos and Bob mentioned that the ICB initials reminded them of Iron City Beer." Audrey offered.

"That's not a bad idea. The task force didn't seem to have a whole lot of information beyond what we'd learned, but they were glad to hear about the location of Stevens's body and the track that you and I followed back into the woods."

"Does it help pinpoint where they might be operating from?" Rod asked.

"We'll see. They're going to send some drones up to give them an overview of the area, but if it's camouflaged, they may not get much."

"They'd be better off with infrared cameras," Rita added. "Although they might not be in the budget."

"Does our department have anything like that?" Smitty asked, but Rita shook her head.

"Sorry, not at this point. I do have a friend I trust who's in an amateur drone club that has them, but I would be cautious about other sources. I'm guessing that other groups with that sort of interest might overlap with the militia groups you're trying to locate."

"Okay," Rod interjected. "Rita, would you give Smitty and the captain your friend's information? And for now, let's focus on the group's activities here in the city and let the Staties work on the woods. We'll scroll through the video you and Audrey got and see if we have any ideas for more helpful camera placements."

They were about to settle in when the captain called them back to his office. A female officer with red hair was standing next to another young officer. "I thought you'd want to hear this." He turned to the young woman. "Katz, you know detectives Rodriguez and Smith. What did you find at the site?"

"Sir, I'm sorry, we didn't turn up anything. The main floor is a big bay, an office, and a small bathroom. Upstairs, there's an unfinished attic space, but it was clean. No sign of anyone there."

"And the truck bed?" Rod asked.

"Clean as well, sir." Officer Katz replied.

Smitty leaned against the doorjamb. "Clean, huh, like they knew we might come looking there maybe?"

"But if they moved them," Rod began, but the captain finished.

"They could be anywhere in the city."

"Or the camp, wherever that is," Smitty added.

Rod turned back to Officer Katz. "Was there a basement? Did you go downstairs at all?"

She looked at her partner and then shook her head as she looked back at Rod. "There were stairs that led down, but they were covered in a thick layer of dust. The door at the bottom was locked and Keller said he didn't have a key. The whole space looked so unused, we didn't push further on it." She looked up at the captain. "Should we go back?"

"No, let's leave it for now." He looked at Rod. "Keep working the camera angle and let me know if anything turns up."

"Hey!" Carlo yelled, once he and John had the beginnings of a plan in mind. "This guy's awake, and he stinks!"

"Thanks for that," John whispered, but Carlo just shrugged.

"Sorry, but it's true, and we want to get you into that bathroom. I'm hoping you'll have better luck with that window."

John was surprised to see that the man who responded to Carlo's yell was not someone he recognized. He appeared with a plastic bag in his hand. John noted a few familiar tattoos, but he was pretty sure the man had not been at the camp.

"Stinks, huh?" The man laughed and kicked the bottom of Carlo's shoe as he entered their area.

"He needs some clean clothes and a bath." Carlo offered as the man stood there staring at them.

"If you ask me, he looked better with the bag on his head." The man waved his hand across his face. "You're right about the smell, though."

"What's going on? Who are you? Why am I being held here?" John pushed.

"Got a lot of questions for someone who's not in any position to demand answers, wouldn't you say?" He tossed the bag toward Carlo, who struggled to pull it open and dig out a box of juice and a package of cheese crackers. "I've got an old pair of overalls and a washroom with a sink in it, but that's about all." He reached down and tried to lift John by one elbow, but the ropes were tied such that John staggered and fell.

"Damn, that hurt. Can't you do something about this rope? I can't even straighten out my legs."

As Carlo tore into the package of crackers, the man knelt beside John and began untangling the rope from his feet. Once he had one end of it free, he re-tied John's legs, this time with about two feet of slack between them. After they were secured, he dug a knee into John's leg to hold him still while he re-tied the other end of the rope around his hands. They had been behind John's back but were now secured in the front.

"Try standing up now." The man ordered. John took his time getting his balance, grateful that the nausea had not returned.

"I'm John Washington. You got a name?"

"I know who you are." Then the man pulled a knife from his back pocket, flicked it open, and prodded John forward with it. He shoved the door against a pile of trash and boxes before stepping forward. "Bathroom's this way. Let's go."

"See you, kid." John offered before moving slowly forward. They entered a short hallway and paused by an office where the man unhooked a pair of overalls from the door and grabbed a T-shirt off a shelf. A key was hanging from the doorknob of the bathroom. He loosened the rope around John's wrist, then opened the door and shoved John in ahead of him. "You have five minutes," he growled and then closed and locked the door behind him.

The fluorescent bulb over the sink blinked twice before deciding to stay on. John caught a look at his face in the tarnished mirror and quickly looked away. They'd done a number on him; that was for sure. And he'd thought that the kid looked bad. It wasn't easy struggling out of the reeking clothes. The shirt had a button front which helped, but there was no way he could get out of the pants or clean himself up as long as the rope was holding his legs together. "Can I at least have the rope off my legs so I can get my damn pants off?" He bellowed. There was no response for what felt like a long time, but then he heard the key turn, and the man stood facing him in the doorway.

He brought the knife up to John's face before dropping down and slicing it through the cords, freeing his feet. "You're down to four minutes." He stepped back and locked the door once again.

It took some time to untangle the length of nylon rope and finally get the wet pants off. A roll of paper towels was sitting on top of the towel dispenser, and he went through half of it trying to get clean. He finished by washing his face and rinsing out his mouth. It was disgusting putting on someone else's dirty clothes, but it was still an improvement.

When he was as clean as he could get, John turned the tap back on to mask the noise as he began working on the window. It had been painted shut years ago, but it was at ground level, so that was a plus. Trying not to make too much noise, he smacked at the frame, loosening the paint at the bottom. It was difficult to get leverage in the small space, but just as he heard footsteps approaching, he felt the bottom section of the window give way. Hopefully, it would be enough for the boy to get through. As a last step, he ripped the camera off the shirt and tucked it under a trashcan next to the wall. He reached to turn off the tap just as the door opened.

"Time's up." The man gestured at a garbage bin by the backdoor where John dropped his dirty clothes. After being ordered to gather up the severed cords, John was forced back into the storeroom at knifepoint. The man pushed him roughly to the floor and re-tied him. "Maybe the kid'll toss you a snack." He laughed and left the two of them alone again.

Carlo did his best to toss the second package of crackers to John, but with his hands cuffed, his aim was terrible. "Sorry." He used his feet to nudge the packet closer.

"Thanks, Carlo."

"How'd it go?" Carlo whispered as John tore at the wrapper with his teeth.

"Good. I think I got it loose enough for you to pull it up. I got the camera in position, too."

"When do you think I should try to sneak out?"

"For now, let me rest and pull myself back together a bit. I want to be able to help if I can, in case something goes wrong."

"Okay." Carlo nodded, reached into the bag, and tossed a juice box over, this time aiming it a bit better. "Around dark, maybe?"

"That sounds like a good idea. You'll have a better chance of sneaking away then, too."

27

Friday morning, Audrey was relieved to see the steady green light on the charger for her aids. She tucked them into place and unplugged the unit, carrying it to the overnight bag that she was packing. Just to be safe, though, she slipped the backups in as well. A slim suit bag hung from the back of the bedroom door. She checked that her second pair of shoes was in the bottom of it before zipping it closed. With a suit bag, an overnight duffle, and two camera bags, it was going to be awkward, but at least they were sending a car for her. The rehearsal dinner was scheduled for seven that evening, so she was glad to have a few hours to work before the car was due just after two.

At noon, Rod returned home for lunch, happy to have the chance to see Audrey before she left for the weekend. After their argument the other day, Rod hadn't said anything more about the photo shoot, but he was sitting at the kitchen counter when she emerged with her bags. She settled everything by the door before sitting down beside him and accepting a cup of coffee. She leaned over and kissed him before taking a sip. "Thank you." Audrey waited to see if he would return to the topic once he saw her bags.

"I'm not going to say anymore, Audrey. I'm not trying to be the boss of you, I just want you to be safe. This resort or lodge or whatever you call it, where you're going, do you know where it is?"

Audrey thought back to the information she'd been given, but when nothing came to mind, she got out her phone and pulled up the couple's wedding website. She turned the screen so that Rod could look at it with her. "The address is a little vague, isn't it?"

"I'll say. Did you notice this note? It's telling people that there isn't much of a phone signal at the lodge."

"Yeah, the bride warned me about that. They want to keep the press away, and she said they may even collect people's phones at the door. They don't want a bunch of people taking pictures with their phones during the events. I've seen that happen at other weddings, and it can be annoying."

"I don't like the idea of your being out of touch, though. It makes me nervous."

"Rod, what do you think is going to happen to me at a wedding?"

"I don't know. That's what worries me. The dad doesn't have the best reputation, you know."

Audrey sensed an undertone to what Rod was saying, but with nothing more to go on, she put her phone away.

"Are you hungry?" Rod asked. He got up from his seat and retrieved a bag from the kitchen counter. "I picked up a couple of sandwiches on my way home."

"That sounds great. Thanks!" Audrey filled glasses at the tap while Rod set the sandwiches on two small plates. "I know you said the search didn't reveal anything. Has more happened on the video feed?"

"Not yet. It's been very quiet. Carlo's mother called me again this morning, and it's killing me that I don't have any more information for her." He looked up. "Like with Rosey, you know?"

Audrey squeezed his hand for a moment. "I know. It's always the waiting that's the hard part."

"Rita talked to some of the tenants in the space across the street and got two more cameras in place, but the angles aren't great, so we aren't expecting too much from them."

Audrey wasn't sure what else to say, so they sat eating quietly. When they finished, they put the plates in the dishwasher, and Audrey went to finish getting ready. She was just slipping on her shoes when he appeared at the bedroom door.

"I need to get back to the office." He squared his shoulders a bit and then pulled Audrey into a hug.

"It's going to be okay, Rod. I've got this."

"I know you do."

"If it's possible, I'll send an email or two to let you know how things are going. I don't want you to spend the weekend worrying about me."

"That'd be great." He kissed her once more and headed out the door.

It wasn't long before the doorbell rang. A graying, older man in a white shirt and black pants asked, "Audrey Markum for the Ellerby wedding?"

"That's me!" Audrey answered. She handed the clothes bags to him but carried the camera and computer bags herself. Her first destination wedding, she thought. She was determined to shake off the unease that Rod's worrying tone had left her with and enjoy herself. "I'm going to ace this and, before you know it, Maui, baby." She whispered to herself before settling into the back seat.

CHAPTER

28

By Thursday evening, John Washington had regained some of his strength, but the meager food rations were of little help. At dinner time, the man had set two small cups of ramen noodles in front of them that they'd each finished in record time. About half an hour later, John signaled to Carlo that it was time to try and get out through the bathroom window. The boy hollered for their guard who then led him out. As the minutes ticked by, John grew hopeful that the boy had made his getaway. He tried counting to see how many minutes might have passed, but before he'd reached three hundred, Carlo was back, a look of defeat on his face.

Their guard handcuffed the boy again and stepped away. "I'm getting goddamned sick of traipsing back and forth, so there'll be no more toilet trips tonight."

John decided to risk pushing the man a bit. "Why the hell are you doing this? You're supposed to be a patriot, right? That's what the Brotherhood is supposed to stand for? So, how's this patriotic? Do you know this boy's father is in the army, stationed in the Middle East right now? As we speak, he's busy defending our country, and here you are beating up his kid, scaring him to death. What kind of patriot does that?" The man guarding them looked at Carlo with a hint of concern on his face, so John pushed once again. "Plus, you're supposed to be all about supporting the thin blue line, right? Backing up the cops? Right? Well, hello, I'm a fucking cop, and look at how you're treating me. I don't know how you expect to recruit people to your cause when it doesn't make any fucking sense!" He'd lost his temper now, and when the tattooed arm came flying at him, the fist connecting with his already sore face, John knew he'd gone too far. He slowly regained his sitting position, and the man raised one finger in the air.

"Enough." He announced and then left.

Once they heard his steps retreating, John whispered. "What happened?"

Carlo shook his head, looking miserable and afraid. "I tried to get it open. I really did. But I only managed to raise it about three inches before it jammed up again. I thought about yelling, but that didn't seem like a good idea."

"No, you're right. I'm sorry I didn't get it loose enough for you."

"I got the camera though, tucked it deep into one of my cargo pockets."

"Good, good. That's the most important thing right there. We'll keep working on the window whenever we get down there. I bet by tomorrow night, we'll have it open wide enough for you to climb through."

"Okay." Carlo paused, a thoughtful look on his face. "What's the Brotherhood, by the way?"

"They call themselves the Iron City Brotherhood. They think they're some kind of patriotic militia."

"What, like during the Revolutionary War?"

"Yep, they think they're exactly like that. But they're wrong."

"Wrong?"

"They're nothing but a street gang with more weapons than an army. From what I can tell, they hate African Americans, women, the whole LGBTQ community, immigrants, college students, anyone they think is the least bit different." He paused, shifting his position to try and relieve some of the tension on the ropes. "Did you study Hamilton in school at all or see the musical?"

Carlo shook his head no.

"I had tickets to see Hamilton with my fiancée, so I decided to read the biography of Hamilton that it was based on. The thing I noticed the most was how modern so much of what was going on back then seemed. The South was trying to hold onto the economic power that it had, and slavery was at the center of it. A lot of the people that we were always told to admire were actually slave-holding white supremacists. Hamilton and some of his friends wanted to stop the southern slaveholders from becoming president after Washington stepped down."

"And did they?"

"Nope, Jefferson and Madison both became president." John gestured around him at the narrow storage room. "I don't think they were patriots, and I don't think these modern wannabes are patriots either. I think a lot of these guys have been tricked or persuaded to fear people who might be different from them."

"And you said they have weapons? A lot of them?"

"Yep, and big plans to haul them out on Halloween night."

"But that's just next week." Carlo looked around him frantically for a moment. "My mom and dad's families are both from Italy. They were immigrants here a long time ago. Are they planning to hurt people like my mom?"

"I don't think so. One of the especially stupid things about them is how contradictory the stuff they say is. Most of our families were immigrants to this country. In fact, unless you're a Native American, your ancestors were definitely immigrants. They've just decided to complain about the more recent immigrants because many of them are people of color." John leaned back against the rough wall. "I'm sorry that we seem to be handing your generation such a messed-up country, Carlo. I wish I knew how to fix everything. I really do." He felt the pain in his jaw and the fatigue washing over him, and his eyes closed without him planning for them to.

"Well, I'm sorry. You'll have to call the car and take me back to the city. I turned over my phone, but I can't do my job without my equipment. It's as simple as that." Audrey had been patient as the driver helped her carry her bags from the car and into the beautiful lodge. But she'd been stopped in the doorway now for more than twenty minutes and, frankly, she'd had enough. As soon as the person at the door saw Audrey's bags with her cameras and computer, he'd taken them from her and started rifling through their contents. If anything was broken, she was going to be even more livid. At some point, the driver had disappeared, and the guard, for he certainly wasn't a butler, picked up the in-house phone.

"Sir, we need you at the front door, please."

Within a few minutes, a tall, tan, GQ-type older man stepped into the foyer. Audrey had seen his face on the billboards plastered around town advertising his run for state representative. The stylishly graying temples and black plastic glasses had become his trademark. "Wade, what seems to be the problem here?"

"Boss, this woman has two bags of cameras, as well as a laptop. We were told not to allow any type of electronics into the lodge."

"Excuse me, Mr. Ellerby. My name is Audrey Markum. Susan Ellerby hired me to be the wedding photographer for this weekend, and this is my equipment. If I can't bring it in, then I can't do my job."

Audrey thought that his voice sounded just as cultivated as his TV persona. "Please, Ms. Markum, step on through. I apologize for the confusion." As the guard attempted to stuff one of the lenses back into the bag, Ellerby reached to take it from him and picked up the entire bag to hand it to her. "I'm sure Ms. Markum would prefer to take care of her own equipment. Have the boy deliver her other bags to her room." He turned to Audrey. "Please, follow me, and I'll show you the layout of our place." He gave her a moment to resettle the camera equipment and then led her into the next room.

Audrey found it hard to reconcile the ease with which Mr. Ellerby began leading her forward and the rough, insolent nature of the man who had first greeted her at the door. He looked vaguely familiar to her, but she was not given a last name and couldn't come up with a context in which she might have seen him.

When they stepped into the great room that appeared to be the heart of the lodge, Audrey was struck by both the beauty and the size of the place, and she paused to remind herself once again that this weekend could be a real breakthrough for her. There was no reason to let the first man's rudeness ruin that.

As they turned the corner toward a large dining area, Audrey heard Susan's voice bubbling from another room. Ellerby waited as his youngest daughter made her way graciously into the room, stopping along the way to chat with the guests who had arrived early.

"You made it!" Susan called out as she entered the dining area. "Has Daddy given you the grand tour?"

Ellerby leaned over and kissed his daughter before turning to go. "I've only gotten this far, dear, but if you'll take over, I'll get back to our other guests. Ms. Markum, again, I apologize for the earlier confusion." With a half bow, he was gone.

Susan looked concerned as she turned to face Audrey. "Did something happen? Was the car okay?"

"It's nothing," Audrey answered, waving her hand as if to dismiss any concerns. "Just a mix-up at the door." She looked around her at the warm wooden walls and the stairway that curved along the back of the room opposite the wall of windows. "If you can show me to my room, I'll get changed and start to organize everything." She gestured behind her. "I'm thinking that stairway would be a lovely spot for us to start, don't you think?"

Susan seemed pleased with the idea and chatted easily as they made their way down a long hallway. Most of the doors stood open awaiting guests, Audrey presumed, and many sported a picturesque view of the woods and mountains surrounding the lodge. When they arrived at her room near the end of the hall, she was disappointed to see that there wasn't quite the panorama that many of the other rooms enjoyed. But she told herself, she was there to work, *not* as a guest. It was only fitting. Quickly, she began sorting through her gear and arranging a workspace for her laptop. There seemed to be enough outlets, but no Wi-Fi at all. This must be even more isolated than I thought, Audrey mused. How odd. She had hoped to send some sort of reassuring email to Rod once she'd arrived, but it didn't look as though that was going to be an option. Oh well, he would just have to trust that she was safe. Once she'd freshened up and changed into one of the easy, flowing dresses that she'd brought, Audrey grabbed her main camera and bag and set out to work.

It was ten thirty that evening before Audrey was finally able to peel away. Her feet, even in flats, were starting to scream at her. She'd had a few bites of dinner, but most of her time was spent circling the various areas that were set up for the couple and their guests. She hadn't expected any sort of maid service, but it was quite a treat to walk in and spot a tray with a small plate of food and a carafe of hot water. A selection of teas had been provided to go along with the food, so she tossed her shoes aside and settled down at the table to recuperate. Breakfast was scheduled to begin at eight, so she planned to make it an early night.

Carlo and John spent a long Friday alternating between desultory talk about simple things and snoozing, both growing more and more uncomfortable with their confinement. With some maneuvering, each could stand and shuffle around where they were anchored, but it did little to relieve the tedium. They'd been offered powdered white donuts that had left them both messy and thirsty, but no other food had appeared during the day. As the light outside the small window began to dim, they were hopeful that some kind of dinner might finally be provided.

Once night had truly fallen and still, no one had appeared, Carlo and John began taking turns shouting for someone to come. Earlier, they thought they had heard arguing between the tattooed man who'd been tending to them and someone else, but the voices had moved out of range before John could get a clear idea of who he was talking to. One snippet he heard made him think it might have been Bo with his distinctive voice, but he couldn't be sure. John thought he'd heard their guard say something about patriotism and the army, but he couldn't be sure of that either. He had little hope that the lecture he'd given the man would make any difference, but he'd felt like he had to try. Rather than helping their situation, though, it seemed to have kept the man away from them. Hence, the donuts and growing thirst.

Finally, there was the sound of footsteps. When the man emerged, he was balancing a tray on which sat two plates of food with steam coming off them and a plastic pitcher of water. He had two paper cups hooked onto one finger, and he maneuvered the tray to hand the cups out first before setting the tray on the floor. "Sorry, I've been gone all day. My wife made this for you and sent it over." With that, he set a plate and spoon in front of each of them and stepped away without another word. That the taunting arrogance had been replaced by a quieter, more serious tone was odd and welcome, but they were too hungry to spend much time thinking about it.

The plates held a generous portion of stew along with a serving of green beans and a biscuit. It appeared to be homemade and tasted delicious, especially in comparison to the packaged junk foods they'd been getting. There was no sound other than their eating until they were sopping up the last of the stew with the ends of their biscuits. "Good, huh?" John asked, nodding to Carlo over his plate.

"Yeah. I was so hungry, though, I'd have eaten anything. Why the change, do you think?"

"I don't know." John shrugged. "I wish we could have heard more of the argument earlier. I was hoping to make a dent in the guy's moronic thinking, but I don't imagine that I did." There was the faint sound of footsteps approaching, so he quickly whispered. "Listen, I'll take the bathroom first and do my best with the window."

Carlo ducked his chin in agreement but said nothing. The footsteps continued and the man appeared once again. "Good food, huh?" He asked, stacking the plates and utensils back on the tray. He refilled each of their water cups and returned the pitcher to the tray as well.

"Yeah, nice change from the junk." John offered.

"Names Keller, Nathan Keller. I figure I owe you that much at least. You need the toilet, now's the time." He set the tray on a wooden bench and moved to untie John, who'd nodded his head.

"I'll be back for you in a minute, kid," Keller added before withdrawing his knife and prodding John in the back as they moved through the dark hallway. Once inside the bathroom, John used the commode, took a moment to wash his hands and face, and then left the water running as he stepped over to the window. He tried to work quickly, shoving at the old, painted frame until finally, it slid up and down fairly easily. He coughed and spat and complained loudly to cover up the noise before using his shoe to scuff away the paint chips that had fallen. He'd done the best he could for the kid. He hoped it'd be enough. He turned off the water just as Keller unlocked the door and looked in. He seemed to be studying the small washroom and John had a brief moment of worry when his gaze settled on the window. But soon he turned away and, with his knife out once again, began prodding John forward. When they reached the storeroom and he could see Carlo, John gave him a wink and settled back down into his seat as Keller re-tied the various ropes.

John noticed that Keller didn't seem to see Carlo as much of a threat. He uncuffed him and held his knife out, but then picked up the tray and carried it with him, the knife held loosely underneath. Again, John started counting the seconds, praying that they would go on and on and that the kid would be able to get away. They'd been there for days, and his growing sense of desperation told him that something had to give. His count had reached over a thousand when he heard a shout. Thank God. It sounded like the boy had gotten away.

As soon as he got into the washroom, Carlo turned the taps on full. He didn't take time to do anything else before moving toward the window. This time, he was thrilled when it slid all the way up. He climbed up onto the commode and began shimmying through the opening headfirst. Luckily, there was a rusted old dumpster not far from the window, so he eased his head and shoulders out onto it and then pulled his legs up after. Quickly then, he slid along the top edge of the dumpster before dropping down onto the ground on the other side of it. For a half second, he thought about looking for his bike, but he heard a shout and decided to take off running. He crouched low until he reached the walkway up to the main street, then began running flat-out, each second expecting to hear footsteps coming after him.

Three blocks in, Carlo was exhausted, his breath coming in quick, hard gasps, but he tried to keep up a steady pace. At one point, he took a wrong turn, the area was so confusing in the dark. His pace slowed, but when he spotted the market where they'd stopped to take care of Jerry's foot, he knew he was on the right track. For a second, he thought about going in and asking someone to call his mom or the police, but it just felt too risky. Instead, now that he had his bearings, he began zigzagging back and forth, trotting when he could, taking a roughly diagonal path back toward his apartment and safety.

With his energy nearly spent, Carlo finally found himself in front of his own building. His key had been lost with his backpack, so he leaned hard on the buzzer before stepping back into the shadows near the door. When he heard the distinctive click, he shoved the door open and dashed inside, slamming the door behind him. He was halfway up the first set of stairs when he heard his mom hurrying down the upper one. "Mom, Mom!" He called, a sudden surge of energy pushing him up and up.

"Carlo! Oh, thank God!" His mom was on the landing, and Carlo rushed into her arms, feeling more like a six-year-old than the teenager he was. They both had tears on their faces as they moved back up the stairs to their unit, Carlo's hand firmly in his mom's.

"Oh, Mom." Carlo threw himself into the first chair he came to. He struggled to get his breath back. "Mom, I . . ."

"Just sit, take a second, and breathe." She went to the kitchen and then returned with a glass of water. He gulped at it greedily while his mom reached for her phone and settled into the chair next to him at the table. "Drink, rest. Give me a second to call the policeman who was here." She pulled a business card out of her back pocket and began dialing. It was answered quickly. "Detective, he's here."

Carlo waited, trying to hear what was being said on the other end, but his mother just said okay and ended the call. "Who was that?"

"I called the detective I met over at Jerry's. He's on his way."

"Is Jerry okay? Is his foot okay?"

She nodded and rested her hand on his knee. "He's doing fine. They operated on him the night he got to the hospital, but he's been recovering at home since then. He's been as worried about you as I have."

"I'm glad he's doing okay." Carlo could feel his breath evening out and a bit of calm started to replace the terror he'd felt on his trek across town. He remembered then to reach down into his pocket to check for the camera he'd hidden there the day before. He panicked at first, not feeling it, but when he dug further, he found it lodged down in the corner. He put it on the table in front of his mom. "The detective is going to want to see this."

"What is it?"

"It's a secret camera that the policeman I was being held with wanted me to sneak out. I don't know what's on it, but he said it's really important."

"Where were you all this time? You said someone else was there?"

"We were in a storeroom next door to a garage that's near Bishops. But I still don't know why." The buzzer for the door sounded, and Ms. Rizzi went to push the release. "Mom, check first who it is," Carlo whispered, still not sure if he'd been followed. She nodded, and he listened.

"Detective Rodriguez, Ma'am." He heard before the release clicked. She waited by the door and then ushered him into the kitchen, where Carlo was still sitting. "Well, Carlo, it's nice to meet you. I'm Detective Rodriguez." He looked closely at Carlo's face and pointed a figure toward his eye. "Looks like you took a beating. Are you okay? Should we call a doctor?"

Carlo reached up and touched the tender area, relieved that the swelling around it had gone down. "I'm okay. I was unconscious for a little while, but I've been feeling all right since then."

The detective looked at his mom. "I think you should have him checked out by his doctor in the morning. I can take some pictures here this evening for our report, but if he was knocked out, they're going to want to check him for signs of a concussion." When she nodded, Rod clicked a few photos and then sat down at the table.

"I'll do that."

"Do you feel up to talking, Carlo? I could come back in the morning if you're not up to it."

Carlo shook his head and then picked up the small device that was lying on the table. "No, you need this now."

"What is it?"

"A man named John Washington was being held with me. He's the one who got the window open so that I could escape. He wanted me to get that to the police."

"John Washington, you're sure? And he's alive? Where were you being held?"

Carlo nodded, but his eyes started to fill with tears. "We were in a storeroom next to the garage. It looked like the back of a restaurant or something. He was alive when I left." He looked up as the detective stood and began dialing his phone.

Rod stepped aside to make the call. "Captain, we need another warrant. A storeroom next to the garage. Maybe the back of the old coffee shop." Carlos could see the detective nodding before stowing his phone and sitting back down. "Go ahead, Carlo."

"At first, I was afraid he was dead, especially when Jerry and I saw him lying in the back of the truck. I was brought there Tuesday night, but it wasn't until Thursday morning that he woke up. His face was bashed around a lot, but he thought he'd been drugged too since he was out for so long. I hope nothing happened to him because I got away."

"Do you think the people who had you knew about this camera?" Rod held up the tiny device.

Carlo shook his head. "I don't think so."

"What can you tell me about what happened to you, where you were held?"

"You talked to Jerry, right, so you know what happened first?"

Detective Rodriguez nodded. "He said you wrapped up his foot and helped get him into his brother's car. Then you were walking the bikes back home, is that right?"

"Yep. I think I'd gotten about two blocks away from the convenience store when this pickup truck came flying out of nowhere and knocked me and the bikes to the ground. I was all tangled up and trying to stand when he hit me in the head. The next thing I knew, my legs were tied and I was handcuffed around a pole in an attic. It was above the garage that's back there in the alley behind Bishops. Later, they moved us downstairs to the storeroom next door."

"I know the place. Can you describe . . . One second." He held up his finger while he answered his phone. "Amos, thank you. I've got him right here with his mom. He's going to be fine." There was a pause, and he nodded as he wrapped up the call. "Thank you for letting me know. I'll follow up with you and Bob in the morning if that's okay. Talk to you then." He hung up and looked back to Carlo. "That was Mr. Wright from Bishops repair shop. Do you know him?"

"A little. I was there before I got taken."

"That's right. He and his partner put up a camera for us, and he saw some movement on the feed. He's relieved to hear that you're home with your mom. We all are."

"So, people were looking for me?" Carlo looked up in surprise.

"Of course," his mom responded. "Detective, what's next? Is my son still in danger?"

"Carlo, did they seem to know who you were or where you lived or anything?"

Carlo thought about it but decided he didn't know the answer. "I don't know. I had my backpack with me, but I never saw it upstairs. If they went through it, I guess they might have figured something out, but there wasn't a wallet or a phone or anything much in it. I don't have a driver's license yet, so there was just a school ID, I guess. They didn't seem very interested to tell you the truth."

"Who is they?"

"I only saw one guy, and it wasn't until tonight that he even told us his name. It was Nathan Keller. But I heard someone else a few times, someone he was arguing with. He had kind of a squeaky voice, but I never saw him." Carlo looked from the detective to his mom. "Could I call Jerry and let him know that I'm all right?"

Rod stood and pushed his chair back under the table before picking up the camera. "I think we're done for tonight, Carlo. I'm very glad that you're home and you've given us valuable information on Officer Washington. We're going to have a car patrol around here tonight, just to be sure you weren't followed. Ms. Rizzi, if we need to talk with you again, I'll give you a call."

Carlo shook the detective's hand and then stepped away to go and find his phone while his mom let the policeman out. Not too surprisingly, Jerry answered on the first ring. "Hey, it's me. How's your foot?" Carlo sat back and listened, so relieved to be home once again.

CHAPTER
32

Rod waited until he was in his truck before calling the captain. "Sir, I've just come from Carlo Rizzi's apartment, the boy who was abducted earlier in the week. Were you able to get the warrant? He says he was held with Washington first in the attic above that garage we were talking about and then in the storeroom behind the abandoned coffee shop next door. Amos Wright called me to tell me he'd seen something on the video feed, but the boy had already made it home by then. Carlo tells me Washington helped him to escape and gave him a camera to bring to us."

He paused, listening to the captain's response. "Got it. I can be there in a few." The streets were quiet at that time of the evening, so Rod was able to drive quickly. The captain had offered to call in Rita Banks, so he punched in Smitty's number as he drove. "Hey, can you meet me at the station? The kid escaped and brought out a camera that Washington gave him." He could hear the surprise in Smitty's voice. "I know. It's crazy to think that he's alive and not that far away. Or," he paused, "at least he was there and okay an hour or so ago. The captain has a team there now." Rod ended the call as he pulled into the precinct lot. The captain met him at the station door. Rod had wished there was some way to reach Audrey and let her know that the boy was okay, but he'd tried earlier, and his call had gone straight to voicemail. He hated not being able to talk to her, especially after the ordeal she went through in the spring. He had to force himself to shake off those awful images as he pushed inside following the captain to his office.

"You beat me here, Captain?"

"Aw, hell, I never got out of here earlier. Rita's on her way in. I didn't want anyone else messing with the camera, since she's the one who set it up."

"Makes sense. Smitty's on his way in, too. Captain, any word?"

"Not yet, I've got officers there searching the place for him but I haven't heard back."

"Should we head over there and help? Was Katz available? She was there earlier and could compare the scenes."

He shook his head. "No, she's tied up with a call out on the east side. And I need you here. We've got to get a look at that camera. What did the kid say exactly?"

"He said they were tied up in a storeroom next to the garage. He said that Washington had been beaten and maybe drugged, but he also said that Washington helped him to escape and wanted him to bring us the camera as soon as possible. It's hard to know what they'll do with Washington once they realize the boy's gone."

While they were waiting, the captain took the opportunity to bring up the surveillance video from the cameras near the garage. Two squad cars were parked at angles around the building, lights flashing. It gave the feed an odd look as the image flipped back and forth between color and gray as the light changed. With no more action apparent, he wound the feed backward to earlier in the evening and caught sight of the boy running down the alleyway to the sidewalk. They could see the man they thought was Keller, open a side door and dash out into the driveway. He stood looking around until the heavy-set man stepped out as well, and there appeared to be an argument. The captain looked up at Rod. "Looks like they were arguing about what to do."

They watched for several more minutes until the men returned inside. Lights came on, but as they watched, the bay doors remained closed, and no one seemed to be leaving. "God, I hope he wasn't in there taking another beating." The captain offered.

"Or worse," Rod added.

In less than ten minutes, both men emerged from the side door and climbed into separate vehicles, first a truck and then an SUV pulling away from the garage. The captain rewound and watched the video several times but in the low light and with no clear lines of sight as the men were moving, it was unclear if there had been an additional body. When the squad cars arrived minutes later, no lights remained.

The two men sat silently, watching as the feed caught up to real-time. Rod switched through to the other camera views, but they offered nothing of interest. Rita and Smitty arrived in short order after that.

"Rita, I don't know what's on this, but the boy says that Washington helped him to escape and insisted he bring this to us. Can you pull it up on my screen?"

Rita set her bag down and pulled out her laptop before reaching for the camera. While she worked, Rod filled them in on what he'd learned from Carlo. Smitty had the same question he'd had. "So, we've got to try and go in tonight for him, right, Captain?"

He waved Smitty into a seat. "We're already doing that. I've got units on the scene checking both buildings. They'll call in as soon as they have something. For now, though, let's see what Rita's got. The boy felt pretty sure that the captors didn't know about the camera, right?" He looked up at Rod who nodded his assent. "So, we don't want to give something away if we don't have to." He looked at Rod once more. "I don't know how they would view their risk once the boy got away, do you?" He gestured toward the feed. "They didn't seem to take any immediate action."

"Without following him, I'm not sure that they'd know where the boy lived. He said he didn't think he had anything but a school ID in his bag. I doubt you could call a school and get anyone to turn over an address for a student. You definitely couldn't learn anything at night."

"Okay everyone, I think I've got it." Rita clicked through some additional keys, and a grainy video appeared on the larger monitor. The audio quality was also poor, but with some adjustments, she was able to make both come into greater clarity. The image coalesced into what looked like a camp. They could see some sort of obstacle course between a gate into the camp and a building. Washington paused, and the camera took in more details, including what looked to be a shooting range toward the back. He moved into the building, past a few open doors and then down a hallway. He seemed to pause before opening the last door, but when he did, they could hear him gasp. It was an armory with racks and racks of

automatic rifles, as well as crates of ammunition, helmets, what looked
to be shelves of protective vests, and a stack of riot shields. The captain
paused the transmission as they all reeled back in shock.

"Jesus." Smitty and Rod offered the same comment.

"My God, Captain. How would they even get all that stuff?" Rita
asked.

"The internet for a lot of it, but those shields, for example" he pointed at the screen, "they look like ours, maybe even newer. You'd have
to have an in with the manufacturer to get your hands on those." He
gestured toward the helmets and vests. "Those too, I bet." He looked up
at the faces around the desk. "There has to be some major cash behind
all of this and a supplier with an inside track. I'm afraid this may be even
worse than the task force was expecting." He gestured toward Rita, and
she resumed the transmission.

The camera stuttered for a half second, and Washington turned as if
he'd been startled. Marconi's face came into view then, and they heard
him say "Pretty impressive, don't you think? We've got a local guy, a
businessman, helping us bring them in." Rita paused it again. "Just like
you said, Captain."

They listened as the conversation continued and something was mentioned about Halloween. They watched as Washington left the building
and headed to what looked like an outhouse along the back fence line.
Then the video feed and audio went black. While they waited, Rod asked
the captain. "Do we have any idea yet where this camp is?" The captain
shook his head and turned to Smitty. "You learn any more about a location from the task force?"

Smitty shook his head no. "They used our coordinates from where
the body was found and the trail we followed back, but there are a LOT
of woods out there." He gestured toward the feed. "I'm not seeing any
landmarks at all. I wish he'd had it on as they were driving there."

Rita responded. "I told him that a camera that small would have
a limited recording capacity, so I think he tried to focus in on what he
thought was the most important information. I also recommended he
keep it off at any security checkpoints in case their electronic sweeps
found it." When the feed began once more, a dim light showed a rough

wooden door. A thin voice whispered, "Please don't let me fuck this up," before the door opened and bright light hit the camera once again.

They watched as he entered the building through a different door and took a seat in the middle of a small room. There were chairs set up in rows and a chalkboard toward the front. They recognized Marconi standing by a short lectern beside another, much more heavyset older man. "Can you pause it a second, Rita?" Rod asked as he pulled out his phone with Audrey's photos of Jerry's sketches on it. One showed a heavyset man standing with a ring of keys. His features were not distinct, but his silhouette seemed to match the man they were looking at now. He showed it to the others. "Could be the same guy."

"Looks like it," the captain offered. "I thought I caught the name Bo. Anyone hear anything else? We got a last name on him yet?"

"Yeah," Smitty pulled up a driver's license photo on his phone. "Names Bo Burns, Address out on the east side of town."

"Okay, good work." The captain nodded and they turned back to the video.

"I know you've all been training, working hard to get ready for our first event." The heavier man began, his voice oddly high for someone of his size, and Rod interjected.

"Carlo said he heard a squeaky voice."

The man on the video rubbed his hands together in obvious anticipation. "You're about to get your wish. Halloween, that's going to mark our debut. It'll be our first mission but not our last. Marconi," He gestured toward the police corporal. "Fill 'em in on what they'll be doing."

As they watched, Marconi flipped the chalkboard over to reveal a map of the city of Pittsburgh, the rivers, and the downtown area enlarged in the center. He pulled out a laser pointer and focused it on the point where the rivers converged.

"Point State Park," the captain uttered. "Right under our noses."

"This is where Iron City's history began," Marconi announced, "and it's where our Iron City Brotherhood is going to make its stand. We're going to mass there, in all our gear, and we're going to occupy the entire area." He gestured at several routes leading into the park, highlighting places where the various teams would assemble. "Once our groups are in position, we will march into the heart of the city and claim it for our own." The men seated around Washington's chair erupted into a shouting frenzy. He joined in as well but took the opportunity to pan the room with his hidden camera before sitting back down.

This time the captain paused the feed and focused a grim look at the group around his desk. As he rubbed his hand over his bald head, Rod couldn't help but notice the wrinkled shirt, the bit of salsa on his old tie, and the general air of dread that filled the captain's voice. "Come Halloween, next Thursday, that park will be packed with kids and families. I saw the parade permit myself this morning. A group that's focused on diversity and providing opportunities for underserved kids is hosting a Halloween party there." He seemed to sink even lower into his chair. "Jesus, someone is going to get killed."

Unsure what else to say, the captain resumed the feed, and they watched as the meeting broke up and Marconi and the big guy sent the members away. They heard a truck mentioned and as the room cleared, they saw the two presenters advance toward Washington. "Oh, shit," Rita gasped as the confrontation ensued and Washington flew backward, chairs flying around him. Then it went dark. Rita fast-forwarded, but there were no more images.

The four of them sat there silently in shock. Smitty found his words first. "Captain, can we stop the parade permit or move that gathering to somewhere else?"

The captain shook his head. "I'm afraid not. Lots of permits get issued for events on Halloween, and we'd have to offer some reason for denying it after it was already issued."

"That could tip them off." Rod gestured toward the screen with his chin.

The captain studied the group for a moment before the radio squawked an interruption.

"*Nothing here, Captain. We've been over both the garage and the shop. There's evidence that they were held here, including what looks like some blood, as well as wrappers and some handcuffs on the floor.*"

"Nothing else?" the captain leaned forward as he spoke into the mic.

"*Nothing, no cars or trucks either. I think we must have just missed them.*"

The captain slammed his hands to the desk. "Dammit all to hell. All right, leave one car there overnight and keep an eye on the place. Pull in someone else once your shift ends, okay?"

"*You got it captain.*"

The captain looked at the faces around him. "I know what you're all thinking, that our priority should be Washington." There were murmurs of agreement, but he lifted his hand to stop them. "I hate like hell not knowing where Washington is now and what shape he is in, and not taking more steps to search for him." The screen switched back to the feed from the garage as one cruiser pulled out and the other adjusted its position.

The captain turned to Smitty. "Get Burns's and Keller's home addresses to dispatch and have them send some uniforms to check out their homes." Then he turned to Rod and Rita. "You two keep an eye on the camera feeds or better yet, go back over to the garage and let me know if you see anything that might have been missed."

They all left quickly, and the captain sagged back into his chair. From bad to worse, he thought, picturing again the way Washington's body had flown into the chairs. When Smitty returned, the captain gestured toward his computer. "We know from this video that this is way bigger than one man. We've got to bring in the task force, maybe even the state police, and work on this together."

"But, Captain, isn't there a chance there's more cops like Marconi being involved?" Smitty asked.

"You're right. It adds to the risk. But Washington gave us a good look at the others in that room, so at least we've got a place to start. I know I didn't recognize anyone else from our precinct. In the morning, I'm going to start reaching out to some other precinct captains that I trust, see if they recognize anyone. In the meantime, check in with the units you sent out and then reach out to the people you've spoken with at the task force. Get someone over here in the morning."

"Of course." Smitty rose and began gathering his things.

Smitty caught sight of the captain collapsing back into his chair and wished he had something encouraging to say. But the reality of the situation was so dire that there were no words of comfort to offer.

"There's no sign of him." Keller returned inside and found Bo stomping around the empty garage bay. He pointed toward the office.

"Go through his bag. Find out where he lives and get him, dammit."

"We tossed it before the cops came. There was nothing in there. No phone, no address, just a school ID. Jeez, Bo, he's just a kid. We don't need him here."

"Don't you get it? The first one already sent the cops sniffing around. With this one gone, they're going to be back. We've got to move."

"Well, what do you want me to do?"

"We've got to get rid of Washington and then clear out ourselves." Keller opened the door to the storeroom while Bo fumbled with his keys.

"You're a fucking pain in my balls, Washington. Do you know that?" The fat man screeched at Washington as he located the key he wanted.

Bo drew closer and leveled the pistol at Washington's face, but the man refused to blink or react in any way. Suddenly, the gun drew back and connected with the side of his head with a crack that echoed in the small space. His head hit the wall behind and left a bit of blood as he slumped to the floor.

"Should have killed him back at the compound, Goddammit," Bo muttered as he tucked the gun back in his belt and then gestured toward the body on the floor. "Tie him up, Keller, tight. Hands behind his back. Then grab him and follow me." Keller did as he was told, struggling to move the uncooperative form as he cinched the knots once more. He dragged him toward the door, finally lifting Washington over his shoulder, and staggering a bit under the weight. Bo led the way from the storeroom back through the garage and then down the dark stairs toward the basement. The thick door dragged, and he used his considerable weight to force it open. Then he pulled a rotted string that hung to the side, and a dim, naked bulb swung in a short arc. Bo reached into his pocket and pulled out a penlight, playing it along the cinder block wall. When he caught sight of a dark, rectangular spot on the wall, he gestured forward.

It was the opening of an unused coal chute, and Keller struggled to get the body inside. Finally, Bo deigned to help, and the two of them forced the body up and out of sight. Bo clicked off his light and started back toward the basement door. Keller paused for a moment, caught between the two men. "We're going to just leave him there?" He asked as Bo pulled the door shut and locked it behind them. Keller followed him up the stairs back into the garage.

"Of course, we're going to leave him there. We've got to get out. The cops'll be here any minute. Clear out anything you've got left in the storeroom or the office, and then take off. But," He paused, leveling a steely gaze at Keller. "Do not, I repeat, do not go home."

"Where'm I gonna go?" Keller rested his hands on his hips, growing angrier and angrier about the situation he'd been forced into.

"A friend's house, a hotel, hell the fucking YMCA for all I care. You just have to lay low until all of this blows over." Bo waved his hand in the air and entered the office, grabbing up items and tossing them into a plastic bag. Keller returned to the storeroom and picked up his wife's tray and dishes. He didn't think he had anything else of value there, so he returned to the garage and looked over at Bo and his frenzied movement. Keller shook his head briefly and then headed out to his truck. He backed out onto the street before turning on his lights and driving away. Where the hell was he supposed to go, he wondered.

Rod and Rita spoke with the uniform out front before entering the wide bay doors. He and Rita headed toward the back hallway where a metal door was hanging open. It led to the coffee shop storeroom that Carlo had described. There was a patch of blood on the wall and wide streaks dragged across the dusty floor, but nothing leading out of the room to indicate where he might have been taken. "Fuck!" Rod uttered in frustration. He began searching through the office while Rita went upstairs, but she came down from the attic shaking her head.

Rod phoned the captain. "Nothing here, Captain. No vehicles either. Any sign at their houses?"

Rod shook his head as he ended the call, and he and Rita left the building reluctantly. He thanked the uniform as they left, and then with one hand resting on the bay door, he and Rita stood staring back into the building. Rita dared to say what they were both thinking. "He could be anywhere by now, dead or alive." She looked around the empty space. "I could stick up an extra camera or two in case anyone comes back." She offered and waited while Rod considered it.

"You got some on you?"

"Yeah, in my pack. I'll get it from your truck and be right back."

Washington heard the first shout from Keller and hoped it meant that Carlo had gotten away. He could hear doors being thrown open and an argument between Keller and someone he was now sure was Bo. "You fucking moron. You didn't think to check the damn window before you let him in there?" The squeaky voice threatened to crack and break as he yelled. There was a long pause and more doors opening and closing before Washington thought he heard Keller come back inside. Then he and Bo entered the storeroom.

"You're a fucking pain in my balls, Washington," Bo spat out. Washington remained silent, glad to hear that he'd accomplished one thing at least. Keller stood beside Bo and Washington couldn't be sure how to interpret his expression. It looked as though he might be as afraid of what Bo was planning as he was. Then, with surprising speed, Bo yanked his pistol from his belt and aimed it at Washington's head. He didn't want to die a coward and worked hard to keep his gaze steady. As Washington held his breath, Bo raised the gun and then slammed it against his head with a crack that he heard as well as felt. Then it was darkness again.

When he awoke, John had no sense at all of how much time had passed. Surprised that he was still alive, he took stock of the situation he was now in. He was lying on his back, bound again by the nylon rope, his ankles tied snugly together with his hands secured underneath him. There was no bag over his head this time, but he was somewhere in complete darkness. It felt as if he was lying on dirt or stone, the smell like that of a recent campfire. He tried to sit up, but as he lifted his shoulders, his forehead bumped into a rough surface just inches above him. Then his foot slipped, banging on a section of wall beside him, and he realized he was lying in some sort of crawl space. It reminded him of his grandmother's house that he'd explored as a young boy. She'd had an old-fashioned coal bin at one end of her basement, and the smell reminded him of that spot.

So instead of being dead, he was now in some sort of basement? Was he even in the same building? Why didn't they just kill him and get it over with, he wondered. He knew their names and he knew what they had planned. What was he supposed to do now? He rested his head on the rough surface, the darkness so complete that he shut his eyes to block it out. Assuming that he hadn't been unconscious for too long, he figured it was still night. Perhaps once the sun came up there would be at least a hint of light to tell him where he was and give him some idea of what to do.

Throughout the night, Washington slept in fits and starts. In the pitch dark, there was no way to judge the passing of time. He was aching, parched and trying not to cough. Anytime he moved within the narrow confines it seemed to set off a cloud of gritty-feeling dust. With his hands tied behind him he couldn't cover his face, so it felt as though he inhaled a lot of it. After he'd lost count of the number of times he'd slept and awakened, the faintest of light seemed to be entering the crawl space.

He leaned his head back and saw that three short slits of light lay ahead of him. Washington slowly scooted himself toward it. He figured he'd moved about four feet when his head banged against a small metal door. He twisted to try and look through the narrow openings but there was little he could see in the dim morning light. He lay listening for a long time, hoping to hear someone walking past so that he could call out, but it remained quiet.

Resigned at having met a dead end, he began trying to scoot through the narrow passage in the opposite direction, angry with himself at having to backtrack. When he judged himself to be back where he started, he took a short break, but the light at his feet was now growing brighter, encouraging him to try again. He took a deep breath, managed to suppress another cough, and resumed his scooting.

Suddenly, his leading foot slipped off some sort of ledge, so he inched farther and farther until both feet were hanging below him. He figured gravity was about to take a nasty hand in the situation, so he hesitated, trying to control both his breathing and his fear. There was no way to know how big a drop was coming and without his hands to brace him, he'd have no control. Try and roll, he told himself as he began scooting forward once again. He felt the ledge against the back of his knees, his thighs, and finally the seat of his pants, but one more scoot and he was airborne. He tried to yank his knees close and curl into a ball, but the drop only lasted a few feet.

He mentally surveyed his body first, sure that he had just collected a few more bruises, but at least nothing felt broken. Then he wriggled into a seated position and began to look around. It did indeed look like the coal bin he'd seen in the old house and, apparently, he had been stuffed up into the coal chute. They really hadn't meant for anyone to find him this time. Exhaustion seemed to pour over him then, and Washington felt tears form in his eyes. He brushed against his shoulder to try and dry them, but the soot just made it worse, so he tried to blink away the worst of it.

Once his vision had cleared, he looked carefully at the area around him hoping to find something that might be useful in getting the rope off. He scraped at the area with his feet, raking them across the dusty floor, hoping something useful would be uncovered. An old metal bucket was propped against one wall, and he tried to move it quietly with his foot. Once it was out of the way, he spotted a bent nail hammered into one of the wall studs about six inches off the floor. It wasn't much, but at least it would give him something to do.

The Saturday morning brunch was lovely, Audrey thought. The guests were so relaxed, and everyone seemed to be enjoying themselves. The Ellerbys had gone all out with a grand buffet and another open bar. Now, with the wedding not scheduled until 5:30 that evening, the guests had scattered to enjoy a variety of activities. The main lodge backed up to a deep looking set of woods but in front, ringing the primary building were half a dozen smaller structures. Audrey had been down to the one housing an elaborate arcade and game room where guests played pool or ping pong, in addition to video games. Another held a small bowling alley where the bride and her attendants were having a friendly match against the groomsmen. Outside, she'd gotten some great shots of guests on the tennis court and in the large hot tub. There appeared to be a sizeable pool but the accompanying pool house looked dark and neither seemed to be in operation on such a cool, autumn day. She walked around the back of the lodge and grabbed some shots of the stunning foliage, but didn't venture far into the woods, although she had heard the bride's older brother offering to lead a nature hike.

During a lull in the afternoon activities, Audrey took a break in the great room. The broad windows looked out over the colorful woods, so she settled into a plush armchair where she could enjoy the view. She slipped her feet out of her shoes, and the relief was immediate. She wiggled her toes surreptitiously as she watched guests drift in and out of the room, many stopping to pick up a snack and a cocktail before gathering in the conversational groups of chairs that were set up in various parts of the large room. Audrey was trying to decide whether it was worth putting her shoes back on in order to pick up a snack when she saw people looking up, while a few stood and began moving toward the windows. There was a bar set up in the corner of the great room, and the kid acting as bartender seemed to be one of the few people who hadn't reacted to whatever was going on. Audrey stepped back into her shoes quickly and then up to the small bar. "Can you tell me what's going on?"

He slid a scoop of ice into a cup and then held it up as if to ask what she would like. "It's just gunfire."

"What?" She asked in alarm.

"Yeah, crazy, huh?" He looked around to check that no one else was nearby before leaning toward her. "You never know what kind of stuff is going on in these woods."

"Really?"

"Yeah, I grew up not far from here, tiny little town. Some of the woods belong to the state, but a lot of it's privately owned like this place, and there are a ton of rumors about what goes on."

"This isn't just a resort?"

"Nah, these people own over a hundred acres. This spot? It's maybe ten or eleven, tops. The woods go way back." He gestured with his arm, indicating the area behind the main building.

He held the cup up again, and Audrey nodded toward the tall bottle of tonic, shaking her head when he paused with his hand on the vodka bottle next to it. "Sorry, working." She grinned and waited as he fit a wedge of lime along the rim. She nodded her thanks and then took her drink, sitting down on an ottoman near the wall of windows. A boisterous group had captured her chair and pulled it into their grouping, but thankfully, the atmosphere in the room seemed to have settled. Audrey took her camera out and began looking back through the most recent shots she'd taken when she saw heads pop up once again. A murmur of conversation started around her. She looked quickly over at the bartender, who caught her eye once more and gestured with his chin toward the outdoors. "More gunfire," he mouthed. Audrey stood and brought her camera up as she spotted their host speaking to Wade, the rude doorman she'd met when she arrived. She snapped a few shots of the two of them and then watched as Mr. Ellerby directed the man out the door. When she saw the host turning her way, she began panning across the room toward the beautiful staircase. She could see him hesitate and then turn away, apparently unconcerned. Audrey took that moment to return to her room.

The hallway was empty, so Audrey made her way back to her room without being intercepted. Once inside, she kicked off her shoes again and propped her feet up on the low table. She was happy to have the hour to herself before heading into the bride's suite where they'd be having hair and makeup done before getting dressed.

Without getting up, Audrey managed to pull her computer onto her lap. She hooked her camera to the unit and began downloading the photographs she'd taken so far that day. When she reached the end, she took a few minutes to study the shot she'd taken of the bride's father and the rude man at the door. It sure looked as if the man was being directed to take care of something. She puzzled over what it might be and why the man still looked so familiar to her. She didn't think she'd have an opportunity to send it, but, just in case, Audrey took a minute to write a quick email to Rod. *'There was gunfire in the woods this afternoon, and it looked like the host was sending this man to deal with it. His first name is Wade. Why does he look so familiar?'* She attached the photograph and noticed that a Wi-Fi signal had popped up. She guessed that someone had managed to sneak their phone in and was using it as a hotspot. She hit send quickly and then watched the signal blink out. Oh, well. She had no idea if it went through or not. She'd just have to wait until Monday to find out.

In the meantime, there was still a lot of work to be done. She set the computer aside and took a few minutes to enjoy an apple and the rest of her drink. Soon enough, it would be time for a shower, a fancy dress, more annoying lady shoes, and then back to work. She'd be shocked if she was back in her room and rid of the shoes before midnight.

Marconi was disappointed that the weekend wasn't more interesting. The guests were all a bunch of wealthy snobs hanging around sucking up Ellerby's food and drink. To make matters worse, the man hadn't even arranged for a room and food for him inside the lodge. Instead, Marconi'd had to go looking until he finally found a spot in the empty pool house where he could at least stretch out on a couch. He was half dozing when he first heard the shots. They'd only left a couple of guys at the camp, so he had no idea why there would be gunfire. If Ellerby caught wind of it, there'd be hell to pay. Luckily, though, the burst didn't last long, and he resumed his seat by the window overlooking the pool. He'd finally found a beer and some chips in the small auxiliary kitchen here and he really didn't want to get up..

He was reaching for a chip when the shots began again. He set down his snack and began hurrying up to the main house. Sure enough, there was Ellerby, standing in the foyer with the door open. He didn't say much, but it was clear he expected Marconi to deal with it. For a second, he caught sight of the photographer woman and thought she was taking his picture, but then she turned and seemed to be panning the whole space. He thought Ellerby had noticed it as well, but since he didn't seem bothered by it, Marconi dismissed it from his mind.

As the crow flies the camp was only about a half mile distant from the lodge but it would take him a good twenty minutes to get there on the back roads, all of them winding and indirect. Luckily, he hadn't heard any more gunfire while he was on his way over. At the entrance, he pushed the button and waited for the gate to drop and the twin doors to open. Then he paused on the other side to make sure they'd resumed their positions correctly. They'd had trouble with the backdoor recently, but now it appeared to be fixed.

When he reached the camp, he wasn't surprised to see a young, bandanaed guy lifting a rifle to his shoulder. "Hey," Marconi yelled and approached the man as he lowered the weapon. The idiot wasn't even wearing ear protection, he noticed. "What are you doing out here?"

"Uh, the other guys are in there watching a football game, so I figured I'd come out and get some practice in before the big day."

"You didn't hear Bo say no gunfire this weekend? He even posted a sign. There's a wedding less than a mile from here. You can hear the gunfire from there. You want to bring the cops down on us when we're so close to our goal?"

The man quickly lowered the rifle even further and pulled off the bandanna. "I'm sorry, didn't think a plain rifle would matter. I thought he just meant the automatics. Isn't it hunting season anyway?"

"Not yet, just antlerless this weekend, and what pussy goes after them anyway? Look, just go back and wait inside with the others. Keep an eye out for any problems today and tomorrow, and then you're all back in the city tomorrow night."

"All right. I'll see you in the city." Marconi watched as the man gave a half salute before he returned the rifle to the rack in his car and traipsed into the camp building. When no one else appeared outside, Marconi got in his truck and returned to the lodge. He found Ellerby in the main hall talking with his wife and another guest, so Marconi just offered a quick nod and decided he'd walk the perimeter and stay out of the way for a while.

For the rest of Friday night, Rod and Rita took shifts watching the camera feeds, a few hours on, a few hours off. Neither one truly slept, but it afforded them some rest. When morning came, they were confident that no one had left or entered the garage. Smitty came into the office just after eight and dropped off coffee and donuts. He took a shift while they each got up and stretched their legs, but at ten o'clock, he needed to head out and began stowing his laptop into his bag.

"Thanks for the food. Where are you off to?" Rod asked as he tossed the cup and began picking up wrappers.

"I've got a meeting with the two guys who started the task force. We'll be in the conference room downstairs if you need us." He said, hooking his thumb over his shoulder to indicate the direction. Then he added. "Captain's still back in his office on the phone. Catch you later."

"Will do." Rod turned to Rita, and they both sat back down, their eyes not straying from the camera feed. Rod shifted uncomfortably in his chair just as an alert pinged on his phone. He was thrilled to see it indicating an email from Audrey. He read it quickly and clicked on the photo before jumping to his feet. "I'll be right back." He said before tearing down the hall toward the captain's office.

The door was closed, so he rapped on the frame and waited a beat. "C'mon in." The captain called out.

"Sir, we've got an even bigger problem than we thought." Rod turned the phone and the photo toward him. "Audrey is photographing Ellerby's daughter's wedding this week. She just sent me this email saying she thinks she's heard gunfire. Look who's being sent off to deal with it."

"Oh, God, not Marconi." The captain looked up. "He must be working security for the wedding this weekend. That's why he wanted off the roster. Will he recognize Audrey, do you think?"

Rod shook his head. "She says she can't remember where she's seen him, and since her powers of observation are light-years beyond his, I'm sure he won't make the connection. Captain, does this mean Ellerby's the money behind the operation?"

"It could very well be. Plus, it may be that his land is where the camp is located."

Rod looked up hopefully. "Maybe that's where they took Washington? Earlier, someone who has an in with the feds told Smitty that Ellerby's going to be arrested on charges of tax fraud on Monday, as soon as they're back in the city after this wedding. It doesn't seem like that would stop the militia's plans, but it might tip them off and make them even more unpredictable, don't you think? We want Washington, but we also want to stop these nutjobs. Can we ask them to delay the arrest for a little bit?"

"I don't know. Is Smitty still downstairs with the task force guys?"

"I think so. And Rita's keeping an eye on the feeds."

Rod nodded, and the captain stood up, rubbing both hands across his head before re-tucking his shirt and moving toward the door. "Okay, check in with Smitty and have him pull up the records that indicate what land Ellerby owns. See if that can help the task force triangulate where this camp might be located. Meanwhile, I have no idea if there's any way to slow the tax guys down or not, but I'm going to have a talk with a couple of my bosses and see if they can pull any strings."

Rod headed down the stairs and knocked on the door to the conference room. "Come on in." He heard Smitty call. "What's up?"

Rod pulled up the photo from Audrey and added the information that he had about possible locations for the camp. Leaving them to get to work, Rod headed back upstairs to his desk.

Once the task force knew the location of Ellerby's land, the search for the compound kicked into high gear. After all the discussion, though, Smitty was a little bit surprised to find himself in charge of the team that was heading out to meet the drone operators and hopefully organize a raid. One of the men he'd been coordinating with all day drove Smitty and the other two in the lead vehicle, while four more vehicles followed behind. Once they'd entered the area, Smitty called ahead to the drone operators and then signaled the other vehicles to hold back.

At the intersection of the main road and a smaller, paved offshoot, they pulled over into a small field and got out. Two women met them there, one holding a controller while the other monitored a computer screen on an industrial-looking laptop.

"Anything yet?" He called out as he approached, and the first woman shook her head.

"No, we're working a grid pattern between the locations you gave us, but we haven't seen anything yet."

"My guess is that it's going to be hidden under a fair amount of canopy."

The woman operating the drone offered, "The infrared should help us see through that." And her partner turned the laptop so that the group could all have a better view. It showed a split screen, one side a mixture of green pines and autumn foliage, while the other side revealed bright red leaves. The drone seemed to make slow but steady progress, but the dense woods offered little variation to the scene. They had been watching for nearly an hour when the woman on the monitor called out to her partner. "There, I saw something. Move east again."

The image continued until a narrow break appeared between the trees, and the thermal screen showed a white-hot streak down the middle. "What's that?" asked Smitty.

"That's a small road, paved, apparently, since it's giving off some heat."

"Good, let's follow it if we can."

On the green screen, the patch of black didn't reappear, but on the other screen, they were able to track it deeper into the woods. Then a black rectangle appeared with two smaller ones nearby.

"I think you've got something," the operator called to her partner.

As Smitty and the others leaned in, the corner of a building appeared along with some other odd-looking shapes. He looked up at the others who'd been studying John Washington's video with him. "That look like an obstacle course to you two?" Then he pointed to the two squares in the thermal imaging, "The outhouses we saw, maybe?"

All the imagery was being fed to the police captain as well, so Smitty put in the call. While he waited for it to connect, he turned to the two women. "Can you tell how far away we are and try to track the road back until it meets another road that we could get to?"

Using the thermal imaging, it was less than a minute before they could see the road dead-end at a building. There was the building and another gap, and then what appeared to be a main road. "Looks like maybe half a mile from here to the entrance there. We can send you the GPS coordinates to pinpoint it for you."

The call connected, and Smitty put it on speaker. "Did you catch that, Captain? We're not too far out."

"Yes. Any sense of how many men are there?" the captain asked, and Smitty turned to the women. They conferred briefly, moving the drone in a wide sweep across the area of the suspected camp.

"We're not reading any bodies, but it could be they're in that building."

"No sentries further out that you see?" Smitty asked. Again, there was a pause while the drone patrolled a wider circle. The woman shook her head no.

"Captain, I think we should go in. We've got the manpower and a route that's paved at least partway."

"All right. You've got the go-ahead form here. Talk to the team and make sure everyone's on the same page before you go in. Have them keep the drone up over the camp so that we can see what's happening."

"Will do, Captain. We'll be in touch." The men headed back to the lead car while Smitty stopped for a word with the women. When they said they were fine keeping the drone in place and would be communicating what they saw, he joined the vehicles to conference with the tactical team.

As they drove the short distance to the entrance point, Smitty's mind couldn't help but go back to the raid he'd been a part of in the spring. They'd gone after three men who had shot up a nightclub, and, although the men were all captured in the raid, it was Smitty who'd taken the bullet. Now, his index finger moved slowly back and forth over the puckered scar as he thought ahead to what was coming next.

Sick of sitting, Rod headed back to check in with the Captain. "Any news yet, Captain?" Rod asked as he leaned in the open doorway.

"I talked with the feds about the arrest planned for Monday, and they weren't feeling much like cooperating, but when I explained about Washington and the rally, they agreed to stay in contact and alert us to the timing of it."

"I guess that's all we can hope for."

"Without anything more specific, you're right."

"And the camp? Any news there?"

"Maybe. With the addition of the Ellerby information, Smitty and the others think they may have a better sense of where this camp is. They're talking to Rita's friend's team. They've got a high-quality drone with regular and infrared cameras on it. They figure they've got about an hour or two of daylight left, so they're hurrying to get it in the air now."

"Are you heading out there?"

"No, Smitty's there with them and, if they do see something, they've got a tactical squad ready to drop in. I'm going to stay here and act as backup on the coordination." He pointed at his computer monitor, and Rod thought he heard a radio crackle. The screen came to life then, a split view between a dark green and orange forest scene and an eerie infrared version of the same thing. "You and Rita learn anything?"

"Nope." Rod gestured toward the screen. "I just hope Smitty finds Washington there at the camp. Otherwise," He shrugged his shoulders. "since they didn't find those garage assholes at their homes, we're back to square one."

"Let's give this an hour and see how it goes."

"Okay, I just feel like the clock's ticking for Washington though, you know?"

"I feel it, too, believe me. Give me an hour."

"Will do, Captain," Rod answered and headed back to his desk. Rita looked up from the screen as he entered.

"Anything new?" She asked.

"They've got a drone out looking for the camp right now, so let's hope they find him there.

They had just resumed their seats when they heard a shout from down the hall and went running. The captain was standing up behind his desk, pointing at the screen.

"They found it! Look! Just like Washington's video, the obstacle course, even the outhouse."

"Looks deserted." Rod offered, and the captain agreed.

"I know. I had a chat with Smitty, and they're about to take it."

"Mind if we watch with you?" Rod asked, and the captain indicated the chairs.

"Of course not."

Rita set her laptop with the garage feed up on a nearby table and settled in with the two men to watch the raid on the compound.

Audrey often thought that one of her favorite parts of wedding photography was the time spent with the women and men before the service as they were getting ready. The mother and father's first view of their daughter as a bride, the parents and groomsmen trying to calm the groom. Even more than the ceremony itself, Audrey felt that this was where the tale was told, where successful and unsuccessful matches seemed to come together. She'd seen the rivalry and teasing at the bowling alley and had wondered how deep the competitive streak went in the group. But that was all gone now, with tears and laughter, mostly laughter, taking its place. Perhaps this one would truly last, she mused as the bride looked up at the woman signaling for them to move to the top of the staircase so that they might begin.

Audrey skipped out ahead of them and set up her position at the base of the stairs. The guests were held back by wide ribbons marking off the makeshift aisle, so it was easy for her to set up her shots. The parents were already in position as the groom and his attendants approached from the other side and took their positions nervously. The music was cued, and the bride's sweet little niece made her careful way down the stairs, one hand firmly holding onto the smooth rail. The rest of them followed until the entire party was in position. As the service was about to begin, Audrey took her seat at the back.

The music swelled to a finish, and in the quiet at the end of the song, Audrey wondered at the odd percussive element until she realized she was hearing gunshots. She looked at the father of the bride, who smiled a bit ruefully but reassured the crowd that it was nothing that should stop what they were doing. There were a few quiet laughs, and the ceremony began. Audrey's eye caught sight of Wade hurrying out the backdoor of the lodge, but there was no other indicator of any concern.

As the couple concluded their vows and exchanged rings, Audrey readied her camera and, with the final word, was on her feet to capture the new couple coming back down the aisle. When the groom caught his new bride up and spun her around unexpectedly, Audrey was right there to catch it. The applause grew louder after that until all the guests began standing up and moving to the next room where hors d'oeuvres and drinks were being served. Once the bridal party split off and joined them, Audrey worked through her list of requested poses, dismissing each group as they finished. She noticed Mr. Ellerby stepping aside to talk on his phone, but nothing else seemed to be out of the ordinary. Audrey finally finished with the bride and groom and then moved ahead to be ready for when they were introduced to the waiting crowd.

It was a very long evening for Audrey, a seated dinner followed by hours of dancing that began with the sedate parent/child couples and ended with a raucous dance scene that had Audrey's head pounding by the time she made her exit. She entered her room and, before doing anything else, took out the hearing aids and put them on the charger. Her head was still pounding with the noise, though, and, for a moment, she was carried back to the night she was abducted, her head pounding from a different wedding dance party. She shook it off and kicked the painful shoes toward the open closet. Then she fell back onto the bed and closed her eyes. Two days down, one more to go. What had made her think she wanted to do a destination wedding anyway? She might have been at home in her own bed with Rod . . .

Marconi was pissed when he heard the gunfire just as the ceremony was beginning. He knew before even looking at Ellerby that he needed to deal with it immediately. He couldn't believe those assholes he'd left at the compound had started shooting again. They must be drunk, he thought.

He started to radio ahead, but then thought he'd prefer to catch the idiots in the act. He moved quickly on the twisting road before turning off onto the gravel drive. He was reaching for the button to activate the gate when he spied the chain lying on the ground, the hasp of the padlock cleanly cut. He backed out, made a quick U-turn, and traveled a quarter mile back down the road before turning onto a grassy lane. It wasn't quite dark yet, so he opened his windows, turned his lights off, and drove slowly down the path that roughly paralleled their paved drive.

The gunfire had ceased by the time he neared the camp, but spotlights and the sound of multiple car engines caused him to stop and back up. The dense woods held little light this late in the day so he drove slowly before tucking the car in behind one of the larger oaks. He shut off the indoor light before easing his car door open. He crouched down low and listened once again. It stayed quiet, so he moved ahead, stepping behind one tree after another as he slowly made his way forward. When he got within fifty yards of the camp's fence, he could see the scene clearly. Three vehicles were parked in a triangle in front of the compound with two more visible in the rear. He watched as the doofus from earlier and four other guys were marched out in handcuffs to the waiting vehicles. Wasn't there one more guy, he wondered? But then he saw two of the officers, one looked like that guy Smith from his precinct, carrying a stretcher between them. Once that was loaded as well, three of the vehicles left immediately while the rest of the officers started to search, some inside the building, others on the perimeter.

There was nothing more Marconi could do now. They wouldn't find much, he knew. The armory had been emptied and was safely in the city, waiting for him to pick it up on Monday afternoon. Without much power or internet service, there were few electronics in the building other than the TV and the closed-circuit feed. He knew that Ellerby and Bo would be pissed, but he felt as though the operation could still proceed as planned. Later, they'd find another spot for a camp, and this would all turn out to be just a hiccup.

Marconi carefully made his way back to his car and sat inside and waited. There was nothing to be gained by hurrying back to the wedding, so he sat quietly until finally, the last vehicle headed out and the woods were silent once again.

Rod, Rita, and the captain were all glued to the computer screen, watching the drone's view as the raid unfolded. They saw a flash that might have been gunfire, but without sound, it was difficult to interpret what was happening on the ground. Then, after only ten minutes or so, the captain's phone rang. He listened for a few minutes before setting down the phone and turning to pass on the news. Leaning back in his chair, they saw a grin creep across his face. "They got in without incident. Only six men were present. One appeared at a doorway and took a shot, so they fired back. He caught a round in the chest, but the others walked out without any trouble."

"Smitty and the team are all fine?" Rod asked, holding his breath as he thought back to what had happened in the spring. He'd only just gotten his friend and partner back to full-time in homicide, and he didn't want a repeat of any of that.

"They're all good. Not even a scrape." Then the captain's tone turned more serious. "However, the armory is empty, just as we suspected, so that means all that weaponry is somewhere here in the city. And," he paused, resting his hands on the desk. "No sign of Washington."

"Dammit!" Rod slapped his hand on the captain's desk. "No sign of Washington, no sign of the truck. What's next, Captain? How do we stop this?"

The captain gestured at the monitor. "I'm assuming the people at the wedding would have heard the gunfire, so presumably Marconi was sent to check on it and will know it was raided. Smitty's group didn't see anyone outside of the compound, so if Marconi saw anything, he would have had to have been watching from a good distance. He'll be reporting back to the wedding, and then who knows what he and Ellerby will do next."

"Can we get someone to follow him?"

The captain shook his head. "They're out of our jurisdiction for now, but when or if he re-enters the city, we can get someone on him. Hopefully, he'll lead us to the truck at least."

"But in the meantime? We can't just sit on our hands here." Rod looked at the feed on Rita's computer as it switched between the outside camera at Bishops and the new ones they'd hooked up inside. Then he pointed at the screen. "It's quiet there now. Why don't Rita and I go take one more look? Maybe there's something we missed when we went in before."

"All right. I'll coordinate with the Staties and have them pick up Marconi's trail if they can. Once Smitty's done out at the camp, we'll regroup here."

Rod and Rita left the captain's office and returned to Rod's desk, where the warehouse feeds were running as well. "You got a buddy here who can watch this and let us know if anything starts happening?" Rod asked Rita as he pointed at the screen.

"Sure do." She pulled her phone out of her pocket and stepped into the hall while Rod gathered up the keys to his truck. She returned quickly. "All set."

"All right. Let's go and take another look."

The warehouse looked just as they had left it, Rod thought, as he and Rita retraced their steps through the storeroom next door and around the big garage bay. Rod climbed the stairs to the attic area and thought back to Carlo's description of it. He kicked at the pole in the center of the space, but there was nothing new to see there. When he returned downstairs, Rita was coming out of the bathroom, but he could tell from her face that it held nothing new. They met in the center of the big space. "Anything?" He asked.

"Nope, you?"

She shook her head and then walked aimlessly toward the staircase that Rod had just come down. As she looked over the edge, though, she beckoned Rod over. "Didn't Katz, the woman who searched this place with her partner, tell us that the steps to the basement were covered in dust? That's why they didn't go down there?"

Rod stepped down with her. "You're right, but someone's been here since then." The heavy door was locked and didn't budge when Rod pushed against it. He withdrew a credit card from his wallet, figuring it was quicker than waiting for a locksmith and at least worth a try. He jiggled it for a few minutes before the latch gave way, and Rod grinned as he looked at Rita. "We're in!" Rod felt beside the door and found a light string. He clicked it on, but the basement remained dim. However, Rita had a flashlight out before he could even suggest it, and they stepped forward into the dark space.

A spate of coughing woke Washington once more. It felt as though he'd spent hours trying to saw at the rope before falling asleep and waking himself up again with more coughing. He tried to feel the rope behind him and guessed that at most he'd sliced through only two or three strands. Without food or water or, to be honest, without any hope, it was hard to keep trying. What was he even hanging on for? No one was going to find him in time. Even if Carlo told them about being held together, no one would know to look down here. Late Monday afternoon, the truck would begin distributing the ammunition and other supplies to the various groups, and then the operation would be unstoppable.

He leaned his head back against the crumbling wall and took a moment to catalog all the places where he hurt. He knew the head injury was the most serious issue but, after the beatings, being hauled in the back of a truck, and then falling out of a coal chute, his arms and legs, as well as a few ribs, were all screaming at him. He coughed once more and then closed his eyes to block out the dark. It was embarrassing how much he hated the complete darkness. He was about to drift off again when he thought he heard a sound. Please, God, don't let those idiots come back at me. Just let me die in peace, he thought. Then a flash of light caught his eye. He blinked, but there it was again, on the other side of the coal bin. He wanted so much to call out, to beg or plead or just wail out loud, but he knew the futility of that. Another cough slipped out before he could stop it.

He waited, the tension tearing at his empty stomach. What is it? Who is it? He wondered. The waiting was too much. Then a light appeared beyond the wall of the bin. "Jesus!" Someone exclaimed. "John, is that you?" The voice called out, and a brighter light appeared around the side.

"Who wants to know?" John's answer creaked out.

"Sounds like he's alive," a woman answered. Then they were in front of him, kneeling on either side as they gently turned him away from the wall.

"It's Rodriguez, John. And this is Rita Banks. I've got a penknife. Give me a second."

John could feel the moment the tension left the rope, and his arms were free to drop down to his sides. The movement hurt like hell, but it was so worth it. They lifted his legs to untangle the rest of the rope and then reached on either side of him to help him stand. He tried his best but couldn't stop himself from falling.

"It's okay. We've got you." They reached under each arm and helped to lift him to a standing position. "We'll take it slow. Are you with us?"

John was so afraid that he was going to start crying that he paused a moment before answering. Then he breathed out, "I'll do whatever you want me to."

He felt a hand squeeze his shoulder gently, and then they arranged themselves on either side of him. His rescuers were of very different heights, but they moved slowly, and it seemed to work. They paused whenever he needed to catch his breath or when a fit of coughing overtook him. They inched their way toward the base of the basement stairs. John could see some light at the top, and the urge to cry hit him once again. They stepped through the door, and then all three of them paused before slowly tackling the stairs. Once they reached the top, they took a moment to sit and rest. He watched Rita pull out her phone and then turn a worried eye toward Rodriguez.

"What?"

Rita looked from him back to Rod. "Bo's just pulled up outside. They're sending Chao and Katz as backup, but we've got to move."

"Shit." Rod spat out. He turned to Washington. "I know you're done in, but we have to move now. My truck is just outside."

Washington nodded and then stood and faced him. "How far are we talking?"

"It's a bit of a hike, about fifty feet on a fairly open sidewalk." John knew the man was trying to be encouraging, so he did his best to pull himself together. They cleared the stairwell and headed toward the side door of the garage, stopping briefly once as a coughing fit made it hard for him to catch his breath. Then they were out the back door, and the cool evening air hit him in the face. It felt glorious.

They walked slowly to the corner and allowed him to peer ahead to see the truck parked in the alley. He could make it that far. He knew he could and nodded at Rodriguez to continue. "Okay, here we go." And they moved out.

Sitting in the dank hotel room, Bo found himself smoking one cigarette after another and churning back through the last few days' events. It felt as though everything was unraveling around him, and he didn't know what to do to stop it. If only Marconi had taken care of the cop out at the compound, they'd have been just fine, but once those kids had seen him in the back of the truck, it had all gone to shit. And, to top it all off, involving that idiot Keller had only made things worse. Who knew what he would even do? What if the cops found him? He and Marconi had kept Keller in the dark as much as possible, but he still knew details that could sink them.

The room had only grown hotter as Bo sat there stewing, so he pushed off from the chair and pocketed the keys to his car. He couldn't do anything about the kids, and the truck was safely parked at the abandoned plant, so that left Washington and the garage. Better to get rid of it all, he decided. He reached into the back of his SUV and lifted the gas can kept for the generator, pleased to find it was nearly full. That should do it, he thought.

It didn't take him long to get back downtown, and he pulled up on the side of the garage. He sat for a few minutes watching for any movement around the sidewalks or back alley, but everything looked quiet. He pulled his hat down low and climbed awkwardly out of the tall vehicle, looking around him once more before hauling out the can. He unscrewed the cap and tossed it on the ground before pouring out a stream alongside the back of the garage. Bo had nearly reached around to the front of the building when he thought he heard a sound from inside.

He hurried back, whipped the door open, and darted inside but didn't see anyone. He set the can down for a minute and stepped into the office, wondering if he needed to remove anything, but there was little to see other than a wad of keys and an old phone. Marconi had a second set for himself, so he picked up the can and began pouring gas around the office before stepping back out toward the stairs to the attic.

He didn't want to have to climb all the way up there, so instead, he turned to toss some gasoline down the stairs to the basement. Then he noticed that the door was ajar. Oh God, how in fuck's name had he gotten out? Bo dropped the can and stumbled toward the front window but couldn't see anything. Then he hurried over to the side door. As he looked out, he spotted three people, or was it two, hurrying toward a pickup truck that was parked behind the repair shop. When the truck's back door opened and the interior light came on, Bo spotted Washington. "Hey!" He yelled and rushed back through the garage to his car.

Bo hauled himself up into the driver's seat and stabbed his key into the lock. "Goddamn it!" he yelled again, fishtailing as he backed out into the alley. He caught sight of the truck speeding down the alley and turning onto the main road. He floored it until he spotted the truck racing ahead once more. Did it know he was following it?

Bo took the turn as fast as he could. Without a seatbelt, his bulk jostled against the door but kept going. Once more, Bo yelled in frustration as he turned. He was driving on a street parallel to the truck's path and then whipped into one more turn. The SUV careened around the corner and was moving flat out when the pickup truck reappeared. With no time to stop, Bo plowed into the driver's side. There was noise, and then there was nothing.

Rita and Rod did their best to hurry Washington down the sidewalk. They were just helping him to slide onto the back seat when a yell erupted from Rita's phone.

The officer's voice shrieked. "He's seen you! Hurry!"

Rod slammed the back door and raced for the driver's side while Rita jumped in on his right. The engine turned over immediately, and Rod took off. "Belt up!" He yelled at Rita while he quickly snapped his into place.

"They're in a gray SUV just behind you. Hurry! We're on the way!" The officer on the phone shouted again. Rod just drove while Rita hung on, not bothering to try and respond. He was heading in the rough direction of the hospital but kept checking behind him for the other vehicle. He saw it turn off, and then it disappeared from his view.

"Where'd it go?" He asked Rita, but she just shook her head. He pushed harder on the accelerator and turned to Rita once more. "Do you see . . ." He asked when he saw her eyes widen, and the world around him seemed to break.

CHAPTER

47

Officers Chao and Katz heard the accident before they saw it. They pulled up to the intersection in time to see both vehicles come to a stop. Rod's truck was curved in an arc between two flattened parking meters, the SUV T-boned into its side. Laura grabbed the radio immediately, barking out, "Get an ambulance here!" She shouted more instructions, including a call for more ambulances, while Officer Chao took off at a run.

Chao could already hear the siren by the time he reached the SUV. It looked as if the driver had been thrown against the windshield. There might have been a groan, but Chao ignored it, rushing instead to the truck holding Rod and the others. He couldn't even see into the driver's window as both the side and front airbags had deployed. He leapt around to the far side, where Rita Banks was still in her seatbelt. She appeared to be unconscious, her head leaning against the window. He tried pulling on the passenger door, but it didn't budge. Then he looked into the back where the man they'd been searching for had slid off the seat and was lying on the floor. He was awake, and as Chao pulled on the back door, he began kicking at it as well. It flew open finally, and Chao just managed to jump out of the way before it hit him. "Oh, my God. Can you move?" He asked once he could see Washington.

Washington nodded and began trying to sit up, carefully sliding toward the door. Then a couple of EMTs arrived, and Chao stepped back. While one of them helped Washington out and onto a stretcher, he and the other EMT worked to open Rita's door. Chao climbed in and pushed as the other man pulled until they got it partially open. A second ambulance had arrived by then, and they brought over tools to open it further.

Gently, they lifted Rita out and set her on a second stretcher. When the EMTs were finally able to reach Rod, there was a lengthy pause. It wasn't going to be easy to get him out without hurting him further. They started an IV and consulted with the firemen who had arrived, while another pair of medics moved the heavyset man from the garage out of the SUV. Chao didn't think he was going to make it.

It was half an hour later, after the captain had arrived and two ambulances had already left the scene, before they were finally able to lift Rod out and onto a stretcher. Their siren wailed all the way to the hospital. Chao had seen the captain climb into the back with him, so he and Laura stayed to help the other uniforms and the wreckers restore order to the neighborhood.

As soon as the captain heard the desperate call from Laura Katz at the scene, he took off, racing through the hallways shouting orders as he ran. His heart was breaking for his officers who had been hurt, but the larger picture was still in the forefront of his mind. He was nearly at the backdoor when Detective Smith walked in. He grabbed the man by both arms and quickly reported what had gone on. "Listen, I know you want to get to Rodriguez. I do too. But we just had a call that they've got a sighting on the truck. They think they found it parked in the back of an abandoned factory. Can you grab some of your team and get over there?"

"Oh, damn! Damn, damn!" Smitty cursed before pulling himself together. "All right, if you've got Rod, I've got this." The captain nodded his thanks and then hurried on out to his car.

He arrived at the scene as the first ambulance was getting ready to leave with Rita and John Washington in it. He got a good look at each of them but didn't let it delay their being cared for. Two more ambulances and a fire truck soon arrived and were working to gain access to the man from the garage, as well as Rod. They were able to get the other man out first, but it wasn't immediately clear if he would survive. The captain made a call to dispatch and sent an officer to the hospital as a guard.

As the SUV was being peeled away and loaded onto a wrecker, the captain's phone rang. He stepped away from the whine of the saws so that he could hear. "Smitty, what'd you find?"

"Captain, the truck is locked up tight, so we think it's probably still loaded. We've located just a few paper records in the cab, but there doesn't seem to be a whole lot else here. The task force has been talking, and they're inclined to stake out the truck to see if someone comes to pick it up. People like Marconi who've been out of the city may not know about the accident yet."

"That sounds like a good idea." He looked over his shoulder to see the EMTs lifting Rod out of the truck on a backboard." Do they have enough men to free you up to head to the hospital?"

"I'll make sure they do."

"Fine, I'll meet you there."

The captain didn't want to do it, but he forced himself to take a look at Rod as he was finally being strapped onto the gurney. They had inserted an IV while he was still trapped and were now positioning a canula in his nose. There was blood everywhere along his left side, making it difficult to assess the damage underneath it all. Once they lifted him into the ambulance, the captain climbed in behind. There was a small jump seat near the back, so he rested his hand on a bare section of Rod's shin and tried to will his energy into the young man. "Stay with us Rod, we need you." He whispered as the siren began again and they pulled away from the curb. They arrived at the hospital quickly, but a long night of waiting stretched out in front of them all.

Sunday morning was much more mellow than the day before, Audrey thought, probably because so many people had been up late partying. Despite being tired, she'd struggled to fall asleep, the headache throbbing until after two. She slept fitfully after that until around seven, when she decided she might as well get up. She showered and dressed, then packed up the bags she wouldn't be needing anymore. A brunch was scheduled to begin at ten, so she thought she'd walk down to see if there was anything to eat in the meantime.

When she stepped into the dining area, she noticed that most of the people who were up early were the older ones. Not surprising since they'd probably had the sense to go to bed before midnight. Luckily, there was an urn with fresh coffee, platters of fruit, and small pastries ready for the early risers. She fixed herself a plate and went to sit at a small table near the windows. It was after dawn, but a thin layer of fog was resting on the treetops around them, muting the vibrant fall colors that everyone had been enjoying.

Gradually, a few more guests began to appear, and Audrey half-listened to the conversations around her. From what she could hear, it seemed as if everything was going well. When laughter and music began spilling in from another room, she decided it was time to get moving. She returned her breakfast things and thanked yesterday's bartender, who was now busy folding napkins, presumably for the brunch. "See you later." She called and made her way down the hall toward her room. As she passed the large entryway, she spotted Mr. Ellerby deep in conversation with the rude man, Wade, but since neither of them turned her way, she kept going without greeting them. She couldn't decide if they looked angry or worried, or maybe it was a bit of both. When she'd seen the man in silhouette, though, it had finally clicked. He was a policeman, a corporal at the precinct where she and Rod worked.

Audrey worked quickly, organizing what she would need for photographing the brunch and then the couple's exit, but the image of the policeman kept bugging her. What was his name? Wade, Wade what? She worked hard at learning and remembering names for her business and was disappointed that she couldn't pull this one up.

When the guests had eaten their fill of the brunch and posed in various groups for more snapshots, they began making their way to their rooms before heading to the circular drive out front. A limousine decorated with flowers and streamers waited by the door. Two small girls with baskets began working their way through the crowd, handing out little packets of birdseed to toss at the departing couple. When they reached the end of the line, Audrey was given a nod, and she made her way into position near the car. The couple was hurrying, so she did her best to capture the moment, bodies moving and hugging while the birdseed flew in every direction.

Then they were gone, and as the guests trooped back inside, Audrey could see the first of the cars being brought to the door. She hadn't been asked for any more photographs, so she returned to her room. She stepped into the shower stall first, brushing off her clothes before bending over and shaking as much of the birdseed out of her hair as she could. Then, she moved to the mirror and took a brush to it, a few more bits flying out as she did. Finally, she finished packing and set all of her bags by the door to her room. She stood in the doorway expectantly, but when no one arrived to help her, she walked back to the main room and was shocked to find it empty. The young bartender/waiter seemed to be the only one left.

"Hello, I'm the photographer, Audrey Markum. I believe someone is supposed to drive me back into the city?" she asked as she looked around the deserted room.

"Oh, that's me. Someone had to go and do something or other, so they asked me to take you."

"Are you old enough to drive?" Audrey asked and was pleased when he laughed instead of taking offense.

"Yup, since April. It's not a fancy car, I'm afraid, but it works. I'm Peter, by the way."

"Well, thank you, Peter. As long as it runs, I'm not very picky. Could you help me with my bags, though?"

"Sure thing." He followed her back to the room, and the two of them carried them to the main entrance. "I'll be back in a second." He called and left through a side door.

As she stood at the entrance, Audrey remembered that she had surrendered her phone when she had arrived. Now, she spotted a wide wicker basket with one phone remaining in its center. Luckily, it was hers. She turned it on eagerly, hoping for a text from Rod, but there was no signal to be had. Peter arrived then, so they loaded up the car together. She started to reach for the back door but turned to the young man. "Shotgun okay?" She asked, and he gladly held the passenger door open for her.

"Okay, where are we going?"

Audrey gave him Rod's address in Brookline, her address, she reminded herself, and he plugged it into his phone. Then they were off. Once they were closer to the city, she could feel her phone vibrating with several alerts. She pulled it out and was shocked to see more than ten missed messages and calls. The first one was her friend Sandy's number, so she dialed it rather than exchange more texts. "Sandy, what's up?"

Immediately, Audrey heard the concern in her friend's voice. "Audrey, you need to get to Mercy Hospital. Rod's hurt."

"What?" Audrey sat up straight and turned to the young driver. "I have to get to Mercy Hospital. Do you know where that is?"

"Yeah, of course."

"Sandy, I have all my stuff with me. My cameras and everything. What'll I do with it?"

"Oscar's there. I'll have him meet you at the entrance. Keep what you need, and he'll get everything back to your place."

"What's going on? What happened?" Audrey asked, her voice catching in her throat.

"I'm sorry. I don't have the details. When no one could get you, Smitty thought to call Oscar. There was some kind of accident last night."

"Last night? Has Rod been in the hospital this whole time? My God!"

"Okay, don't freak. This is going to sound bad, but you couldn't have seen him anyway. He's been in surgery and then the ICU. But Oscar says there are cops all over the hospital, so he's not alone."

Audrey turned to the driver. "Can you go any faster?"

When they pulled into the circular drive at the hospital, Audrey was out of her seatbelt before they'd even stopped. True to Sandy's word, Oscar was waiting at the curb when they pulled up. Audrey jumped out of the car and was enveloped in his warm hug. Then he stepped back. "Okay, I'm going to take care of your stuff so you can get inside. Rod's captain is there, as well as Smitty and a rumba line of guys in blue donating blood. Keep Sandy and me posted, will you? You're both family to us, you know."

"I will, Oscar. I will and thank you for taking care of all of this." She turned back to the car and pulled out just her purse and the overnight duffel. Then she took off running for the entrance.

A check-in desk was located near the front entrance, so she dashed over and gave the attendant Rod's name.

"Stanley Rodriguez remains in ICU. That's on the second floor above the ER department. Just follow the green arrows on the floor." She stamped a visitor badge and handed it to Audrey. A bank of elevators lay ahead, but a line of people was already waiting, so she dashed for the stairs. She emerged on the second floor where the arrows snaked along one hallway after another until Audrey was about ready to scream. Then she spotted the nurses' station and recognized the two men camped in the waiting area nearby. She raced up to the captain and Smitty who gave her a quick hug before walking her up to the desk.

"She's here for Rodriguez."

"Another one?" The nurse asked with an irritated tone, but Audrey interrupted.

"We live together. He's my boyfriend."

"Oh, in that case, let me call the doctor. She'll fill you in on how he's doing."

Audrey thanked her and stepped back to join the two men. "Can you tell me what happened, sir?"

The captain gestured first toward Smitty. "A *lot* has happened while you've been at that wedding. The boy, Carlo, escaped from the garage and is home safe."

"Oh, thank God."

The captain nodded and then continued. "Smitty was in the mountains and led a raid on a militia compound not far from the wedding you were attending. In fact, that email you sent Rod with the photo of Marconi was a key piece of the puzzle."

"So, it got through. I wasn't sure. I saw Marconi leave during the service. Was the gunfire that we heard the raid? Was anyone hurt?"

"One of the men who was there was killed, but no one on our team was hurt," Smitty answered before turning it back over to the captain.

"Once his team was safe, and they determined that Washington wasn't being held there, Rod and Rita went back to the garage to search again. It turned out Washington was being held in the basement. They managed to get him out to Rod's truck, but they were spotted and chased down by the guy who'd held Carlo and Washington. Audrey," He rested his hand on her shoulder, "the man T-boned his truck on the driver's side."

"Oh!" She gasped, her hands flying to her mouth in shock.

"Rita and Washington are both here, too. They're not in too bad a shape, just being held for observation." He looked up then as the doctor approached. "This is Audrey Markum, Dr. Singh."

"Ms. Markum, I'm sorry to be meeting you under these circumstances. Please come with me, and I'll fill you in. Mr. Rodriguez's sister is in with him now."

They turned a corner into an area with six rooms, a square with patient rooms on three sides, and a small waiting room on the fourth. Wide, sliding glass doors fronted each room and allowed the central nursing station to see into the ICU rooms. Dr. Singh led Audrey to the third room on the left. Several machines partially blocked Audrey's view of Rod, but she could see Emma, pulled up close to the far side of his bed, both of her hands cupping his. Audrey thought she saw tears in her eyes.

"When Mr. Rodriguez was brought in last night, he was immediately taken into surgery to deal with the breaks in his left arm."

"Breaks? Plural?" Audrey asked in horror.

"Yes, I'm afraid it was broken in two places, one of them an open fracture. Our orthopedic surgeon was able to stabilize both breaks and repair the wounds. In the morning, you'll want to talk with Dr. Edmonds who did that operation. The collarbone was broken as well, and he reset that once he'd finished with the arm. Mr. Rodriguez has a severe concussion; however, imaging has not identified any significant bleeding. There were multiple lacerations to Mr. Rodriguez's face and neck, and he's gotten some stitches. His hip and left leg were both bruised severely, but there were no additional breaks to the lower body. Let me give you a moment to take all that in."

Audrey had no idea what to think of the list she'd just been given. "Is he still in danger?"

"Yes, I make it a policy not to sugarcoat things. His body has been badly traumatized. Taken individually, his injuries would not typically be life-threatening, but the blood loss, the shock, and the combination of injuries are what's concerning me. Right now, he's still sedated. We're going to monitor him closely through the night, and in the morning, we'll reassess everything."

"Can I see him?" Audrey's face was wet with tears, and she swiped at them impatiently.

"We only allow visitors in one at a time and only for a short while. His sister knows to come out in another minute or so, then you may go in."

Audrey wasn't able to pull any more words together, so she just nodded at the doctor and stepped to reach for some tissues on a nearby table. When she shifted her position, Rod's bed came into view, and she felt her breath stop. It looked as though he had cuts and deep dark bruises everywhere. His right arm had an IV inserted in it, while his left arm was held slightly away from his body in a sling. A thick white cervical collar held his head in place and matched the bandages on the left side of his face. Nothing about the body in the bed looked like Rod.

As she studied him from the window, Audrey caught Emma's eye. She smiled ruefully, kissed Rod on the hand she'd been holding, and then stood. When she came through the sliding door, she and Audrey practically fell into each other, tears and quick, short sobs coming from both of them. "I'm so sorry I wasn't here earlier, Emma," Audrey said as she stepped back.

"Oh, Audrey. It's so hard. They called me in the middle of the night. I'm not even sure how I got here. Then there were hours of waiting through the surgery and recovery. Even now . . ." She paused, and Audrey reached out and held her close again.

"He's tough, Emma. We just have to count on that now."

"I know. I keep telling myself that. You go and be with him now. I'm going to go home for a little while and get cleaned up. Then I'll be back."

"Okay. Hug Gina and Far for me." Then she was gone, and Audrey was faced with entering the room alone. She didn't know why she felt so afraid. But Rod had been there for her when she needed him in the spring, so she was determined to stand by him now. She took a moment to blow her nose and dry her eyes once more before stepping inside.

The sounds and smells were overwhelming at first, the sharp bite of the cool antiseptic air, and the beeping and whooshing of machines. It felt as though she had to make her way through a forcefield before she could reach his side. Once she did, she stood there silently, running her hand gently down his right arm before picking up his hand as Emma had. "You kept warning me about my weekend wedding and look what happened, Rod."

After the doctor had spoken to Audrey, she returned to where the captain and Smitty were standing. "Gentlemen, I don't think I'll have any more news for you today. He's stable. We've got him sedated and under observation for now. I believe Ms. Markum and Mr. Rodriguez's sister will both be with us this afternoon and evening, so I imagine they'll keep you updated."

"Thank you, Doctor." The captain nodded, and he and Smitty stepped toward the front door. "I don't think there's any more we can do for him, Smitty."

"All right, Captain. I understand. Have you had any updates on Washington and Banks?"

"They were both held overnight, but they're expected to be released soon. A lot of bruises for Rita, and the concussion is the main issue with Washington, but I know they did a scan on him and didn't find any other concerns."

"That's good to know. Think I could go up and try to speak with him?"

"Check with the nurses first to see if it's okay."

"Will do. I'll let you know what I find." Then his tone of voice hardened. "And the guy who hit them?"

The captain shook his head. "Didn't make it."

"Well, I have the cell phone you found in Bo's SUV and the little paperwork we collected from the truck, so I'll see what I can find out when I talk with Washington. If we need to move tonight, I'll let you know."

The captain rested his hand on Smitty's arm before he stepped away. "Good work yesterday, Smitty. I'm sorry I didn't have a chance to say that earlier. A raid like that isn't easy to pull off. I'm proud of you." The captain released him then and watched as Smitty headed upstairs before pulling out his phone to check in with the precinct. There was nothing new with the truck, so he made his way to the lower level to see if they were still accepting blood donations. Thinking about the work that his team had done, the courage they'd all shown. It was a squad to be proud of, he thought. Wouldn't hurt to give back a bit.

When Smitty reached Washington's room on the fourth floor, just a few doors from the elevator, a young woman with long blonde hair stood and motioned him forward. "How's he doing?" Smitty asked.

"A nurse and the doctor are talking with him now." The young woman responded anxiously but then added, "He looks terrible, but they tell me he's improved a lot since they brought him in. I'm Sylvia Brown."

"Demetrius Smith. Pleased to meet you." She reached out her hand, and he shook it just as the door opened and the medical staff stepped out. They gestured for Sylvia to come with them, but she hesitated until a weak voice spoke up.

"Sylvie, can you give us a minute?"

She and Smitty stepped into the room, and Sylvia patted Washington's leg. She picked up her purse and left. "I'll talk with them and go and get a cup of coffee." She nodded to Smitty before walking out, closing the door behind her.

Smitty moved to the far side of the bed and took the seat she had been using. "How're you . . ." He started, but Washington was already speaking.

"I am so sorry for acting that way the other day. That idiot Marconi was . . ."

Smitty raised his hand, and Washington stopped. "Listen, you don't owe me any apologies. It can be hell going undercover. I know. I've done it and hated it the whole time. Let's you and me start fresh. That alright with you?" Smitty reached out his hand, and Washington offered his. "All right then. I'm really here to ask you some questions if you're up to it. How are you feeling?"

Washington held down the button to raise the head of the bed and shifted into a better position to talk. "I'm okay. The beatings were bad, but for some reason, the coal dust is what's getting to me now. I can't seem to quit . . ." A deep cough erupted from him, and Smitty handed him his cup of water once it subsided. "Coughing." He was finally able to finish. "I heard that your partner was hurt pretty bad in that accident. How is he now?"

"It's too early to tell, I'm afraid."

"Do you know who was driving the other vehicle?"

"It was Bo Burns, the big guy we'd been seeing at the garage."

"He make it?"

Smitty shook his head. "No, his airbag went off, but he wasn't wearing a belt, and it wasn't enough to save him. By the way, did you know that the boy got your camera to us as soon as he got out? That was some amazing footage you got."

"Oh, what a relief." He let his head drop back against the pillow. "The kid's okay?"

"Yep, both kids are going to be fine. That's how we knew to put the garage under surveillance. Your footage also gave us details about the camp, but it took some sleuthing to figure out where it was. Did you ever hear anything at the camp about an undercover officer out of Butler?"

"No, the captain had me on the lookout, but I never heard anything about him, sorry."

"We found his body on the far side of the camp, and a blood trail that led back into the woods. Then we got another tip that helped us narrow our search for the location. Do you know Audrey Markum, our police photographer?"

"Yeah, I actually missed two appointments with her for our engagement photos. Did Sylvia contact her when I didn't show up?"

"She sure did. That was smart thinking on your part, and it helped us put two and two together when the boys reported seeing a body in the back of the truck at the garage. Anyway, this weekend Audrey was up in the mountains photographing a wedding at the Ellerby Lodge, and she spotted Marconi doing security. She heard gunshots yesterday afternoon, and that helped us to locate the camp."

"What happened then?"

"Once we had the general area, we had a drone crew help us find the camp itself. A group of us took it yesterday, but there was only a handful of guys up there. Any idea where the others are?"

"I think they were planning to return to the city in preparation for the demonstration on Halloween." He paused and looked at Smitty. "So, Bo is dead?"

"Yep."

"Any sign of the other guy, Keller, the one with tattoos? I never saw him up at the camp, though, so he may not have been privy to much information."

"No, they're still looking for him. We found a cell phone in Bo's SUV. He seems to have spent all day yesterday calling people."

Washington nodded. "The plan was for him to check in with the various lieutenants around the city and set up the deliveries for Monday afternoon."

"What deliveries? You mean what's in the truck?"

Washington nodded again. "Yeah, just before I was knocked out at the camp, Marconi was telling the guys to take the small arms with them and load the other, bigger items into the truck. I think the plan was for him to pick up the truck and then deliver the heavier arms and shields and things to some locations around the city."

"Do you know when he was going to pick it up?"

He shook his head. "No, sorry. Could be anytime between Saturday and Monday afternoon. I was out for a while, and after I woke up, we were next door and too far away to hear much. After the kid got away, I was knocked out again and didn't know anything until I woke up in that damn coal bin. I know that on Halloween night, they were to set up at the three or four parks that are closest to Point State Park so that they could walk to the central meeting point quickly. What happens next?" he asked, pushing himself up so he was sitting straighter in the bed.

"We've got video and personnel on the truck keeping watch. It's still locked, and we're sitting on it, hoping it can lead us to the larger network." Smitty pulled the phone out of his jacket pocket. "I've got a hold of Bo's phone. He also made a lot of calls today."

"I can help with that." Washington leaned forward, coughed momentarily, and reached for his water.

"Man, you don't seem . . ." Smitty started, but Washington overrode his comment.

"I'm fine. I won't know everyone, but I can put names to faces and help you locate at least some of the people here in the city."

"Did you know a park permit was issued for a Halloween party to a group focused on diversity here in the city?" Smitty asked. "Did Bo and Marconi know that?"

Washington swore under his breath. "That's . . ." He stopped. "Someone's going to get killed." He offered finally, and Smitty nodded his head in agreement.

"My thoughts exactly. We know that Marconi was not picked up in the raid, that presumably he returned to the lodge and the wedding. There's no way to know when or if he's heard about your escape or the accident. What do you think he'll do once he finds out?"

"It's hard to say. His first priority will be the truck. Is someone watching it now?"

"Yes, in person and on camera."

"You haven't seized it?"

"No, not yet."

"Why, for God's sake. Do you know the kind of arsenal that it contains?" Washington's eyes darted from Smitty to the door. "I have to get out of here. We have to do something!"

Smitty rested his hand on the man's shoulder. "What'd the doctor have to say?"

"He gave me the concussion protocols and a prescription for an expectorant. That's all. Please. I want to help."

"What do you think we should do first?" Smitty asked just as Sylvia stepped back into the room and Washington pulled her over.

"Please, go and ask for my discharge papers. I have to go."

"But Sweetie, I . . ."

"Now, Sylvia. A lot of lives are riding on this. I have to go. I promise I'll rest once this is done." Reluctantly, the young woman bent over and kissed Washington before gathering her things and heading out the door.

"You're crazy, you know?" She asked, but there didn't seem to be much heat behind the statement.

Once she was gone, Smitty pulled a chair up next to the bed so that he could share the phone screen with the battered officer. "If you're sure?" He paused, but when Washington said nothing more, he dove in. "All right. I've got the call logs pulled up here, starting at eleven. Tell me what you know."

It was almost an hour later when Sylvia returned with a handful of paperwork. From the closet, she pulled out a backpack and began reaching in to pull out fresh clothes. "Can you take a quick shower, do you think? There are grab bars in case you feel a little unsteady."

Smitty had noticed the soot and odor still emanating from the man. "Go ahead. Take your time. I'm going to call the captain and let him know we're coming in if you're sure you're up to this." Smitty stood and leaned over to shake Washington's hand one more time. He held onto it for a moment longer as he spoke. "I appreciate everything you've done, man."

Washington's face was horrified. "Oh, my God, did you see the camp? The targets they used for practice?"

"I did indeed. That's why I'm telling you how much what you've done matters. We have the truck. We have leads, and we're going to make sure this demonstration never gets off the ground."

Washington was already sliding his legs to the side and preparing to stand when Smitty stepped out and closed the door behind him, his phone in his hand. "Captain, we're coming in."

Captain Fischer hadn't heard any more from Audrey about Rod's condition but had been trading texts with Rita Banks's boyfriend. She was being discharged, and he was going to take her home for some additional rest. Although it was Sunday, Fischer knew there was too much riding on what happened next to even think about going home. He had no way of knowing where Marconi was or what he would do once he discovered the absence of the hostage and the men who had been set to guard him.

He had just finished reading a text from his counterpart in the task force when Smitty appeared at his door. He waved him in. "Smitty, what've you got? Is Washington really planning to come in?"

"I couldn't stop him, Captain. He wants to help finish this. His fiancée is going to bring him by in a few minutes."

"Were you able to get into the cellphone?"

"Yep, unless there's something that we've missed, they don't seem to be a very tech-savvy group. The phone had no more encryption on it than one you'd pick up in a store, and the camp had little surveillance beyond the few cameras that we found." He spread his hands wide. "I guess it's possible that they have some sort of massive presence on the dark web, but at least at first glance, I don't think that's the case. What the phone did have was a long call list from yesterday."

"Bo's phone? He wasn't tipped off about the raid?"

"I don't think so."

"Who was he calling? Could you tell?"

"Washington and I spent some time going through the call log while he was waiting for his discharge paperwork. He doesn't know all the names, but he's confident he can help us zero in on at least some of the folks here in the city."

"Did he have any idea who would get the truck and when they'd start their deliveries?"

"He said his first guess would be Marconi, but he couldn't say for sure. He confirmed that they planned to muster at the city parks closest to Point State Park."

The captain leaned back in his chair, his eyes on Smitty but his thoughts scrolling through that day's duty roster. "We're still looking for the second man, Keller, but until we find him, that list is about all we've got to go on."

"Plus, Washington had never seen Keller at the camp. He figures he's a lower echelon guy who wouldn't have access to much useful information."

Just then, the captain's phone rang. It was a brief conversation, and he hung up quickly before turning to grin at Smitty. "The Staties have spotted Marconi and are on his tail now. We'll see if and when he goes for the truck. In the meantime, what do you think we should recommend to the task force?"

"Captain, I would love to bring that truck in, get those arms safely off the street, but . . ."

The captain leaned forward, resting his elbows on the desk. "We need to follow it, don't we? Scoop as many people up in its wake as we can."

Smitty nodded. "I think that's the only hope we have of finding some of these lieutenants. Washington's video showed them being told to take the small arms in their cars. That means there's more firepower in the city than just what's in that truck."

"It's going to take some real organization, though, to manage this without tipping the driver off to what's going on."

"Is Marconi on the schedule today? Is he supposed to be coming in?"

He shook his head. "No, he's not on the schedule until Tuesday. You think that makes him the driver?" He watched as Smitty looked up, pondering the question. Then he turned back, and the captain was interested to see the certainty in his expression.

"I think that's a pretty good possibility."

"He's going to be monitoring our chatter on the radio if that's the case."

"Yup, which makes the coordination even harder."

Captain Fischer stood up, pulled his phone out of his pocket, and held it up. "Looks like we'll be using these. Were you able to pull any full names or addresses off the call log?"

"Only a few. When Washington gets here, we should be able to pin down more, enough to help us sketch out some of the destinations, maybe." He looked up at the captain. "We're going to want to get warrants for the homes and vehicles of the ones we identify. Do we have enough to ask for wiretaps too?"

"I hope so. If we could get Marconi making contact about the deliveries, it'd make a difference. You get me a list as soon as you can, and I'll interrupt a judge on their weekend."

"All right. I'll get tech support to round up some phones that we can use. As soon as Washington gets here, we'll see what we can put together as far as a list of names and addresses."

"You know, I wasn't able to shift the tax guys from picking Ellerby up tomorrow, so we really do need to get this done today. I'm going to get on the phone and see how many people I can pull in to help us."

"I'll take Washington back to my desk to work. We've got a couple of monitors, and I can pull up the videos he shot while we go through the log." The captain watched him pause at the door. "Sir, Washington and me, we're fine. I wanted to let you know. The poor guy was rushing to apologize to me from his damn hospital bed. I've got no problem with him."

"That's good to know. I figured you'd see it that way once you had the whole picture." Smitty stepped out and the captain went to talk with his assistant and the dispatcher. He'd need some firm numbers before he went begging for more from the task force.

Just after noon on Sunday, once the wedding guests had left and Ellerby was on his way home, Marconi took the time to drive back over to the camp. He followed the same route that he'd used the day before, driving in on the grassy track. He didn't know why he wanted to see it again. Especially since it seemed possible that it might still be under surveillance. He kept his distance, standing next to another wide old oak as he studied the scene. Then he turned and called Bo.

When the phone failed to find a signal, he drove slowly back down the track and onto the main road that would take him into the city. After about ten minutes of driving, he made the call again but it went straight to Bo's voicemail. He was supposed to pick the truck up on Monday to make his deliveries, but Bo's silence was making him edgy. He figured he'd go home and get cleaned up first, then if he still hadn't heard from Bo, he'd head over to the garage where the truck was parked. As he drove, Marconi considered what anyone might have learned from the raid on the camp. The few people they'd left there were newer and younger than most of their members and knew comparatively little about their operations. The bigger worry was Washington, and it helped knowing he was safely under wraps at the garage. Marconi had no stomach for killing another cop, but he felt a little foolish remembering how easily he'd been able to interest the young officer in their camp and their cause. Of course, it had been a set-up, probably another bleeding-heart liberal hoping to move up in the ranks.

At four-thirty that afternoon, Marconi had still not been able to reach Bo, so he pulled into a parking area at the side of the garage. He was reassured to see the bay doors still padlocked, but once he'd parked, he saw that the side door was hanging open. He stepped inside the darkened bay, spotting a gas can laying on its side. He called out. "Bo! Keller! What's going on?" He paused, but there was no response. He pulled out his phone and dialed Bo's number again, listening to see if it was ringing somewhere in the building. Silence. This didn't look good. What the hell was going on?

He got back into his car and took off as quickly as he could. There were a few backup plans in place, including an alternate site for hiding the truck. Marconi took a circuitous route away from the garage, backtracking more than once before heading to the abandoned factory. He pulled up to the entrance and then waited, his eyes searching the area around him. When he'd been there a good five minutes and nothing had moved, he figured it was safe enough to approach the truck. He pulled up beside it, turned off his truck, and dug into his glove box for the extra set of keys.

Once inside the truck's cab, Marconi took another few minutes to look around it carefully, but nothing caught his eye. It looked like it had when he dropped it off at the garage. He didn't like the silence from Bo, though, and decided that the timetable needed to be pushed forward. He needed to get everything in place if they were to be ready for Halloween. With that in mind, he punched in the first number he had on his list.

The first call to Bo's phone registered around two o'clock that afternoon. Smitty and Washington had turned it off so that any calls would go directly to voicemail. The caller hadn't left any messages, but they'd called again at 2:30 and again at 2:45. Bo's phone ID'd it as Marconi's number, and Smitty wondered again at the lack of technical sophistication in the group. Even someone who got their information solely from movies would know what a damn burner phone was, he thought. How had these idiots not figured out the simplest steps to follow in a secret operation?

The most recent call had come at 4:35, just before one of the agents on-site at the garage called into the station. "We've got someone at the side door now."

Smitty listened in as the captain responded. "Keep your eyes on them but don't intervene."

"It's Marconi. He seems to be searching the place." The voice whispered again.

Smitty heard Washington snort in derision. "That guy."

Smitty nodded and continued to listen in as he watched the feed from the black and white cameras Rita had installed inside the garage earlier. He could see Marconi's anger and bewilderment grow. Then the man darted out the side door and back into his car. Smitty and Washington had come to sit at the table in the captain's conference room and were able to hear him order one of the units to follow Marconi.

By cross-referencing the video that Washington had shot with the phone logs from Bo's cell, Smitty and Washington had put together a list of the ten most likely candidates for deliveries. Their homes and businesses had been plotted out on a city map in the conference room. Smitty had heard the captain's impassioned plea to the judge who had signed off on the requested wiretap orders, as well as the search warrants that would allow them to go into their homes and vehicles after the smaller arms. Now they hoped it would begin to pay off. As the tracker on the truck blinked its location, the men around the table waited anxiously to see if its path would take it to one of their suspected targets.

"First call coming in." One of the techs they'd enlisted put the call on speaker.

"*McCarthy, coming to you early for delivery. Be ready.*"

"*Got it.*"

Washington motioned to the spot on the map corresponding to one of the suspects they'd identified.

"Looks like he's going ahead with the deliveries." Smitty offered.

The captain barked out orders for the nearest team to be ready. "He's on the move. Now remember, you've got to hang back and wait until he unloads, and someone accepts the delivery. Then wait for the truck to pull away before going in. Is everyone clear on that?"

Again, Smitty could hear the various officers responding via cell phone. Now they just had to wait. Smitty hated pacing so he walked back to his desk and dug in the drawer for a box of cough drops. He stopped to pour a couple of cups of coffee and then returned to the table, placing a cup and the box in front of Washington. "You okay, man?" Smitty asked.

Washington looked up and smiled. "Thanks, yeah, I'm okay."

"Another call, sir." The tech announced just before one of the agents reported in.

"*Stuart, coming to you now. Be ready.*"

Again, there was an almost immediate response, but this time it wasn't a welcome one.

"*No, not now, I've got company, you gotta give me a half hour at least.*" A panicked voice answered.

"*Half hour, that's it.*"

Smitty heard the officer at the first location give his men the go-ahead. He looked up at the captain. "What do you think Marconi'll do in the meantime?"

The captain shrugged. "He seems in a hurry. Maybe he'll . . ."

"*Westfall, you ready? Materials are coming now.*"

"Move on to another target." The captain grinned as he finished his sentence. "We got Westfall on the map?"

"Yep, it's not too far," Washington responded, and the captain reached out to that team. Then they continued to wait.

After a few more minutes, the first team reported in. "Captain, we're good. We've got McCarthy in custody as well as the goods. The team is searching his house and cars for other firearms while we take him in."

"Excellent. Westfall team, same procedure. Be ready."

Smitty turned to Washington and grinned. "One down."

"So many more to go," Washington answered, and the two men continued to wait.

If only Rod was here, Smitty thought, then this moment would really be complete. He checked his phone, but there was still no more news from Audrey. He said a silent prayer for his friend and continued to watch the truck's progress.

Within the hour, the teams had picked up both Westfall and Stuart. The next hour brought in Jones and Baker, but they knew their luck was over when one of the younger officers mistakenly reported back over the radio. Smitty's gaze locked on the captain.

"Shit, there's a scanner in that truck."

"All units, move in, I repeat, move in." The captain announced as the tracker they were following began picking up speed. "Please let us take him." Smitty heard the captain whisper, and everyone at the table sat transfixed. Smitty knew there were multiple units on the truck, lights and sirens would be running now as they hurried to box him in and stop the old truck.

"It's a piece of shit truck, Captain, hopefully it'll . . ." Smitty offered just as they spotted the tracker pausing on the map.

"Have you got it?" The captain barked out.

"We have the truck. Marconi took off on foot."

Smitty watched as the captain tore out of the room toward the dispatch desk. "All units, all units in the vicinity of . . ." The order went out along with a full description of Marconi and the warning that he was most likely armed.

Thirty minutes later, the captain returned to the conference room, collapsing into his chair. Smitty could see the despair washing across his face as he shook his head. "They couldn't find him."

"Dammit to hell," Smitty grasped both of the arms on his chair and shoved back, the tension and frustration spilling out..

"I used the phone to contact the rest of the teams and had them move immediately on the rest of the names in our list. They won't get them all, but they'll get some."

The group continued to monitor the rest of the raids, listening to the chatter and ticking names off the list as they went. Only one house had been empty, while all of the other houses and vehicles had yielded arms and militia men. It was a good day, a very good day if you discounted the role that Marconi's escape played in it. But no one could do that and no one was gloating.

By nine o'clock that night, the truck, the goods it carried, and all of the intended recipients that they'd identified were in custody, but Marconi was not. News of the coordinated arrests and the thwarted plans for the Halloween demonstration just days away filled the airways and social media and was being carried by national as well as local stations. The faces of more than twenty militiamen were being paraded across the country. News of the manhunt for Marconi, though, was being kept much quieter.

Just after ten, the captain sent everyone home. "You did good work today, all of you. Together, we stopped something that could very well have been catastrophic. But now we need rest, all of us. I don't know when or how we're going to track down Marconi, but we will. You have my word on that."

Smitty looked over at Washington as the captain finished speaking, and the exhaustion on his face was unmistakable. He set his hand gently on the man's shoulder. "C'mon, let me give you a ride home, John. You look like you could use some rest."

The captain came up behind them and echoed Smitty's remarks. "We couldn't have done this today without you, John. Now I'm ordering you to go home and rest. I don't want to see you back in here before Thursday. Are we clear on that?"

Washington nodded at both men before taking his time standing up and pushing in his chair. "I think I'll follow that order, Captain. And yes, I'd love a ride."

"Get some sleep, all of you!" the captain called out as the chairs scraped and the room gradually emptied.

Marconi was pleased with the delivery business so far. Only Stuart had put him off, and that had been easily dealt with. There were just three more on his list, and then he could get some rest and actually sleep in his own bed again. Ellerby's lodge was a great place, but he hadn't been able to enjoy the luxury accommodations it had to offer. After roughing it in the pool house for two nights, he was looking forward to a steak on the grill and a long, hot shower. "Finishing up here, Captain." The truck's scanner scratched out. Finishing what? Marconi wondered when it occurred to him that the scanner had been unusually quiet for a weekend. A sick feeling began rising in his gut as he quickly dialed Baker's number, his last delivery.

It went straight to voicemail, the same with Jones's. "Shit, it's over." He thought, slamming his hand against the steering wheel. "Goddammit!" He shrieked as he threw the truck into gear and gunned the ancient motor. It moved from a slow grind to a grudging hum, but he was too far from any highway to make decent time. Forced to take one surface street after another, soon he could hear the sirens over the noise of the truck. They were coming from more than one direction, he realized, just as an idiot with a rental truck pulled out in front of him and began to reverse. Marconi stood on the brake and slammed the wheel again and again before throwing it into park and jumping out. The sirens were almost upon him when he ducked into a laundromat and out its back door. He kept to the alleys, moving as quickly as he could, zig-zagging his way along. When he hit an open stretch, he doubled his speed before ducking back into a restaurant and again making his way out the back. The kitchen staff had looked startled, but he ignored the yells and kept moving.

Finally, as he stood hunched beside a rancid dumpster, trying to catch his breath, he realized he didn't hear any more sirens. He'd run for nearly thirty minutes, and it was taking him a while to recover. He stepped away from the smell toward a low bench that extended along the back of an apartment building. He sat, his head held in his hands as he focused on calming his breathing. What the hell was he going to do now? He reached into his pocket and pulled out his phone, tossed it onto the sidewalk, and crushed it under his boot. He stood, tossed the broken phone into the stinking dumpster, and took off again, this time at a slower pace. He was pleasantly surprised when he realized where he was. It wouldn't be safe to head to his own place, but his mother's house was just a few blocks ahead.

Marconi covered the distance quickly and paused across the street, studying the scene. He didn't think there was any way the cops would have her place on their radar, at least not yet, so when he saw no movement in the block around him, he hurried down the driveway and grabbed the key that rested above the side door. His mother's car was gone, so he felt sure he could get in and out quickly without alerting her to what was going on. The side door opened directly onto a set of stairs to the basement. He took them two at a time and hurried into the far corner where he'd stashed some emergency supplies. His mother had emptied his childhood bedroom more than a decade ago, converting it into a combination sewing and exercise room, but he'd never finished collecting the boxes of junk and memorabilia that she hadn't felt comfortable throwing away. Instead, he'd hidden an emergency bag in the mess, stocking it with a few clothes, a hat, a fake ID, and a throwaway phone, as well as a pair of pistols and a thick wad of cash. He knew he had enough to disappear while he figured out what he wanted to do next. He took a moment to change his shirt and put on the hat before settling the pack on his back and heading up the stairs. There was still no sign of his mother, so he headed out to the back end of the yard. Night was falling as he disappeared into the busy neighborhood.

Audrey couldn't remember when a night had ever lasted so long. The staff was busy constantly, with little change in their activity level between daytime and nighttime. After a while, the sounds around her blurred as she grew accustomed to the frenzy. Audrey wished she could position a chair right outside the big glass door of Rod's room, but of course, that was not allowed. Instead, she and Emma developed a sort of routine as they took turns sitting with him, walking the nearby halls, and dozing in the small waiting room.

Dr. Singh returned to meet with them before going home for the night, but there was no change to report. The new doctor, a brusque-seeming older man, stopped in at 1:00 A.M. and again at 4:00, but his curt nods and few words offered no new information. Around 6:30 A.M., an unfamiliar woman entered and spent some time with Rod as Audrey and Emma stood eagerly at the door. She was a tall, African American woman with a warm smile and a faint tattoo chain down her arm. "Let's talk a minute over here." She said as she pushed the glass door closed behind her. They moved to the waiting area, and she took a seat across from Emma and Audrey, who both perched on the edge of the sofa, their equally anxious expressions turned to the woman.

"Good morning. I'm Sonia Lee, one of the PAs from Dr. Edmonds' office. I'm pleased with what I'm seeing in there. The arm is looking very good. We're going to keep it splinted for just a little while before we cover it with a hard cast." She paused, her gentle gaze moving between the two women. "The collarbone is going to hurt a lot, I'm afraid, but restricting movement is about all we can do for that. I'll be consulting with Dr. Singh when she comes in, but I'm cautiously optimistic at this point. Do you have any questions for me?" She asked both women.

Emma leaned forward. "Can you tell what the long-term impact on the arm may be?"

"Not at this point." She shook her head. "The breaks were serious, and there's no way to know what kind of damage may have been done to the nerves in the arm. Physical therapy may be a difficult journey, I'm afraid." She looked up and stood. "Here's Dr. Singh. Let me go chat with her."

The two women watched as Dr. Singh and the PA stood talking. Then the PA left with a wave, and Dr. Singh stopped in the doorway to speak with them. Audrey and Emma both stood. "Ms. Lee had a good report, and I talked with the doctor overnight, but I want to get a look at Mr. Rodriguez myself for a few minutes. Then I'll be back."

Rather than sit back down, Audrey and Emma moved to stand by the door to Rod's room and watched as Dr. Singh reviewed the notes on her tablet. She spent some time listening to his chest and checking his pupils and the various bandages before entering her notes and stepping out.

"He looks good. His vitals have been steady throughout the night, and his chest sounds clear. We're going to decrease the sedation and let him wake up. We'll assess him again after that, but I'm hopeful we can move him to a step-down bed and get him out of the ICU." She looked at both women and maintained her level tone. "I told you I don't sugar-coat things, and I won't now. It appears he may be beyond the worst, but that doesn't mean there isn't a tough road ahead. Once he wakes up and you both have a chance to speak with him, you need to go home and get some rest. Let them get him moved and settled in a new room before you come back." She gave each of them a steady look before stepping away to talk with the husband of another patient.

Emma and Audrey fell into each other's embrace, tears flowing once again. Finally, Emma stepped back and pulled out her phone, as Audrey did the same. Emma reached out to Gina and Far, while Audrey contacted the captain and Smitty, as well as Sandy and Oscar. Once they'd communicated with everyone, the nurse led them both into the room as she stood on the other side and touched him on the shoulder. "Stanley," she called, and both Emma and Audrey burst into unexpected laughter.

"Call him Rod," Emma offered and took Audrey's hand as they waited.

Smitty appreciated the captain's kind words but never really expected to sleep through the night. Instead, he kissed his wife as she went off to bed. "Don't be up too late," She cautioned.

He knew she still worried about him after the shooting in the spring. He held her close and said softly, "I'm fine. Don't worry about me. I promise not to stay up too late."

"Will we have time for a run in the morning?" She asked as she stepped back. They used to always head to separate gyms, but when he was recovering in the spring, Lise had started walking and then running with him. He didn't need the supervision anymore, but they'd both come to enjoy the company, so they'd kept it up when their schedules permitted.

"I doubt it, I'm afraid. There's still plenty of work to do, and I'm anxious to get in and see Rod as soon as I can. I'll try to get out quietly in the morning."

"Alright." She kissed him once more and then headed up the stairs. "Remember, not too late now."

He smiled and sat back down at the table and worked until after midnight on the paperwork and other details that he and Washington had collected. It had led to a successful operation, but with Marconi in the wind, he knew their work wasn't done.

He exchanged a few texts with Audrey as he was working, but there didn't seem to be any new information, so around one-thirty, he dropped onto the couch and closed his eyes. At 5:30, they popped back open, so he stepped into the shower before making a pot of coffee. As he stood letting the warm water course down his face, he found himself reviewing the events of the last two days. He'd gone into the raid at the camp doing his best to appear confident and in charge of the team, but inside had been a different story. There was so much ugly history surrounding raids on camps of militia types that his heart had been in his throat as they crept up to the place. They had deactivated three cameras as they drew nearer, but there was no way to tell if they'd gotten them all.

When they reached the fence, one of the men from Erie plucked a long piece of grass and touched the tip to the wire grid. With a nod, he confirmed that it was electrified, and they steered clear, then approached the gate with caution. They tested again and found the gate itself without a charge, so they breached it quickly. They surrounded the building and, in unison, entered the three access doors. As the men inside scrambled to get out of their chairs, one man with a rifle got off a rapid shot that whizzed past Smitty's head. He fired back immediately, and once that man lay on the floor, the others quickly raised their arms in surrender. It was over almost before it started.

In the shower, Smitty took one more deep breath and blew it out before cutting off the water and reaching for his towel. His thoughts strayed then to Rod and the hospital, and he hurried to dress. When he stepped out of the bathroom at 6:00, he was shocked to see that his wife already had the pot of coffee started and was putting a second breakfast sandwich into the microwave for him. "I'm sorry I woke you, Lise."

She turned and wrapped him in a hug. "I have an early meeting, so no worries. Did you get any sleep last night?"

"Mmmm, some. There's still an awful lot hanging in the air at this point, so . . ."

"I understand. What's first then?"

"I'm going to meet with the captain and see what leads he has on tracking down Marconi."

"And Washington, the man you were working with, how is he feeling?"

"He was beat up pretty bad, and he was concussed and dehydrated. He'd been shoved up a coal chute if you can believe that."

"My God, buried alive almost."

"I'm not sure how 'almost' it was. Anyway, I couldn't believe he wanted to come in, but sure enough, he came straight from the hospital to the station."

Lise stood next to him, her hip resting against his as they ate their sandwiches. He was so lucky to have her, Smitty thought, so lucky. When he'd finished his last bite, he poured a generous amount of the coffee into a tall thermos and went to brush his teeth. Once he was ready, he stopped to hold Lise once more, soaking in the warmth and love that he'd come to depend on for so long.

She kissed him once more and said, "Give Rod and Audrey my love. I'll be thinking of them today."

"I will. I'll be in touch once I have a sense of what my day is going to be like." He pulled on a jacket and headed out the door. The clock on the dash indicated it was not yet 7:00.

58

Rod was beginning to notice a few sounds when he heard an unfamiliar voice say, "Stanley." He tried to force his eyes to open, and then the same voice leaned in closer and said, "Rod." He felt his eyelids finally come under his control, and he blinked a few times before he was able to hold them open. An older woman in scrubs was looking at him, and he lifted his head to try and see where he was, but the pain drove a spike through his brain. He could feel a gentle pressure on the back of his head as someone lowered him back to the pillow. "It's okay, I've got you." He heard.

He felt his head sink back into a pillow. He wanted to fall back into sleep, into the inviting darkness he'd been swimming in, but then a more familiar voice spoke. "Rod, it's Emma."

He opened his eyes again and looked to his right, where Emma was leaning toward him. "Hi, Ems. What happened?" He managed to croak out hoarsely.

"You're in the hospital, Rod. There was an accident." Emma offered.

Audrey sat down on the very edge of the bed and rested her hand on his leg. "You were rescuing John Washington when an SUV from the garage slammed into your truck."

He felt a piece of memory start to slide back into place, but it was still so fuzzy. Who was John Washington, he wondered? Then a memory of black dust and hard coughing shifted more memories into place. He looked up at Audrey. "Is he okay?"

"Yes. Rita Banks is doing well, too."

He was struggling to put a face to the name Rita when an image of a woman holding a video camera came to mind, and suddenly the entire setup fell into place, and panic set in. He tried again to rise, but Emma put her hand on his shoulder. "What day is it?" He asked, desperate to know how close to Halloween it had come. "The truck . . ."

"Rod, it's only Monday morning. It's okay. The captain and Smitty are both on it. I don't have any of the details, but they'll come and talk to you when you're ready."

Rod heard a door slide open, and a woman wearing a white coat came up to the end of his bed. "Mr. Rodriguez?" She asked.

Rod started to nod, but at the first flicker of renewed pain, he spoke instead. "Yes, that's me. People call me Rod."

"It's good to meet you, Rod. I'm Dr. Singh. It's Monday morning, and you're in the ICU at Mercy Hospital." Rod looked around, taking in the details of the small room filled with machines. His eyes traced along the line of an IV and then across his body to where his arm was being held up in the air. He tried to wiggle the fingers of that arm, but they didn't seem to be answering at all.

"My arm?"

"Your arm was broken in two places. One of the breaks was an open fracture, so Dr. Edmonds operated in order to set it. It's in a splint temporarily to keep it stable and allow the wound to start to heal. His physician's assistant was just in, and she said everything looks very good." He watched as she drew her hand up to her throat and gestured. "There is a break in the collarbone as well, and it was set, but we can't do too much more for that."

As she spoke, Rod started to catalog the different pains that seemed to be waking up all over his body. *My God. It must have been some accident.* He tried to think back to the rescue. *Was it Saturday night?* He started drifting then, trying to picture Washington and the staggered walk they'd made to his truck. *Oh God, his truck.* He looked back at the doctor, but she had turned to Emma and Audrey. "I'm going to authorize his transfer out of ICU and into a bed down the hall." He heard her say. "Take a few more minutes with him, but then I want both of you to go home and get some rest." She turned back to him. "Rod, I know everything hurts like blazes. We're going to keep you on something strong for the rest of today, and then we're going to back it off. Do you understand?"

"Yes. Do you know when I can go home?"

"Your legs are very bruised, but I don't anticipate you having any difficulty with mobility. However, you've had a severe concussion, and we want to monitor you for a little longer. Once we've got you shifted to a regular room, we're going to get you up walking a bit." She paused and waited until he focused on her face once more. "I'm going to tell you right now, it's going to be hard, harder than you expect. You're going to have to be patient with yourself."

Rod watched as she made a few notes on a tablet and left. Then he looked at Emma and Audrey and realized that they looked terrible, their faces tear-streaked and tired, their hair and clothing rumpled. Monday morning. An accident Saturday night. They must have been at the hospital for a long time, he thought. The pain was growing steadily more noticeable, but he was still moved by them. He wanted to reach up and bring them close, but with one arm in the air and the other anchored by an IV, he was unable to move much at all.

"Thank you both for being here." He managed to say, his voice feeling slightly steadier. "You should listen to the doctor and go home for a while. It'll be okay."

Emma leaned in. "I will, but only because I promised Gina and Far that I would. Far really wanted to come and see you."

"Give my little buddy a hug for me and tell him I'll see him as soon as I can," Rod responded as she leaned in and kissed him on the cheek.

"I will. And I'll be back before you know it." She gave a quick wave to him and Audrey as she slid the door open and left.

Audrey scooted up the bed until she was sitting much closer to him and took his free hand in hers. He expected her to say something since they were alone now, but she just sat there, stroking his hand and looking at him. They were quiet for a moment, looking into each other's faces. Even disheveled, she was still so beautiful. Rod hated to think what he looked like. Finally, she broke the silence. "I don't even know what to say. I've been so scared."

"I'm glad you're here now. I think I'd be a lot more frightened waking up this way if I couldn't see your face." She leaned in and kissed him gently, cupping his cheek as she did. Then she sat back and took his hand once more. "I hate to ask this," he said, figuring he already knew the answer. "My truck?"

Audrey just shook her head. "Sorry, my friend. I'm pretty sure they had to take a can opener to it to get you out. Think there's any chance the force will spring for a new one?"

"I doubt it. I liked that truck, too."

"Well, it took good care of you. Emma said that they told her the side airbag is what protected you from the worst of the hit."

"Do you know what happened to the guys from the garage? Did they survive?"

Audrey shook her head. "I don't know any more details. Smitty and the captain are going to be coming to see you as soon as you're out of the ICU, and they'll fill you in." She paused, uncomfortable still with the way things had played out. "I'm sorry I wasn't here right away after the accident happened. They weren't able to reach me at the lodge. I was on my way back into the city yesterday when all the texts finally hit my phone. Oscar met me here and carried my gear home for me. Smitty called them when he couldn't reach me." The door opened, and a man in blue-green scrubs came in.

"Ready to move to your new room?"

"Well, that's my cue." Audrey offered and stepped back out of the way. "Can you think of anything you want me to bring you from home?"

Rod could feel his bare butt pressing on the hospital sheet beneath him. "Maybe just some shorts? He asked, and Audrey grinned.

"Not liking the ventilated hospital fashions?"

"No, not so much." Fatigue began washing over him then. "You go and rest, now. I know I'm going to sleep once I'm moved, so take your time."

He watched as she touched her hand to her mouth and mimed blowing a kiss before she stepped out the door. He felt his eyelids closing in almost the same moment.

CHAPTER

59

Captain Fischer wished he'd been able to take the advice that he'd given Smitty and the others about trying to sleep. However, at fifty-five, sleeping had become much more difficult than when he was a younger man. He longed for the days when he could come home from a late shift, tumble into bed, and be asleep within minutes. Now, he was more likely to toss and turn, stewing over the events of the day while trying to ignore the small aches and pains that seemed to have arrived with his fiftieth birthday.

He'd had a bite to eat and taken a warm shower, but sleep hadn't come until after four. Then, before the faintest bit of early light filled the sky, it was over. He'd gotten up, showered again to wake himself up, and slipped quietly out of the house in order not to wake his wife. She'd had to put up with his crazy hours for so many years now that when the opportunity came to slip away and leave her in peace, he did. He left her a brief note on the kitchen chalkboard and then drove to the old-fashioned diner that wasn't far from the precinct station. The waitress knew him on sight and led him to one of the booths near the front. She settled him in with a cup of coffee before going to put in his usual order.

He had his phone out immediately and began scrolling through Audrey's texts about Rod, as well as additional notes from the task force team. As he was finishing his food, the morning news came on the TV hanging against the far wall. He couldn't hear it, but he certainly recognized the visuals. There was footage from the training camp with its despicable gun range and a warning to TV viewers about the explicit nature of the images. Then it shifted to footage of the truck, its back door lifted to show the contents, followed by driver's license photographs of the dead man, Bo Burns, and his partner, Nathan Keller. He had yet to be located. The captain reached into his wallet and fished out a tip for the waitress as the station showed photograph after photograph of the men they had arrested. There were stock photos of some of the men who'd received the truck deliveries, followed by shots of the others who were picked up at their homes once Marconi took off in the truck. Where the hell was Marconi? That was what ate at the captain now, what took the shine off the successful confiscations and arrests.

He'd reached his desk by the time he received the note from Audrey with Rod's new room number. He'd do his best to get over there before lunch, he thought. The captain was still haunted by the sight of Rod trapped in his truck, bleeding and unconscious, the bone sticking out of his arm at that horrible angle. He was sure it was going to be a long while before that image left his brain. He looked up just as Smitty passed by his door.

"Hey Smitty, you're in early too, I see." As Smitty stepped into the room, the captain could see the fatigue on the man's face and knew that they shared the same set of worries. "You get any sleep last night?"

"Not much, Captain. You?"

Captain Fisher stood and moved to a table next to the wall where he kept a coffee maker. "No, not much. Care for a cup?"

"I've got some already," Smitty responded, briefly holding up his thermos. He waited while the captain added a packet of sweetener to his mug. "Any idea what we do now?" Smitty asked as he took a seat across the desk from the captain.

"Cops hunting a cop is not an easy thing, I'm afraid. I've sent someone out to speak with his mother. She's here in the city, but I haven't found any siblings or other likely contacts. Did Washington say anything about Marconi having friends here?"

"Washington described him to me as being pretty much a loner. Marconi was never easy to get along with. But we all knew that already."

The captain nodded and watched as Smitty sipped his coffee thoughtfully. "There's something else on your mind."

"Does Marconi seem like someone who'd give up easily to you, Captain?"

"Definitely not. Why, what are you thinking? Do you think he'd target someone, one of us maybe?"

"I'm not sure. There are plenty of us he could blame. But I'm also thinking about the big plans they'd made for Halloween. I have a hard time picturing him just slinking away, letting all of that go."

The captain leaned forward, alarm building in him once again. "The Halloween event you mean?" Suddenly, he could picture the crowds, parents and children in costumes, tents filled with people doing activities. The thought of a gunman going after that type of gathering made him feel nauseous. He gestured over his shoulder to the TV on the wall in the next room. "All of these news reports are going to have people dropping their guard. They'll think everything's fine. They may get even more people after this kind of publicity."

"We have to find him before then, Captain." The two men stood. "I'll give Washington a call in a little while, pick his brain some more. Will you let me know if you learn anything from Marconi's mother?"

"Sure will."

"Then I'm going to head over to the hospital."

"I figured. I may see you there." The captain's eye caught on the TV newsreel again. So far at least, they'd kept Marconi's name out of the reporting, but as he was watching, Marconi's face appeared on the screen. Well, dammit. That wasn't going to help.

As she left, Audrey took a moment to text Rod's new room number to everyone. She had reached the lobby before her sleep-addled brain realized she had no way to get home. She pulled her phone back out and began calling for a ride but paused before listing a destination. Well, no time like the present, she thought, and entered the address of the car dealership.

Once she arrived, she knew she didn't want to make an entirely crazy snap decision, so she took the time to meet with her contact again and test-drive several models. In the end, though, it was still the hatchback that she liked the most, so she felt comfortable filling out the paperwork to clinch the deal. Within the hour, she was pulling up to the house in her brand-new car. It was fun and exciting to buy her first car, but even more, she loved the wash of relief that flooded over her knowing she could jump in it at any moment and be at the hospital in just a few minutes.

With that peace of mind, she tried the side door of the house and was relieved to find it unlocked. She stepped inside and immediately spotted her gear in the hallway near the front door. She didn't remember having given Oscar her keys, but there they were, sitting on top of the larger camera case. Thank God for good friends, she thought, and went to find clean clothes to put on after a long shower.

With her hair clean and a fresh shirt and pair of jeans on, Audrey fixed herself some coffee and toast and sat down to call her parents. She hadn't wanted to call and frighten them in the middle of the night, especially when she was still so scared.

"Hello?" Her father answered, and when she saw his face, Audrey was surprised to feel tears filling her eyes once more. It took her a second to be able to speak. "Audrey?"

"Hi, Dad. Sorry about that."

"What's going on Audie? Is something wrong?" She saw her mother slide into the seat beside him.

"Mom, Dad, Rod was in a really bad accident on Saturday night." She began and gradually filled them in on the sequence of events from the wedding through to her recent car purchase. They waited patiently as she worked her way through it all, allowing for the tearful pauses along the way. Only when she'd run out of steam and tissues did her father step in.

"Well, that's a lot to take in, Audie. I won't kid you. What can your mom and I do to help? Is there anything you need? Can we bring some food by for you, maybe?"

Audrey had just taken stock of the kitchen cabinets and refrigerator, so she knew she was set. Plus, with Rod in a regular room now, she figured she'd be there with him for the next day or two. "I'm fine for now, Dad. Thank you for offering. Can I check back in with you two once I'm able to bring him home?"

Her mother answered for both of them. "Of course, of course, Honey. If you want to bring him home here, that'd be fine, too."

"Thank you, Mom, I appreciate that offer. I'll keep you updated on everything."

"Okay, Audie. We're here whenever you need us."

"I count on that, Dad, I really do."

Audrey took the time to call Sandy, but since she was working, they made a plan to talk more that evening. She didn't feel at all like sleeping, so Audrey went about packing a bag to take with her to the hospital. She rounded up some shorts and a pair of soft pajama pants for Rod, as well as some slip-on sandals, a cloth robe, and a toiletries kit. She gathered a few things for herself, collected a few snacks, and lastly, tucked in her computer. She knew Rod would be sleeping a lot for a while, so she thought maybe she'd be able to work. Luckily, her photography schedule that week was clear until Friday afternoon. She called to let the police department know she'd be missing her shifts that week, but they weren't at all surprised and sent warm wishes for Rod's recovery. Audrey took a moment to fit her house key onto her new car's fob before heading out.

After just a bit of searching, she arrived at Rod's new room, this one with a wide wooden door and a second bed, empty behind an open curtain. A chair was set up on Rod's right side, and she wasn't surprised to see it occupied by Captain Fischer. He looked so tired that Audrey felt bad for interrupting his visit. He stood up quickly, though, offering the chair to Audrey. "Well, Rod, looks like the reinforcements have arrived." He held out his hand to Audrey and rested his other one on top of it. "You look after our boy for me, Audrey. I've got to head out." He turned back to Rod. "I'll put in a claim for that truck of yours, but I don't think I'd hold my breath there, son." Audrey was glad to see the smile light up Rod's face, even if it was only for a moment. The captain stepped out, and Audrey saw the fatigue take over Rod's features once more, accentuated by the deep bruising.

She leaned in to kiss him before resting her hip on the side of the bed. "Hey, buddy. How're you holding up? The captain looked almost as tired as you."

"I know, Scout, he's got the weight of the world on his shoulders right now. But I feel better, now that you're here." He squeezed her hand.

"Have you had many visitors?"

"Smitty was in before the captain got here, and I texted with Emma, so she's taking a break."

"Did the captain fill you in on everything that's happened? I saw some of it on the news."

"Yeah, we're not out of danger yet, though, I'm afraid. There's still no sign of Marconi." Audrey could see the frustration on his face as he lay there, unable to help. She remembered when they'd been on one of their first dates and he'd gotten the call that his partner Smitty had been hit.

"Hard to have to sit on the sidelines, isn't it?"

"Yep. How are you doing?"

"I'm fine. I had a chat with my mom and dad, and they said you're welcome to come home there to recuperate if you'd like. My mom's a nurse, you know."

Rod grinned. "Your folks are so nice to offer that, but . . ."

She held up her hand. "I didn't agree to it. I figured you'd rather be in your own home when you're feeling bad, not someone else's."

He looked up at her with a smile. "Don't you mean 'our home'?" She leaned in to kiss him.

"Yes. Our home. Now," she sat back. "How can I help? Have they had you walk around yet?"

He grimaced. "Actually, I was putting that off until you came back with some clothes. It's really embarrassing, though, because I think you're going to have to help me put them on."

Audrey smiled at him before pulling the backpack up onto the end of the bed. "Lucky for you, I've seen that bod before, so I don't imagine I'll be overcome by the vapors or anything."

"The vapors. Who even talks like that?" He laughed as he looked over the offered clothes. "Let's just go with the pajama pants for now. I think they'll be easy enough to operate one-handed."

"You got it." With one arm still elevated and the IV in the other, it wasn't an easy task. It seemed to take forever for him to sit all the way up and then swing his legs to the side of the bed. As he swept the gown aside, Audrey was shocked at all the bruising and smaller wounds that the gown had been hiding. She had drawn her hand up to her mouth before realizing it. "My God, Rod. How are you even moving at all? You must hurt all over. Let's not worry about the pants."

He rested his hand on her arm and made her sit back down beside him for a moment. "Audrey, it's okay."

"No, Rod, you're . . ."

"It's okay. The captain filled me on some of the details from the crash, and Audrey, I'm so damned glad to be alive that I'm not going to let the pain stop me now. C'mon, help me get my feet through and then we can pull them up together."

"Alright, but slowly."

"Of course." He smiled at her, and she could almost see the familiar face through the damage. She slipped the pajama pants over each foot, bunched the rest up in her hands, and inched them up Rod's battered body. It took every ounce of energy he had to lift his hips up and allow her to pull them up into place, but finally, they were on.

"I think I might need a little more rest before I tackle that walk, but at least my bare ass won't be hanging out when I do it." Audrey grinned and positioned his sandals by the edge of the bed so that they'd be ready when he was. As he slowly settled back into the bed, Audrey pulled the chair up close and leaned in. It was time to lighten the mood, she figured.

"Guess what I just bought?" She pulled out her phone and showed him the few shots she'd taken of her new car. "Like it?"

"Wow, I do. You know, I've never bought a new car. I got my truck used from a friend of a friend. Were you intoxicated by the new car smell?"

Audrey laughed, "It's so funny that that's a real thing. One part of my brain knows that it's just off-gassing chemicals from the interior or something, but it still got me." She rested her hand on Rod's once more. "The best thing, though, is that I was able to get back here so easily." They clasped hands, but she could see his energy fading. "Close your eyes now and get some rest. I'll be here."

"You sure?" he asked, already sounding groggy.

"I've got my laptop and snacks, so I'm set." She pulled her computer out and set it on the bed's swivel table as she watched his eyes close.

With the pack from his mother's house in hand, Marconi felt more confident as he made his way through the adjacent neighborhood. The evening was growing steadily darker, and he stepped into a convenience store to use the bathroom and pick up some food. In the flickering light of the small restroom, he put on an additional shirt, pulled a jacket on over the gun he had tucked into the back of his waistband, and then squared the baseball cap down over his face a bit. As he stood there studying himself in the mirror, he relaxed his legs and hunched his back. The baggier clothes added up to a good look, he thought, at least ten to fifteen pounds heavier and a few years older.

Continuing with that posture, he moved over to the hot food section where he picked out a double slice of pizza. As it warmed, he filled a tall cup with ice and soda and covered it with a lid. He picked up a bottle of water, chips, and a package of cookies before carrying them all to the register and paying with some of his cash. A man he'd met at the camp had told him that his brother was spending the football season on the road with one of the southern teams, so Marconi headed to the brother's townhouse. He'd been there once for a game months ago, so it wasn't hard to find it again. When no one answered the buzzer, he easily opened the door with a credit card. He didn't turn on the lights, in case a neighbor was watching over the place, but plenty spilled in from the streetlights outside. It wasn't a very big place, but it suited Marconi perfectly.

He spread his dinner out on the coffee table, but as he was starting the second slice, he spotted a TV hanging on the wall in the bedroom. He stepped into the room and found that those drapes were already pulled, so he flicked on the set. It wasn't immediately clear how to pull up the news, but once he saw it, the punch to his gut registered. He sank onto the end of the bed. So many plans, all for nothing, he thought as face after face of the men he'd spent months training flashed across the screen. Even the houses where he hadn't made deliveries seemed to have been raided. It had to have been Washington, but how had he . . . ? Just then, the screen changed to the scene of an accident between two vehicles. He recognized Bo's SUV as soon as he saw it. So, Bo was dead, and Keller was in the wind. Shit. Rodriguez, that asshole Smith's partner, seemed to still be alive. That he and Washington should be alive while Bo wasn't? He slammed the end of the pizza into a nearby waste can. It fucking wasn't right. Marconi had had a few issues with Bo while they worked together, but the man had spent his whole life working in the steel industry just to be left high and dry when production left the city and pensions were slashed. Rodriguez and Smith had benefited their whole lives from the work done by people like Bo, and now the man was dead. He hadn't gotten to see even a glimpse of the revolution he'd been preparing for.

Marconi had stopped paying attention to the newscast until the screen suddenly filled with images of Point Place Park. There was news of a party and parade planned for Halloween night. Marconi raised the volume as the program showed images of the groups who were sponsoring the event. He was on his feet with outrage as the list began to scroll. Every fucking minority and gay-assed bastard seemed to be represented. Well, that fucking well wasn't going to happen. No way. If the brotherhood couldn't be there to stop that kind of replacement trash from taking over the park, then he sure as hell would. He just needed to put together a plan.

Audrey was pleased that Tuesday morning, when she arrived at the hospital, Rod was sitting up in bed, his broken arm now in a cast and an elaborate sling, rather than hanging up in the air. "Well, this looks like a good step. How did it go?" She asked.

"It was no picnic while they did it, but now it feels much better." He held up his other hand. "They took out the IV, too, so I'm way more mobile than I was."

"And all of the bruising and the pain?"

"They took me off the hard stuff once they finished with the cast, and I'm just taking Tylenol now."

"That's all so fast, though. Shouldn't they be doing more?" Audrey sat on the edge of the bed and took hold of his free hand.

"It's what I want, Audrey. I want to go home. I want to be clear-headed. I know I need to rest, but I'd much rather do all of that at home."

"What do the doctors say?"

Rod grinned. "They're working on the discharge papers now, maybe mid-afternoon, if I pass one more check-in with the PA from Dr. Edmonds' office."

"Okay, well, in that case, I think I need to go and get things ready for you at home. We'll need some groceries for sure. Have they given you any instructions for home care?"

"Not yet." He shook his head. "That should be in the discharge paperwork. I think sleeping is going to be the hardest thing." He gestured at the hospital bed, the head and knees both propped up partway. "I slept like this last night, and it was easier than being flat."

"Why don't I fix up the recliner in the living room with some bed-clothes and a table that you can reach?"

"I could see the TV from there." He joked but held her hand tightly. "I hate the idea of not sleeping next to you, but I think that plan makes sense, at least for the short run."

She leaned over and kissed him, lingering for a moment before some-one at the door cleared their throat. Audrey looked up and grinned at Smitty. "Hey, you." She laughed and walked over and hugged him before shouldering her pack and offering the chair. "I've got some things to do to get ready for this guy coming home, so I'll leave now." She looked at Rod. "Call me when you're ready."

"Do you need a ride?" Smitty offered. But Audrey mimed steering a car.

"I have my own wheels now, Smitty." She laughed and then, with a quick wave, was gone.

"Well, my friend. You seem to be in good hands."

Rod laughed in spite of the pain. "It's her first new car. Apparently, she left here yesterday morning and went straight to a dealership then drove back here in the afternoon." He hung his head briefly. "Given the state of my damn truck, it seemed like a pretty good idea."

"Yeah, sorry about that, man. From what I hear, though, the next one should have side airbags like this one did."

"No kidding, right? What's the latest on Keller from the garage?"

Rod watched as Smitty shook his head. "Still no sign of him. They're keeping a watch on his house, so we're hopeful he'll show at some point." He shrugged his shoulders and sat down in the chair beside the bed.

"Any word on Marconi? Any sightings?"

"Not yet. There was some thought that he might have gone into his mother's house, but it's not clear at this point. We're looking at cameras all around the city, but our guess is that he's put together some sort of disguise and is avoiding places with a lot of cameras."

"Makes sense. You have any ideas about what he'll do next?"

"I'm not sure." Smitty raised his hands to indicate uncertainty. "I told the captain, I don't think he's someone who'd quit. He's got too much invested at this point."

"So will he target one of us, do you think?"

"Possibly. I'm more worried, though, about the event on Thursday. It's exactly the kind of crowd he hates. Some of us will be there keeping an eye on things, and he can shoot us or the crowd, both if he's got an automatic or two on him. He may see it as an opportunity to get a twofer."

"Is the media warning people away from the event?" Rod leaned forward in the bed.

"Nope. In fact, I think the publicity may mean they draw an even bigger crowd."

"Oh, shit."

"You're not supposed to say that word, Uncle Rod." A small voice spoke, and Rod looked up to see Emma and Far poised in the doorway.

"Hey, little man!" Rod smiled at Far but tensed for a moment when the little boy hurried toward the bed. At the last second, Emma scooped a hand around Far's waist and held him still.

"Remember what we talked about." Rod's heart broke a little to see the fear that washed over Far's face when he got his first look at Rod. Tears formed in the little boy's eyes, and he didn't seem to be able to say anything.

"It's okay, Far. Come sit on the bed right here beside me." Rod patted the space beside his hip.

"Are you sure?" The small voice asked.

"I'm sure. Far, have you met my partner, Demetrius Smith? We like to call him Smitty." He looked over at his partner. "I think you've met Emma before. This is her son Far."

"It's good to see you both," Smitty said as he shook hands with the little boy and then nodded to Emma. "I'm going to go and let you all visit." He pointed at Rod. "You take it easy now, and let me know once you're home, okay?"

"Will do. Thanks for coming in."

Smitty nodded his head before leaving, and Rod turned his attention back to Far, using his free arm to hug the little boy close. "Uncle Rod, you look really terrible." Far said, looking up into Rod's face.

"I know, little buddy, but I'm going to get better. You'll see." Rod looked up at his sister. "I'm hoping to be discharged this afternoon."

"So soon?" She asked.

"That's exactly what Audrey said. It's time, though. It's so hard to sleep here. I really want to be home."

"If you're sure . . . What can we do to help?"

Rod managed a one-shouldered shrug. "I'm not sure. Audrey went to pick up some groceries, and she's going to fix up that recliner in the living room so that I can sleep there."

"That sounds like a good idea. Do you need a ride?"

Rod laughed. "Nope, Scout went and bought herself a new car when she left here yesterday! Since my truck's totaled . . ."

"Oh no, your truck, Uncle Rod? The blue one?"

"Yep, they had to cut it open to get me out." He could see Emma's eyes bug out, and Rod thought perhaps he'd said a bit too much, but Far was running with it.

"When you get a new truck, will it have a back seat for me again?"

Rod grinned down at his nephew. "Of course. I have to have a place to put your car seat, don't I?"

"I'm so big now, all I need is a booster. But my little sister will need one when she's born."

"That's right. How's Mama G feeling?"

"Good, just a little tired, like you said. We're going to take her some lunch."

"That's right. So, we'd better get going." Emma leaned over and eased Far off the bed before kissing her brother on the cheek. "Make sure Audrey knows we want to help."

"I will."

"Uncle Rod, are you going to the Halloween party with us on Thursday?"

"What party?" Rod asked his sister, a sinking feeling in the pit of his stomach.

"The one at Point Place. Gina's office is one of the sponsors," Emma answered. Then she looked down at Far. "Uncle Rod may not be up for that kind of thing, though, Far. Since he's hurt."

"I'll see what I can do, Far. No promises, but I'll try."

He watched as Far and Emma left, the list of possible dangers growing in his mind.

CHAPTER

63

"He's heading home this afternoon, Captain." Smitty filled in his captain once he returned to the station from the hospital. They were seated on opposite sides of the captain's desk, trying yet again to sort out the best next steps.

The captain shook his head. "They just don't keep people in hospitals very long anymore, do they? Women go right home with their babies. I've even heard that people who get hip replacements are walking the very next day. That's a little terrifying, don't you think?"

Smitty couldn't help but agree with the captain, but he also understood Rod's point of view. When he'd been shot in the spring, he couldn't wait to get home. Now, though, it was time to focus back on the topic at hand. He nodded in agreement before asking. "Any sign yet of Marconi, Captain?"

"Nothing. We interviewed his mother a little more thoroughly, and she doesn't seem to share his views."

"But you think she'd still protect him?"

"It's hard to say. But I don't think she'd be of much help to him. When we searched her place, they didn't turn up any weapons at all."

"And when they searched Marconi's place, any weapons there?"

"No, which makes us think he may have some stashed somewhere else. We just don't know where."

"We cleared the camp on Saturday. There hasn't been any action back up there, has there?" Smitty leaned forward, his elbows resting on his knees.

"No, nothing."

"Did the tax guys pick up Ellerby? Is he talking at all?"

The captain shook his head. "They got him, but those feds are so tight-lipped I'm not sure they'd tell us if the building was on fire."

"Captain, that Halloween event is the day after tomorrow. Are you sure we can't stop it?"

"I checked with the mayor's office, but they just won't. It would look like we were caving into these people. The best they would do is authorize overtime for some additional officers to try and patrol the park."

"Well, I guess that's something. But a bunch of uniforms at a diversity-focused event won't look good either."

"They'll be in plain clothes, but I get what you're saying. The organizers are going to be setting up tables, as well as a big tent to house a music area, a kids' art space, that kind of thing. It's going to be a security nightmare."

Smitty leaned back in his chair thinking. "Captain, we need to provide him with a target that's separate from the kids."

"What are you thinking?"

"Bait. I'm thinking we need to offer him some bait that's so juicy he won't be able to pass it up."

"You mean you, don't you?"

"I'm thinking me, Washington, Rita Banks, Laura Katz, Chao. A frigging police diversity smorgasbord."

"Jesus, Smitty, that's a terrible idea."

"What else have we got, Captain? If we haven't found him by Thursday, we're looking at a pretty desperate situation."

"I'm going to have to think about that. In the meantime, I'm hoping we'll catch a break and pick him up well before then."

Smitty stood. "Agreed. I'll check in with the techs who're studying the video surveillance."

"Okay, I think Rita's back in, so check on her for me too, will you?"

"Will do, Captain," Smitty answered and moved toward the door but not before catching sight of the captain's worried face.

Late Tuesday afternoon, Smitty picked up Lise after work. They stopped for some pizzas and salad, and the two of them headed to Rod and Audrey's. When she got in the car, he told Lise about the offer he'd made the captain. She hadn't had much time to react before they pulled in, but the look that she gave him could have peeled paint. He opened her door and took the pizzas from her, balancing them in one hand as he offered her his other. "Don't you act all gallant on me, mister, this discussion is not over." She wagged a finger at him before stepping onto the sidewalk.

When they reached the door, Smitty heard Rod call from the living room, "Come on in!" He handed the food over to Audrey as he stepped inside.

"He's in the living room. Go right on in." Audrey let them pass and she set the food on the counter. "Can I get you something to drink? We've got wine, beer, some lemonade, I think."

Smitty opted for a beer while Lise picked wine, and they both turned to face Rod. Smitty's heart sank seeing the deep bruising that still covered so much of his friend's face. "How're you doing, man?" He spread his hands to indicate the recliner. "Looks like Audrey fixed you up a throne." It was good to hear Rod laugh.

"She's been taking good care of me, in spite of my constant whining. What's the latest news?"

Smitty wasn't surprised that Rod already wanted to talk shop. But Lise beat him to the punch line. "He has a terrible idea, Rod. You need to talk him out of it."

Smitty and Lise sat on the couch opposite the recliner while Audrey brought them each a drink and then took a seat herself. "What's the terrible idea?" She asked.

"Mr. Demetrius Smith here thinks it would be a good idea for him to act as bait for that crazy cop on Halloween."

"The event is still going forward?" Rod asked, leaning forward a bit in his seat. "They couldn't stop it?"

Smitty took a sip of his beer and leaned back against the cushions. He shook his head. "Nope, Captain couldn't persuade the mayor's office to call it off. So, I suggested we offer Marconi a target, keep his eyes off of the kids and the rest of the crowd."

"I'll join you." Rod offered. "I can't walk around much, but I could sit at a table with you."

"That's what I was suggesting to the captain, a table with a bunch of us types that Marconi can't stand. Me, Washington, Chao, Katz, you, if you're up to it. The captain's got a bunch of plain clothes coming out, but it'll still be risky, I'm afraid." He looked at his wife before shrugging his shoulders. "I just hate the idea of him going after a bunch of kids."

"Wait, do you mean the Point Place event?" Audrey interjected. "I had a call from Jerry's mother, Mrs. Kaminski, asking if I'd photograph it. The Art Institute is one of the sponsors." Audrey looked toward Rod. "I hadn't decided when you were still in the hospital, but now that you're home . . ." She noticed the look on Rod's face. "Don't give me that look."

"What look?" Rod asked. Smitty didn't think his innocent face was very convincing.

"You warned me off photographing the wedding and look what happened. I'm not the one sitting in a recliner trying not to spill beer in my lap." She looked up at Smitty. "If I'm photographing the event, then I can wander around, be everywhere. I can help keep an eye out."

"That's a terrible idea . . ." Rod said just as Smitty spoke.

"That's a wonderful idea . . ."

"Hold on now, you crazy people," Lise interjected. "Why don't we eat some pizza and take some time talking about all of this before anyone goes making a bunch of loony-tune decisions."

Late Wednesday morning, Marconi figured he'd pushed it with the apartment long enough. It'd be too easy for the guy to drop by home during a break in the schedule, so he'd taken time to stop at one of the big hardware stores and pick up some cheap camping gear the day before. In planning for their demonstration, Marconi had spent a lot of time checking out the various parks around the city. Many had mostly public spaces that were far too open, but a few had larger wooded areas where he knew he could hide unseen. He took a long shower and thought through his next steps. Afterward, he shouldered the new pack and exited out the back of the building, walking through several neighborhoods before stopping in a convenience store to pick up a few more supplies.

He had wanted to get another good look at Point Place Park, but with all the media coverage, he figured it was bound to be under heavy scrutiny. Instead, he took his time walking to the other park that he'd picked out, his eyes alert for any sign of patrol cars or street cameras. Avoiding all of that was adding considerable time to his movements, but he had to play it safe. He munched on an apple as he walked and thought over what he was planning to do on Halloween.

His first idea had been to pick up a long-range automatic like the ones they'd had stored up at the camp. It'd be easy enough to set up a perch that would give him ready access to the crowd. He figured he'd be able to pick off dozens before taking off. He didn't intend to die for this after all, he was just going to strike and get out, then maybe move east a bit, see if he couldn't hook up with another militia group, maybe one that was a little more modern and tech-savvy than the one he'd been saddled with in the city.

There was something unsatisfying about the plan, though. It felt too impersonal. He wanted to see the motherfuckers he was hunting, especially the assholes from the police department. He had the two handguns on him and good-sized clips for each. If he were to blend in with the crowd, get close to the people he was after, that'd be even better, he thought. He began imagining the sort of crowd that might attend something like that. He'd seen the news items about it, and it seemed like it was going to be focused on families. He didn't have a kid to drag along, he thought, but what about looking like a grandparent?

As he began sorting through what he'd need for the disguise, his mind also began making a list of the people that he'd aim for first, a who's who of the cops that'd stood in his way, preventing him from moving up the way he'd always intended to. That pussy of a captain'd be high on the list, he thought, along with Washington, Smith, and Rodriguez for sure. He laughed to himself for a moment, since what he'd seen on the news made it look like Bo had already done a number on Rodriguez. One less that he'd have to take care of.

It was nearly dark by the time he reached the outer edge of the park. He watched as the sole ranger made a wide loop in his golf cart before parking it for the night next to a building housing bathrooms. Marconi watched as the man filled in something on a clipboard, hung it on the side of the building, and moved toward his car. As the car headed out in the growing darkness, Marconi moved in. He walked deeper into the wooded area on the east end of the park and was happy to see it grow even darker once he was inside the broad grove. He risked a small penlight and noted that soft pine needles covered the area. Perfect, he thought, as he set down his pack and spread out his sleeping bag in a nicely covered area. He ate a cold dinner before stretching out inside the warm bag and drifting off to sleep as he considered the next night. He'd need to be up early to hit the medical supply store for the items he wanted.

CHAPTER

65

Thursday morning, Captain Fischer was having an early breakfast with his wife before heading into the station. "I really hate the whole idea." He muttered as he set the coffee cup back on the saucer. "But I just can't come up with an alternative plan." He'd told his wife about the scheme to set up a group as bait, the sick feeling settling into his gut. His wife listened as she sipped at her coffee.

"You're not doing this alone, Hon. You told me you've got a lot of people who'll be helping with the whole operation."

"I know," he nodded. "They're a good group, but I'm not familiar with all of them and that makes me nervous."

"Anytime the public is at risk, you worry. I know that about you. I also know you'll do your best for your officers, as well as the crowd."

He leaned back in his chair. "It isn't easy being a cop's wife, is it?"

"No, sir, never has been. But I'm not planning to give up the gig anytime soon."

He stood and took his dishes to the dishwasher, then turned and kissed his wife on the top of her head. "All right. I've got to get this day going." He said as he picked up his wallet and keys. "Keep a light on for me."

"Always." She smiled up at him, returning to her breakfast before pausing to watch him leave.

When he arrived at the station, Captain Fischer checked in with dispatch and the night duty cops who were heading home then took a few minutes to himself at his desk. The bait, as they were calling themselves, were due in at 9:00. He'd lain awake half the night trying to come up with a different plan, one that didn't put the people he cared about at so much risk. But nothing had come to him, and now, they were out of time. Nearly four days in and still no one had caught sight of Wade Marconi.

When the group gathered around the conference room table just after nine, the captain had to laugh. There was John Chao, the TV-handsome Asian cop, and Rita Banks, a shade or two darker than Smitty, who was on her left. Rod, his light brown Hispanic coloring only partially masked by the bruising, sat next to Laura Katz with her bright red hair. Audrey, John Washington, and himself finished out the table. "Diversity smorgasbord is right, huh, Smitty?"

Smitty spread his hands, indicating the group around them. "We could use a few Italians in the mix, but overall, I don't think it gets much better than this, at least not in this area."

"All right," the captain started. "I do hate this idea completely, but since we haven't come up with anything better, let's get to it. Audrey, I wanted you here because I think you've talked the most with Mrs. Kaminski about the organization of the event. Can you fill us in on some of the details?"

"Sure," Audrey began. "When I heard 'parade permit', I thought it was going to be some sort of a march, but apparently, parade and assembly permits are kind of the same thing. Rather than march anywhere, they're going to be setting up tables and a large tent in the grassy area in front of the fountain." Someone had cleared a whiteboard for them, so she stood up, and as she spoke, attempted to draw a crude map of the park and the planned event. "There will be a small speakers' podium near the tent, but they don't plan on having anyone give any real speeches, more like just a greeting of some kind. They want to focus on providing a fun time for kids and their parents, so under the tent, there'll be a bunch of different craft tables, face painting, a small music area, a variety of games, and some food stalls. Outdoor tables will be spread around the outer perimeter of the tent with the idea that people will take their food out there to eat and move freely in and out of the area. On the outer edges of the grassy area on either side, they're allowing organizations to set up information tables. She couldn't tell me exactly how many she expected, but they were only going to provide six or eight tables for them. Like I said, they're trying to focus on kids and families, not make it some kind of overly political event." Audrey set down the marker and returned to her seat.

"Any idea what sort of numbers they're expecting?" The captain asked.

Audrey shook her head. "No, when I talked with Kalisa yesterday, Mrs. Kaminski, that is, that was her main concern. The news has given the event a lot more publicity than they were expecting, so they've been fretting about what quantities of food and craft supplies they should have on hand."

"Don't most kids just go trick or treating in their neighborhoods on Halloween? That's what we did." John Washington asked, looking around the table at the others.

Laura Katz responded. "People seem to have gotten a lot more anxious about that lately. My brother teaches at one of the elementary schools and, for the past few years, their PTA has been organizing what they call 'Trunk or Treat' nights where parents all meet up together and kind of control the whole operation."

Audrey nodded. "That's what Kalisa said as well. They'd like to make this an annual event, so I think they're trying to go pretty big. Not thousands of people, but hundreds for sure, is what she's expecting."

Rod turned to Smitty and shook his head. "What a nightmare."

"You got that right." Smitty agreed, and heads around the table nodded.

"You're planning on a mix of uniformed cops and plain clothes, is that right, Captain?" Rod asked.

The captain stood and moved toward Audrey's rough map. "We have to keep the uniforms at a distance. It's just not the right look at an event like this for us to be standing around like a bunch of hard-assed sentries." He took up the marker and gestured at the outer perimeter of the event. "There are trees on either side of the open area, so my first concern is the possibility of Marconi setting up in one of those with some sort of automatic." He sketched in a rectangular building at what was the bottom of the triangular park. "He could set up a perch on top of this, but it's a low building and pretty exposed, so it wouldn't offer much of a prospect."

"If the uniforms are focused on the area outside the tent and tables, then we've got to have the plain clothes mixing, moving in and out of the tent." Smitty offered. "If we choose a table here," he stood and moved toward the whiteboard, pointing in arcs around the tent. "Not the ring closest to the tent but the second or third ring out, that might draw Marconi away from the greatest concentration of kids, don't you think?" He asked, turning to look at the group.

"Kalisa will let me have whatever table or space I need, so I could easily pick one like that." Audrey offered.

"The key is going to be spotting him, though, isn't it?" asked Chao. "He must be wearing some sort of disguise that we haven't caught sight of him at all."

The captain returned to his seat. "That's the key. You're absolutely right." He turned then to Rita. "How are you feeling, Rita?"

She smiled. "I'm good, boss. Don't worry about me."

"Okay, then. Communication between our team is going to be essential, but before we get to that, do you think you and your techs could come up with some possible looks that Marconi might use, doctor his photo, or whatever?"

"Sure, Captain. We can put those together quickly." She paused, then continued at his nod. "Regarding communication, we can set everyone up with some inconspicuous mics and earpieces. We don't have enough to put them on all of the uniforms, but people would expect them to have their radios and be in communication that way. These will be much more subtle."

Rod lifted his casted arm. "I won't be good for anything more than spotting." He gestured toward Washington. "And he shouldn't be doing much more than that either. We can set up on opposite sides of the table."

"Could I have a set as well, just in case I see him?" Audrey asked as she sat down in the empty chair next to Rod.

A brief fit of coughing hit Washington, serving to underscore Rod's point. "Jesus, I should make the both of you go home right now." The captain stood, his hand resting on Washington's shoulder. He looked over at Rita. "You too, if I were in my right mind." Then he looked at Audrey. "I'm sorry, but it's not protocol to have you included that way,

Audrey. I know you want to help, but I just can't involve you any more than we already have."

"Captain, we have an advantage that Marconi doesn't, though. He's just one person. My guess is he'll be focused on us, especially given what sitting ducks the two of us are." Rod pointed at his own chest and gestured toward Washington. "We're going to look mighty vulnerable, and I think he's going to zero in on that. He knows police tactics, so he'll expect plainclothes to be in the crowd."

"If our uniforms on the perimeter spot him, they're going to do their best to scoop him up. But they're going to be looking at hundreds of people passing by, so if he's not setting up in a tree, there's a good chance he'll get by them. Especially if he mixes in with family groups." He looked at Rita again. "Communication, it's all going to come down to that." The captain walked back around the table as he spoke. "All right, the event starts at 5:00 and sunset is at 6:00, so we're going to have to be ready. Rita, will you put together those images and then start gathering up what we're going to need and distributing it to the group?"

"Sure thing, Captain," Rita said as she stood up and pushed her chair back.

"Rod, Washington," He pointed. "I want to see you two heading home for a while now. The rest of you, get ready." He paused and rubbed the top of his head once more. "God help us all, people. God help us all."

Audrey and Rod headed home after the morning meeting, and Audrey was relieved to see Rod settle back into his recliner. He was so close-mouthed about the pain that he was in, it was hard for her to get a sense of what he needed. She waited until he was settled in the chair before leaning in to give him a kiss. "Are you hungry? Should I fix us some lunch now?"

He looked up, his face a bit pale after the morning's exertions. "Give me a little bit of time first, okay? It's too early for another pill, so I'm going to try and close my eyes for a while. Is that all right with you?"

"Of course. I've got things to do to get ready for tonight." She pulled the old afghan up over his legs and stepped away, watching as his eyelids began to close.

Upstairs in her office, Audrey sat down and went through her email first. She had an inquiry from a couple who were planning on an early spring wedding, and notes from her mom and dad, as well as Sandy. She communicated with the bride-to-be and then took a few minutes to compose a note that would be sufficiently vague and reassuring that she could copy it to her family and friends. She reported hopefully on how Rod was doing but omitted any references to that evening's activities. She would be busy with a wedding Friday afternoon and all day on Saturday, so she made a tentative plan to stop out at her folks' neighborhood on Sunday.

Then she sat back in her chair and released a sigh. That was provided they all lived through tonight. She had watched the group at the conference table that morning, the fear and worry that crossed all their faces, the shadow that seemed to come over the captain especially. What a difficult job, she thought, glad that he was there leading it all, but even more glad that it wasn't her responsibility. She knew Rod was worried too, especially since he hadn't been able to dissuade Emma and her family from attending. With Gina's firm as one of the sponsors, they'd felt obligated to go.

Once the emails were sent, Audrey moved to the folding table that she'd set up and began sorting through the gear that she might need. She wanted to keep it to a minimum so that she could move easily in and out of the crowd, but she also had to take time to think about the lighting she'd be working with before the sunset and then how she'd fill in the shadows after the sun went down. If only she'd thought to ask Kalisa what type of lights they were planning to set up. She tapped her foot for a moment and considered calling her back but decided against it. She figured the woman had enough on her plate. She didn't need some less-experienced photographer pestering her with questions. Audrey had only seen two pieces of Kalisa's work, but she was eager to impress her.

It was frustrating to Audrey that the police wouldn't include her in their communication setup. She wanted to help and knew it was going to be hard to keep her attention on the photography while sensing danger all around. However, if she was forced to make a choice that night between her photography and the needs of the police, there'd be no contest. The safety of everyone there was her first priority.

At midday on Thursday, Marconi greeted the young woman who was behind the checkout desk. "Bill Waters here. I'm sorry I don't have an appointment, but I just found out my gramps is getting out of the hospital this afternoon, so my aunt sent me to pick up some things he'll need."

"That's all right." She stood up and came around the desk, gesturing to the walls on either side of the medical supply shop. "Does he require mobility aids, toileting supplies? Do you know what sorts of needs he will have?"

Toileting needs, Marconi almost peed himself at the thought. Hah, he knew he was right to come to a small shop like this rather than one of the bigger stores associated with a hospital. This was going to be perfect. "Well, I might want to look around a bit first. He's not sure if he wants a walker or a cane. Can you show me what you have?"

"Certainly." The woman was eager to please and quickly began setting up several styles of walkers along with a variety of single- and triple-pronged canes. He wanted to try them out, so he pretended to move like he thought a grandparent might, and she went right along with it. "This model," she demonstrated the flip-down seat on one of the walkers, "is great if stamina is an issue. The user can easily pause and rest. If it's balance that's more of an issue, though, this three-pronged cane offers wonderful stability."

He tried the walkers, checking out those with a seat as well as the difference between the ones with wheels and the ones without. He could definitely move quickly with those, but he felt they might be a little too cumbersome. He wanted to be able to shift easily in and out of the crowd, so he tested out the different canes, even the crutches with fore-arm cuffs. "I think this one feels like the best bet for my gramps," he said, holding up the lightweight aluminum cane with the wide base. "I think it's balance more than anything with him."

"Great, will we be completing some insurance forms for this today?" She turned toward the checkout desk.

"Nah, I'm going to cover it. He's had enough expenses already."

"Wonderful. Well, feel free to look around and see if there's anything else you think he might need."

Marconi smiled and then took his time building the disguise in his head and searching the shelves for items that might help. He spotted an inflatable cushion and some cloth tape that he thought would work for a false gut, as well as some loose-fitting pants. There was also a zippered fleece jacket that he picked in a particularly plain beige color. He could see it all coming together now. He carried the items to the counter and, once the bill was settled, ducked out the front door and across the street to a cosmetics store that he'd spotted on his way in.

"Good afternoon. How may I help you?" This time, the clerk was a woman in her mid-forties with a wide purple streak in her jet-black hair.

"Hi there, I'm hoping you can help me out with a costume for tonight."

"Oh sure, we do lots of Halloween looks. Come sit here and tell me what you're after."

She settled him on a tall chair at a makeup counter and then went around to the other side. He grinned across at her. "I'm working on a big surprise for my wife. We're arriving at a party separately, and I want to see if I can fool her."

"Oh, how fun!"

He held up the cane and bag from the medical supply shop. "I thought I'd go as an old man. Could you help me figure out how to do that?"

The woman laughed with delight. "Of course, that sounds like so much fun. Okay, I think I have a kit here that will work like a charm."

She looked through some things under the counter and pulled out a pre-packaged Halloween makeup kit, but Marconi shook his head.

"Nah, I wouldn't know how to put all of that on." He breathed out a sigh of disappointment and made to get up from the chair when the woman leaned over the counter a bit.

"We're not too busy now. If you're willing to pay cash, I could do your makeup for you now and spritz it with some stuff that would keep it in good shape?"

"Would you really? That would be wonderful." He pulled out his wallet, still thick with bills. "Cash it is." He grinned, and she returned the warm look.

"All right, let's get this show on the road!"

She did an excellent job, and he was especially pleased that she didn't mind him going out the back door in case his 'wife' spotted him on the street. With the great makeup job, he was a little less worried about being spotted, but he didn't want to take any chances now that he was so close to his goal. He ducked into one of the larger library branches, checked for internal cameras, and was pleased when he didn't see any. He made his way toward the back until he found a quiet area not far from a small, handicapped bathroom. Perfect, he thought. He'd kill some time, eat a quick snack, and then get ready. He laughed to himself, figuring he could take a cab to a handicapped entrance to the park and be right where he needed to be.

Marconi studied his image in the library's bathroom mirror and was pleased with what he saw. The loose pants over the fake gut and the ugly fleece jacket were perfect with the makeup while also managing to hide his guns well. He'd had to tidy the makeup just a bit, but for the most part, it was holding up well. The grey powder that he'd used to lighten the wig seemed to have gotten everywhere, covering the small counter. Who cares, he thought, it wasn't his mess to clean up. He stuffed his things back into his pack and shrugged it onto one shoulder before opening the door. He took a few practice steps with the cane and then moved toward the front of the building.

"I don't suppose I could trouble you to call a cab for me, could I, young man?" He leaned on his cane as he spoke to the middle-aged man at the circulation desk.

"Certainly, just give me a minute." The man set a stack of books on the counter and then picked up a desk phone. He seemed to have memorized the number and was able to dial it quickly.

When it was picked up, he covered the mouthpiece for a moment. "Where to, pops?" He asked.

"Oh, Point Place Park. I'm meeting my grandsons for a Halloween party there!"

The man smiled and gave the information to the cab company before returning it to its cradle. "Just a few minutes, sir. They'll pick you up right in front at the handicap entrance."

Marconi smiled but didn't feel like risking any more conversation, so he nodded and moved away toward the entrance. Just a few minutes later, a cab arrived and pulled up alongside the low spot in the curb. A young black man hurried around to the passenger side and held the door while Marconi acted out a struggle to get into his seat. The driver waited until he was settled before closing the door and returning to the wheel. "Thank you so much, young man." He squeaked out in an effort to sound older. "If you could just let me off at the park's handicap entrance, I'd be much obliged."

"Sure thing!" They were off and moving quickly and Marconi couldn't help but congratulate himself. This was going to be a piece of cake. He was going to get in, mingle with the crowd of lowlifes and deviants, pop as many cops and perverts as he could, and then take off running. No one would suspect an old man, and once he ditched the wig and jacket, there was no way anyone would recognize him. He was going to enjoy this.

They pulled up to the park entrance and once again, the driver hurried around to open Marconi's door. He paid with a ten that he had ready. "Keep the change." He smiled and waved at the young man who didn't look quite as eager to help once he'd gotten his 45-cent tip. Fuck it, all the geezers Marconi knew were tightwads, so why shouldn't he be one too?

The entrance placed him right near the low park building and made it easy for him to join the crowd that was making its way toward the tent and the tables. He found a large, chaotic-seeming family and trailed in their wake. He was invisible. No one gave him a second look.

"It looks like a good crowd, Kalisa. Are you pleased with it so far?" Audrey asked as she and Kalisa stood near the fountain looking at the grassy area now filled with a very diverse group of people in a wide variety of costumes.

"It's more than we expected originally, that's for sure. The news about the militia's foiled plans really brought people out." She gestured toward a set of tables on the side that offered information on gay rights, Planned Parenthood, and other organizations, several of which had a small line of people gathered around them. "I think people want to get involved. They want to fight back and have their voices heard."

"I certainly understand that. Let me get a few photos of you by the fountain here, and then I'll head over to the tent and the kids' area."

"Sounds good." Kalisa smiled and reached her arms out in a welcoming gesture that would make for a great photo, Audrey thought.

"Got it!"

"Great, okay, let's mingle!" Kalisa Kaminski led the way back into the crowd, and Audrey shot photos as they moved, but she was finding it difficult to focus on the job at hand. Knowing Marconi might be there somewhere, that Rod and the others were vulnerable, was eating away at her. She scanned the crowd anxiously, watching for the man who'd been so rude to her before the Ellerby wedding. The sun was setting behind them as she wove in between groups of children at the various activities. One group was creating rhythm instruments and playing along with a guitarist, while others were building fanciful masks at a table filled with a variety of scraps, including cloth, paper, pipe cleaners, and paint. She spotted Far, his concentration focused on a wild-looking piece that made

Audrey laugh. Emma was standing behind him talking with other parents. She looked around for Gina but didn't see her.

As she continued to move around, Audrey was a little surprised to see the number of grandparents in attendance. An area near the entrance to the tent had been cleared, and the tables raised so that wheelchair users could access the area. An older man with a cane was making his way in behind them when a group of five or six kids broke loose from the crowd and chased each other through the tent on their way out. Audrey held her breath, watching as the man with the cane stepped quickly out of their line of movement. She expected him to have a firm grip on the cane and be anxious as the group passed, but instead, she noticed him lift the cane and move easily to the side out of the way. That didn't look right.

She lifted her camera and zoomed in to get a better look at the older gentleman. She took a few shots of his face and then focused in on his hand where it rested on the cane. The fellow looked to be in his late seventies at least, but the hand on the cane was that of a much younger man. He looked up, and she panned her camera away into the crowd, but when he turned away from her, she watched as he shuffled along, lifting the cane, waving it a little before carefully setting it down again. She lowered the camera and clicked back to look at the first images of him that she'd caught. She used her fingers on the viewfinder to magnify it as much as she could. She studied the face, and at that magnification, it was clear that the wrinkles were makeup, not true age lines. Her breath caught. It was him. He looked nothing like any of Rita's altered sketches that Rod had shown her. Shit, this was why she'd wanted a mic and an earpiece.

Audrey watched as he started to make his way toward the kids' craft table. She spun around quickly, panicked at what to do to alert the police. She fumbled with her camera and lights, trying to reach the phone in her back pocket, but then Kalisa called out to her. "Audrey, we need you here! We're starting the costume parade!"

Damn it, Audrey thought, but suddenly she caught sight of a pair of teenage boys, one of them on crutches. It was Jerry and Carlo. Of course, Jerry's mom was in charge. It made sense he'd be there. She hurried ahead and caught up to them, whispering in Jerry's ear so that no one near them could hear. It was a desperate idea, but it was the only one she had.

70

"God, I hate this." Washington looked at Rod. "The waiting . . ."

"That's the worst part, isn't it?" asked Chao, who looked at the group and then rethought what he'd said. "Well, I mean, apart from getting shot at, that is."

Rod laughed at the awkward conversation but kept his attention on the chatter in his earpiece. The cops on the perimeter had seen nothing yet, and the sun was nearly down. They had to assume that Marconi was somewhere mixed in with the crowd already. Smitty had wanted to walk around and look for him, but as one of only three able-bodied cops at the table, he'd been convinced to stay. He sat next to Rod while Chao and Katz went to pick up food. When they returned, they'd all had a bite or two, but no one was hungry. Rod leaned toward Smitty. "It's killing me that Audrey and Emma and her family are all in there, maybe even right next to him." They were quickly losing what little light they had, and the darkness was only going to increase their vulnerability.

"Detective?" A young voice spoke to Rod, and he turned to see Carlo Rizzi standing beside him.

"Carlo, how are you doing?"

He held a folded piece of paper out to Rod and leaned in. "The lady with the camera told me to bring this to you." He said it quickly and then headed toward the tent where a kid with crutches met him. Rod unfolded it and studied the sketch for a moment before he realized what it meant. "Guys," he hissed. They turned to look at the paper. "This is what he looks like. Audrey must have spotted him." Smitty was up quickly and began moving toward the tent. Rita pulled out her phone and took a photo of the sketch before immediately sending it out to the captain and the others. "You got it, Captain?"

From the table, Rod had two plainclothes officers in his line of sight already, and he saw them each look at their phones before turning to scan the crowd. Rod spoke into the mic. "Can anyone see him?"

"I thought he was moving toward the art tables, but then I lost him." Answered Smitty.

Rod called out, shooing the boys away. "Carlo, you and Jerry get out of here. Move toward the trees." He tried Audrey's phone but got no answer. "He's gotta still be in the tent area, Captain. Has anyone seen him yet?" Rod called out to the group desperately.

As he moved through the crowd, Marconi was struggling to decide who he wanted to kill the most. The uniform cops on the perimeter would be a nice, easy target, but he took satisfaction in passing right under their noses instead. He walked by some tables where people were spewing shit about abortion rights and gay marriage. He wanted to take all of them out, but it was too soon. He knew he'd only have a few minutes to act before panic would set in and he'd have to take off. He wanted to take time to savor the experience. For Bo and all of the others, he had to make it count.

The end of the tent that he came to first was set aside for wheelchair use, with a couple of higher tables and a wide aisle between them. He was just moving past one of the tables when a handful of kids came rushing toward him. Instinctively, he stepped back out of their way before remembering to place his cane and walk more slowly. He saw a flash go off and realized that the same bitch of a photographer from the wedding was here as well. She seemed to be photographing the crowd, but it still made him uneasy. He turned his back on her and made his way toward some kind of art crap activity.

As his path took him closer to the outer edge of the tent, he spotted the tables that were set up outside. He looked them over quickly before his eye caught on a pair he recognized. There he was, that damned Rodriguez, and shit, there was Washington, too, the motherfucker that had caused all of this. Marconi was starting to move toward their table when he noticed two people looking at their phones and then at him. He was trying to ease out of their line of sight when he noticed a third figure coming toward him. It was the captain. "Come along quietly, Marconi. Let's make this easy."

The captain reached out to put his hand on Marconi's left elbow, so he dropped the cane and used his right to whip out his gun. He yanked his left arm out of the captain's reach and grabbed a little kid around the neck. He pointed the gun at the captain and then the child, back and forth, all the while stepping slowly back toward the open side of the tent. A young woman leapt toward them but was held back by another. "No! Far! You bastard, let go of him!" She shouted.

Panic began to hit the crowd then, as more and more plainclothes officers fought their way toward the captain. Chairs were scraping, and a table crashed as people pushed against one another to escape. "Stand back, now!" Marconi ordered, and they did try to stop, but the momentum of the frightened crowd behind them was pushing people from the side as well as the back. Marconi's eyes shifted from the captain to the others and then to the little boy. He yelled louder, "I swear, anyone gets closer to me, and this kid is dead. Do you hear me? Dead!" The boy's mother was screaming incoherently now, plainclothes cops staggered into a ring in front of him, but Marconi noticed that the child had gone silent. Shit, if he'd already strangled him, he wouldn't make much of a bargaining chip. He loosened his hold on the boy just slightly, and the child ducked from his grasp. Marconi spun, aimed for the captain, and fired. He felt a sudden sting on the back of his neck and then nothing.

Smitty leapt from the table as soon as he'd seen the drawing. Running, he reached the outer edge of the tent just as he saw Marconi sweep Far up, angling his gun at the child's head. Smitty spotted the captain in front of Marconi, so he pushed aside one of the tables and quickly angled to get in behind him. In the instant he saw him drop the boy and raise his gun, Smitty brought the taser to the back of his neck and fired the charge. Marconi dropped immediately, but when his line of sight cleared, Smitty saw the blood blooming on the captain's shoulder. He felt nauseous when he realized he hadn't been quick enough. He lunged forward, grabbed a fat stack of napkins from a nearby table and pressed them into the wound as he lowered the captain into the nearest chair. Smitty barked at the plainclothes as three of them hurried to handcuff Marconi, pressing his face into the ground in case he were to wake up.

"Get him out of here," Smitty gestured with his chin before turning to another cop. "Get the ambulance over here, now!" he bellowed and watched as the rest of the crowd continued to push and shove their way clear of the tent. One man out on the left side was crashing back and forth, flipping chairs, and screaming, "I can't find my daughter!" Smitty was about to yell for a pair of uniforms to go help him, when he spotted Officer Katz carrying a little girl and settling her into the father's arms. The ambulance was bringing the stretcher toward the captain when Smitty spotted Rod's sister Emma, her arms wrapped tightly around Far as Gina knelt next to them, tears covering all of their faces.

Kalisa was standing next to them and catching a nod from Smitty, she got on the microphone and tried to calm the crowd. She called out over and over again for people to stop, that the danger had passed. Some listened, but most of them had shaken loose from the group and taken off running for the park's perimeter. The uniformed officers did their best to keep anyone from being trampled and helped to guide the frightened crowd toward the park's exits.

Inside the tent, there was chaos. People had been pushing and shoving at one another, chairs and tables were knocked over, and art and music supplies had been tossed everywhere. Many of the people who'd had tables on the perimeter, as well as a few other volunteers, were now coming in to help with the cleanup. In the aftermath of the shooting, an ambulance that had been on hand dealt with the captain first and whisked him to the hospital. A second one arrived shortly after that and dealt with the line of people who'd been injured in the crush to get out. Thankfully, none of those injuries appeared to be too severe. The open nature of the tent had allowed people to scatter quickly.

With the clean-up finished, the crowd at the table that Rod and Smitty had been sitting at had grown as the few people who were left pulled up chairs and sat down. While Chao and Katz had gone to help with the crowd, Audrey, Jerry, and Carlo had joined Rod, Washington, and Rita. Emma and Gina were there, Far in Gina's lap, leaning against her chest. Smitty had overseen everything, first seeing that the captain was put into the ambulance and then watching as Marconi, still unconscious, was loaded into a cruiser. In the captain's absence, he seemed to have taken charge. He made his way over to the table and sat down next to Rod. He leaned forward. "Audrey, it was genius sending that drawing to us."

She pointed to Jerry, who couldn't help the smile that crept across his face. "Jerry's the one who deserves credit."

Just as she said that, Kalisa Kaminski joined the table, squeezing in beside her son. "He sure does," she smiled, kissing him on the cheek. "Well, it's been altogether too much excitement as far as I'm concerned."

"Amen," added Washington.

Rod leaned over and put his hand on Far's shoulder. "You were so brave, little man, but I'm so sorry that happened to you."

Far sat up then. "I stayed quiet, Uncle Rod, even though I was scared."

"You were great, awesome, brave . . ." various voices around the table joined the chorus.

"Well, it's past bedtime for this brave little guy." Emma reached to take Far from Gina's lap. He was a big handful, but she managed to settle him in her arms, and the family ambled back toward their car.

"That was some event you put on, Mrs. Kaminski." Smitty offered.

"Good Lord." She muttered. "They couldn't pay me enough to take this on again next year. Some other unwitting soul will have to step up." She looked around at the group sitting at the table. "I'm just a mom talking here, not a doctor, but I'm seeing an awful lot of facial bruising around this table." She paused, her face taking on a sterner look. "Exactly how many of you are supposed to be at home resting right now?" Smitty watched as the hands went up around the table, first Rod, then Washington, Rita, Jerry, and Carlo all raised their hands.

Smitty stood up, reaching a hand out to Rod and then the others as they all prepared to go. "When a mom says it's time to go home, we need to listen. I'm going to check in on the captain and then finish the paperwork. You all go home. Nice work, everyone."

There were handshakes and hugs as they began to make their way back toward their cars. Smitty couldn't be sure who it was, but he thought he heard someone say, "He sounds more like the captain every day, doesn't he?" Smitty grinned. If he was going to stay in this line of work, he might as well keep aiming upward.

The next morning, Audrey was still in her bathrobe when she leaned over to kiss Rod good morning. "Hey there, how'd you sleep?"

With his good hand, Rod managed to pull her into his lap. "I hate sleeping without you, but I managed okay. What about you?"

"Same here." She shrugged. "What's up for you today?"

"I've been ordered to take it easy, and I don't think I'm going to fight that order." He pointed at the set. "I think there's a game on later this afternoon. What about you?"

"I'm going to get the shots from last night to Kalisa, although I'm not sure what she's going to do with them, especially since it's all over the news. Then I have a rehearsal dinner tonight and a wedding tomorrow."

"Busy lady, I like it." He grinned. "Would you have some time later this morning to go with me to see the captain at the hospital?"

"Sure. I'd like that."

"And a truck dealership?"

"Really? Are you going to go with a new one this time?" She mimed catching a good scent in the air. "Did the smell of my brand-new car win you over?" She laughed.

"It sure did. Plus, I have very strict instructions." He lifted one finger. "First, everyone is insisting I get one with front and side airbags."

"Of course, that's a no-brainer."

"And second," He lifted the other finger. "Far made it very clear that I need to have a second seat so that he and his little sister can ride with me."

"Well, all right. That sounds like a good list. Come have some breakfast with me, and I'll see if I can't wrap up what I need to do before lunch."

After breakfast, Audrey retreated to her workspace upstairs and got busy organizing the photographs she'd taken the night before. There were a lot of great pictures from before the nearly disastrous conclusion, so she sorted through them and sent them off. It was hard to get the image of Marconi's arm wrapped around Far's neck out of her mind, but so far, at least, there weren't any actual photos of that, not even from the news organizations. It seemed as though people in the crowd were too busy running away to pull out their phones and take videos. Midway through the morning, she took a break and went to get a drink of water from the kitchen. She caught sight of Rod snoozing in the big chair, so she made her way quietly past him.

Once she'd put in another hour and a half, she heard Rod calling from downstairs. She hurried down and found him in the kitchen searching through a drawer. "Have we got another plastic bag that I can put over my cast? I want to get a shower."

"I think so." Audrey opened a second drawer and found a long bread bag. "I think this will work. Can I help you?"

Rod pulled her into a hug. "Kind of the reverse of where we were in the spring, isn't it?"

Audrey nodded. "When you helped me take a bath after the attack?" She wrapped her arms tighter. "I was awfully glad I had you to help."

He leaned his head back to look at her more clearly. "You were so battered and bruised, and now here I am needing help. We're quite a pair, aren't we?"

"Come on, sport, I'll help you get a shower."

They moved down the hall, and Rod collected the clean clothes he would need. He looked up at Audrey suddenly. "Did I tell you that Kalisa called me?"

"No. What about?"

"She told me that the art institute has started offering some art therapy classes. Jerry is going to take them after what happened to him, and she wanted to invite Far to participate too."

"Wow, I think that's a great idea. Poor little guy. He's had a tough couple of weeks, hasn't he?"

"He sure has. I'm going to help Emma write a letter to his principal excusing him from any more of those stupid lockdown drills. He's been through enough as it is."

She helped pull his shirt off around the thick cast and, once he was ready, she used a couple of rubber bands to fasten the bag around his cast. "I think that's a great idea."

As he stepped into the shower, he grinned. "May even send it on Gina's law firm's letterhead, just to make a point, you know? Team Far," he chanted, his bagged hand held triumphantly in the air.

Audrey laughed and closed the door behind her.

After lunch, they made a remarkably quick stop at the truck dealership. Rod had decided to go with the same brand, so it was just a matter of choosing a newer model and selecting the features he wanted. It wouldn't be ready for a week or two, but that suited them just fine. From there, they drove to the hospital.

The captain had been hit squarely in the shoulder, and it had required a lengthy surgery to repair the joint. As they entered his room, Audrey was surprised to see Sonia Lee from Dr. Edmond's office standing by his bedside. "Hey there, we meet again. Rod, do you remember Sonia Lee, the PA you met with?"

"He was pretty groggy when I saw him," Ms. Lee laughed. "You're looking good." She touched Captain Fischer on his good shoulder and took her leave. "You hang in there, Captain."

He smiled, but Audrey could see the pain washing over his face. "Audrey, Rod, have you met my wife, Beth?"

"I don't think we have." Rod extended his good hand, and she shook it. "Captain, what's the word?" Rod asked as he sat down on the edge of the bed.

"Rehab, same as you, I'm sure." Then he looked up at Rod. "But we both know we're so damned glad to be alive that we'll do whatever it takes, isn't that right?"

"You got it, Captain. Do we know where things stand with Marconi and the case?"

"He's being charged with attempted murder, first."

"Amen!" his wife echoed from her chair, making the captain grin.

"The rest is taking some sorting out. Keller finally went home, so they scooped him up and got a few more details about the operation at the garage. They've also traced the ICB company back to Ellerby, so if it turns out he was providing the weapons and gear, he'll face a lot more than just tax charges."

"And the others from the camp, the ones who accepted his deliveries or had guns at their houses?"

"That's trickier since they didn't follow through on their plans. There's talk of some weapons or conspiracy charges, but that may all disappear, I'm afraid. We'll have to wait and see."

"Well, that's hard to hear, but with the leaders and the money out of the picture, perhaps it'll be okay." Rod paused. "Anything we can do for you in the meantime?"

The captain looked over at his wife. She was sitting in the chair next to the bed, a dog-eared paperback in her hands. "No, I've got everything I need. You take your time getting back to the station, you hear me? I've put Smitty in charge for the time being and, from what I hear, he's got everything under control."

Rod stood and shook the captain's hand gently. "Good choice, Captain. You couldn't have picked a finer man for the job. You take care now, too."

When Rod stepped back, Audrey took a second to kiss the captain on the cheek. Then she turned to his wife. "Let us know if you need anything."

"We will." She smiled as they left.

Rod took Audrey's hand as they slowly walked the long, winding hallway toward the entrance. When they were back in the car, Audrey reached to press the starter, but Rod laid his hand on hers to stop her. "Audrey, there is absolutely nothing romantic about where we are, how beat up I am, how much trouble we've been through, or anything, but will you marry me?" He took her hand and held it next to his heart. "It's been a ridiculous journey from how we met to where we are now, but I wouldn't have wanted to go through any of it without you. What do you say? Are you ready for more?"

Audrey leaned in and, with her other hand, gently cupped his bruised and battered cheek. "I would love to marry you, Rod. Being alive together feels pretty romantic to me. I think the rest is just extra."

Audrey loved the old dining table at her parents' house. It was solid wood, and with the leaves in place, it created an oval big enough to seat eight, even ten in a pinch. Most of the time when she was growing up, though, with just the three of them at home, the leaves remained parked in the basement under an old sofa, and the small table rested up against the windowsill. Her mother and father had always sat on either end with Audrey in the middle, across from the window. It was a habit that was hard to break, but since Rod had come into her life, the table had been pulled away from the wall and a chair had been added, backing up to the window. On Sunday evening, though, with a cold wind blowing outside, the light fading early, and the fear still so bright in their memories, Audrey pulled the chair from around back and settled beside Rod instead, holding his uninjured hand as her dad started cutting a cake. Audrey's mother Brigitte carried in a mismatched set of mugs and set the coffee carafe on a battered trivet before sitting down as well.

Audrey's father Mitch, set a big slice in front of Rod before dishing out smaller ones to his wife and daughter. "I hope you've got an appetite, Rod, especially after all you've been through."

Rod released Audrey's hand, used his cast to nudge the plate closer, and picked up his fork. "I'm pretty sure I can handle a slice of cake. Thanks, Mitch." He took a big bite and smiled at Audrey's mother. "Delicious!"

Brigitte laughed, "Don't look at me. It came from Prantl's. I tried to make a burnt almond torte a few years ago, but it involved so many steps that I just gave up. Luckily, they're easy to pick up!"

Rod wiped his mouth with his napkin before taking Audrey's hand once more. He looked at her and raised his eyebrow encouragingly.

Audrey looked at him and smiled, before turning to look at one parent and then another. "We have some news."

"Good news, I hope, after this week?" Her dad nodded before taking the cup of coffee his wife had filled.

"The best, actually. Rod and I, we want to get married." She looked at Rod again as she spoke. "We knew before this all happened that we wanted to be together, but this week reminded us that we don't . . ." She paused and wiped a tear away with the back of her hand. Then she forced a smile. "What I mean is, we don't want to waste any more time. We want to be together, to make it permanent." She looked from her mother to her father and was relieved to see broad smiles across both of their faces.

"Oh, honey!" Her mother chuckled before pushing her chair back and reaching to hug first Audrey and then Rod.

"Audie, Rod, that sounds wonderful to me." Audrey's dad looked at her mother. "I can testify that being married is the best." He pushed his chair back and began to stand up. "I think there might be some champagne in the fridge, should I get it out?"

Audrey and Rod laughed. Audrey rose and gave her dad a quick hug before sitting back down and gesturing him back into his seat. "There's a little bit more before you start toasting here, Dad."

Brigitte took a sip of coffee. "When are you thinking about getting married? Have you made any plans yet?"

"That's the thing," Audrey answered. "I've been to so many weddings, big ones, small ones, formal, casual, personal, impersonal, and nearly every variation in between. I love it. I love my work. I love the flowers and the ceremonies, all of it. I wouldn't do this work if I didn't. But somehow, no matter how many weddings I photograph, I never imagine myself in the bride's position. It's just not what I want. It's not me."

"Well, what do you want, honey? We've got some money set aside if you're worrying about that." Her father offered.

"Thanks, Dad, I appreciate that. What I'd really like is for us to get married here, next weekend."

"We thought we'd have just a few friends and family over and celebrate quietly together," Rod added before resuming his cake.

Audrey couldn't tell if her mother looked just puzzled or hurt. "Mom, are you all right with that?"

Brigitte set her napkin by her plate and reached to hold Audrey's other hand. "Of course, I'm all right with that. I'm all right with whatever you want. I'm just surprised, is all. I know we've never been church-going folks, but I thought you might want something a little bit fancier than this house. Are you sure?"

Rod laughed. "Believe me, I've pushed and pushed, Brigitte, but she hasn't budged. Our friends and family all live in the area, so if you two wouldn't mind hosting us, we'd love to have it here."

"But promise me, not too much fuss, Mom, Dad. We could have it on Sunday, maybe around three-thirty or four, then have some drinks and snacks, and everyone could get home to their dinner. Dad, could we use some of those funds for that?"

"Of course, if you're sure that's what you want. I'll make some calls in the morning."

"Mom, would you be able to brave a few stores tomorrow to help me find a dress?"

Brigitte laughed. "Of course, but you are more than a little bit crazy, I think, to imagine that you're going to find a wedding dress that quickly!"

"Well, I'm not planning on anything too fancy, and I have something I can wear, if we don't find anything, but I thought it would be nice to do at least one bit of wedding planning together."

"Audrey, you're lucky I'm not the sort of mom who's been secretly planning her daughter's wedding since she was born." Her mom grinned as she shook her finger at her daughter. "Heck, your dad and I got married on a rainy Thursday afternoon at the courthouse, so we have no right to comment one way or another on your choices. Do you know how many people you want to invite?"

"It's a pretty short list. We haven't told anyone else yet, so we'll get on that in the morning and get you a list as soon as we can."

"Sounds good to me," her dad responded before resuming his cake.

Rod looked at his soon-to-be in-laws. "Do you think we could get another cake like this? It's excellent!"

"I'll put in an order tomorrow morning," Brigitte laughed, and the table settled into a planning session as they sipped their coffee and relaxed.

Once they were back in the car heading home, Audrey loosened the scarf around her neck and reached to touch Rod's earlobe, rubbing it softly between her fingers. "That went well, I thought. What about you?"

He took her hand and kissed it before returning it to the wheel and placing his hands back in his lap. "I think they're the best, I really do. Frankly, though, I care a lot about the married part and not so much about the wedding. I would like it if we could find a friend to marry us, though, rather than some stranger. While you're out with your mom, I'll see what I can find."

"Sounds good," Audrey smiled and started the car.

Unlike the previous week, this Sunday morning dawned bright and clear, a cool breeze moving through the few leaves still on the trees, light pouring into the bedroom window to wake them. Audrey lifted the covers out of the way and curled her body around Rod's back. It was so nice to have him sleeping next to her again that she couldn't help taking a few more minutes to themselves before the busy day began.

When she couldn't spare another moment, Audrey got up and took a shower, then slipped on a robe before going to start some coffee. She and Sandy had plans to meet for breakfast that morning, but Rod wasn't planning to leave until after lunch. She sliced open a bagel and dropped it into the toaster for him when he came into the kitchen.

"Hey, I could have done that." He waved both his arms in the air. "I'm getting the hang of this. Look." He wiggled the fingers on his casted arm.

Audrey was thrilled to see the movement, especially since the doctor hadn't been able to predict the extent of any possible nerve damage. Rod was still covered in bruises that ran the length of his body in a full spectrum of colors, but in the most important ways, he was becoming himself again.

"That's great!" She kissed him on the cheek and left him to sort out the rest of his breakfast while she went to get dressed. When she returned, he was sitting at the counter, watching something on his phone, which he'd propped against his cast as he ate his bagel. "I'm off. What time do you think you'll get there?"

"Smitty said he'd have me there by 2:00. Is that early enough?"

"Works for me." She pulled her coat on and then bent in for a kiss. "Hey, happy wedding day, Stanley."

He grinned. "Happy wedding day to you, Scout."

After breakfast, Audrey and Sandy drove to the house to help with the preparations. Her mother had bought two large bunches of flowers, so she and Sandy began dividing them up and distributing the smaller bouquets around the living/dining room area. While they did that, her father added the table leaves and spread a white cloth with a beautiful, red-flowered runner over the old table. Audrey opened the refrigerator door and was surprised to see a separate small bouquet nestled on top of a covered cheese platter. She pulled it out and looked at her mom. "It's beautiful, Mom."

Brigitte tucked a piece of hair behind Audrey's ear and rested her hand on her shoulder. "You needed a little something special, I thought."

"I love it, Mom. Thank you."

She hugged her mom, but Brigitte jumped back when she heard a car door slam. "That's Rod now. You hurry upstairs so he doesn't see you." Audrey laughed, but when her mom started shooing her away, she took off for the stairs. Sandy followed, and the two of them fell down on Audrey's old bed, laughing.

"She does know you woke up in the same bed this morning, right?" Sandy giggled.

Later that night, Audrey and Rod were sitting up in bed, enjoying the last of the champagne and chatting about the day.

"I thought Gina did a great job officiating, don't you?" Rod asked as he poured a bit more into Audrey's glass.

"I do. I liked it a lot. It was so personal, and having Emma and Sandy give little readings was sweet too." Audrey shrugged in satisfaction as she looked at Rod. "It was just for us, not some formulaic spiel."

"I liked that your dad put on some music and got everyone dancing afterward, too."

"He's an old-fashioned romantic, my mom always says. I think he probably loved us having it there." Audrey turned toward Rod and waved her hand just above the length of him. "So, when do you think this whole situation might be resolved so that we can go on a honeymoon, after Christmas maybe?"

"That sounds great. Amos and Bob talked about going to Bermuda for Christmas. Someplace warm would be nice."

"Yeah, but after the holidays. I want to have them here, in our place this first year."

Rod clinked his glass to hers. "Sounds great to me. I love holidays."

"Me too, the lights, the decorations, all of it." Audrey started but then paused. "I have to make a confession."

She watched Rod's face to gauge his reaction. "Uh oh."

"I like all of the other holidays, but I flat-out hate Halloween. I mean, I never liked it much as a kid, but now, after what we just went through? Now I actively hate it. I will not be gladly sewing up princess or lion costumes for little whoozits." She waved her hands to emphasize her point.

Rod burst out laughing. "Little whoozits? You think we'll have some little whoozits one day?" He pulled her closer, and Audrey giggled. "I'd like that."

Audrey snuggled in next to him. "Me too, but not right away," She paused, picturing the chaos of Sandy and Oscar's twins over the past year. "And hopefully just one at a time."

"Sounds perfect to me."

ACKNOWLEDGMENTS

Once again I would like to especially thank the wonderful M. Karen Brawn for her patience and insights which early on, made a tremendous difference to the story. I'd also like to thank my editor, Gabrielle Kirk, from Sunbury Press whose guidance was invaluable as well.

I'd like to thank my expert consultants once again as well. They include Suzanne Biermann M.A., CCC-SLP and Carol Fast MSPA, CCC-SLP, both Speech-Language Pathologists. Their understanding and expertise were especially welcome. Former Chief of Police for Ann Arbor, Carl Ent, was also vital to the writing process given his expertise in the workings of police investigations and procedures.

Finally, none of this would have been possible without my wonderful family and friends. I love and appreciate every one of you!

ABOUT THE AUTHOR

LINDA COTTON JEFFRIES grew up in Carlisle, Pennsylvania. She attended the University of North Carolina at Chapel Hill and taught special education for over thirty years. Her novels, *We Thought We Knew You* and *Who We Might Be*, were published by Fifth Avenue Press in Ann Arbor, Michigan. *Seeing in the Quiet* and *Picturing the Dark*, the first and second books in the Audrey Markum trilogy, were published by Sunbury Press. Strong women, suspense and romance are the elements that she most enjoys writing about!

www.Linda-Cotton-Jeffries.com